Thea had almost forgotten what it was like.

Waking up in the morning, knowing you belonged in this place.

Watching your children drift up slowly from sleep, gradually becoming eager for the new day.

Peace was a familiar kitchen, the coffee already made, a steaming cup poured and ready for your first sip.

Peace was the smile of the man who greeted you, his eyes warm and steady and welcoming.

Thea had almost forgotten that peace was made of little things, all the little things that were born of love.

ABOUT THE AUTHOR

Kay Wilding lives in Atlanta, Georgia, with her husband, Bill, and their two children. The family enjoys swimming and sailing together at nearby Lake Lanier, working jigsaw puzzles and playing Pictionary.

Rainbow's End is Kay's debut for American Romance, and is her fifth novel.

RAINBOW'S END

KAY WILDING

Harlequin Books

TORONTO • NEW YORK • LONDON
AMSTERDAM • PARIS • SYDNEY • HAMBURG
STOCKHOLM • ATHENS • TOKYO • MILAN

To Virginia and John,
who got me started in the first place
by having the courage to live their dream
instead of merely talking about it

Published April 1990

First printing February 1990

ISBN 0-373-16340-1

Chapter One

"Are we almost there, Mom?" Alan asked. "It's hot in here."

"Yeah," his brother Max agreed. "And I'm thirsty."

Thea Cameron looked into the rearview mirror at the reflection of her two sons in the back seat of the car and felt a pang of guilt. Seven-year-old Alan and five-year-old Max had handled being confined in a moving vehicle for days on end pretty well, but she knew what they were thinking now. Enough was enough.

"I'll tell you what, boys," she said. "We'll stop at that service station up ahead and get some soda and freshen up a little before we head out to Aunt Maudie's. We don't want her to think we've been living in the car."

"But we have been!" Max protested.

"Yes, but we don't want her to know that. Remember what we agreed. We're on our way to Florida and just stopped off in Georgia for a visit with her." A long, *long* visit, Thea fervently hoped.

Pulling into the station, Thea spied a sign offering a free car wash with each fill-up. The car's gas gauge was almost on Empty, but so was her pocketbook, and she'd been planning to drive out to Aunt Maudie's place without squandering any more money on gas.

Now she changed her mind. The dusty Ford needed a sprucing up, too; otherwise her aunt might think they were flat broke and desperate. They were. But Thea couldn't afford to let anyone else know it. She headed for the self-service island.

"Alan, take Maxie to the men's room and make sure he does a good job of washing up," she instructed the older son. "You both have to pass inspection before I spring for soft drinks."

After the boys left, Thea pumped gas into the car, keeping a watchful eye on the meter, then went inside to pay. "Pump number two," she told the portly attendant with a smile. "And I want to use your free car wash."

The man frowned. "It's free with a fill-up. You only bought a dollar and seventy-five cents worth."

"That's all it took to fill my tank," she lied. "If you want to set a dollar limit to qualify for a free wash, you should change your sign." She held out three one-dollar bills. "I'd like some coins for the soda machine, too."

The man silently handed her the coins, along with a token for the free car wash. Walking back into the bright sunlight, Thea saw no sign of the boys, so she headed for the ladies' room.

She was pleased to find it clean; they'd stopped at some real dumps along the way. Glancing into the mirror above the lavatory, she decided that the rest room was a lot cleaner than she was. Turning on the faucet, she cupped her hands to catch the cool water and splashed it onto her face. Then she reached for several paper towels, wet them and scrubbed her face, neck and arms, trying to remove as much grime as she could.

She really hated what she'd had to put the boys through these past few days. She felt guilty as sin that they'd had to sleep in the car and subsist on junk food. But she'd had no choice. Besides, the ordeal was almost over. They were almost safe. Nobody would think to look for them in the tiny town of Planters' Junction, Georgia. No one probably even knew the place existed.

Thea could already feel Aunt Maudie's welcoming embrace, could see herself soaking in a tub full of soapy water, sleeping between cool, clean sheets, and eating.... *Stop!* she told herself sternly. *Don't think about food. Not yet, anyway.* She extracted a comb from her purse and tried to smooth her tangled hair.

The boys were waiting impatiently beside the soda machine when Thea went outside. She gave each of them a couple of quarters, then lifted Max so he could feed the machine and make his own selection. Alan was extremely proud that he was finally tall enough to operate the machines without help.

She watched them drink thirstily, loving them both so much that it almost hurt. They were worth every pain, every hardship, every risk.

Thea looked into her change purse again and saw that she had enough money for a bag of corn chips the boys could share.

"Want some, Mom?" Alan asked a moment later, after he'd torn open the bag and greedily crammed a handful of chips into his mouth.

Her mouth watered at the thought, but she swallowed and shook her head. "No thanks, sweetie. I'm going to save my appetite for all that good food we'll have at Aunt Maudie's house."

She stuffed her hands into the back pockets of her jeans and grinned. "Now, do you two want to stand around here all day, or do you want to hop into the car and go through the car wash with me?"

"Car wash!" Max exclaimed, running for the Ford with Alan right behind him. "And I get to sit in front this time!"

"No, you don't," Alan said, grabbing the door handle and giving his brother a shove. "It's my turn."

"Alan, Maxie. Stop it!" Thea reached the car just in time to prevent a major brawl from developing. "You can both sit in front."

Driving past familiar landmarks on the way to Aunt Maudie's house, Thea experienced a wave of nostalgia. She'd visited Aunt Maudie, her father's aunt, actually, every summer from the time she was younger than Max until she was sixteen, when her parents had divorced and she'd moved to California with her mother.

Even though the visits had stopped after that, she'd still kept in touch with her great-aunt. During the past few years their correspondence had been limited to exchanging Christmas cards, but she was sure the old lady would welcome her warmly, as she always had.

Or would she? After all, Thea hadn't let her know she was coming; she hadn't known herself until they were already on the road, halfway across the country. Would her aunt understand?

"There it is, boys!" Thea exclaimed as Aunt Maudie's home came into view. Situated in a grove of pecan trees several hundred yards back from the road, the big old Victorian house looked warm and welcoming. Safe. That was the operative word. It was a safe place for them to hide.

Pulling the car to a stop in front of the house, she felt an almost overwhelming sense of relief. "Well, boys, let's go say hello to Aunt Maudie."

At the front door Thea hesitated, then decided to ring the bell, rather than go barging inside when she wasn't expected.

"Maybe nobody's home," Alan suggested a few moments later when there had been no response.

Thea reached out to punch the bell again, but the door swung open. "Aunt—" she began, and stopped. That wasn't Aunt Maudie. In fact, the person standing there was about as different from Aunt Maudie as another human being could be.

He was tall, and his broad shoulders almost filled the doorway. His thick, black hair fell across his tanned forehead, and the expression in his blue eyes was so intense that it made her nervous. Of course, it might not be the intensity of his gaze that was unsettling her as much as the fact that she had a lot to hide.

She saw him peering at her as if he thought he might know her, and that disturbed her even more. So she looked at him more closely, too, and his handsome face suddenly seemed familiar. Did she know him? She was almost certain she'd seen him somewhere before.

"Hello," she finally mumbled after they'd stared at each other for some time.

Thea felt a quick rush of panic when he didn't answer. If she grabbed her sons' hands and pulled them along, could they make it to the car before he stopped them?

"Do we know each other?" he asked at last.

His deep voice immediately called up a memory. She smiled. Of all the people she'd thought about and never expected to see again...

"I'm Miss Maudie's niece," she said, repeating the same words she'd said to him the first time they'd met, so long ago.

His black brows shot up. "Theodora Anne Patricia Cameron!" he exclaimed, his face breaking into a blinding smile. "I can't believe it!"

"Believe it. Hello again, Quint Richards."

"Good grief!" He reached out and took both her hands, giving them a warm squeeze. "It seems like forever since the last time we saw each other."

It didn't seem like forever to her. It seemed like only a short while ago, although they both had changed, of course. His body was now that of a man, and his dark hair was lightly sprinkled with gray. She could see laugh lines etched around his eyes, too, and a suggestion of remembered pain in those eyes.

But standing here now, her hands held tightly in his firm grasp, she thought he looked just as handsome and romantic as she had thought when she was sixteen and madly in love with him.

"It has been forever," she said. "Thirteen years, to be exact."

"And look at you. All grown-up."

Thea laughed nervously. "I should hope so. I'm a mother now." Tugging gently, she extricated her hands from his. "These are my sons, Alan and Max."

Quint bent to shake each boy's hand. "Alan. Max. I'm very happy to meet you. Your mom and I used to play together when we were kids and she visited here in the summertime."

"No, we didn't," Thea corrected him. "Aunt Maudie used to pay you to let me tag along behind you and your friends when you went fishing."

"Is that the way you remember it?" Quint gave her a lazy grin that warmed her right down to her toes.

She cleared her throat. "Speaking of Aunt Maudie, how is she? Are you over here for a visit?" Quint's family used to live just down the road, and he'd made regular visits to Aunt Maudie's house for the peanut butter cookies she'd always kept in generous supply.

The grin disappeared from his face, and a frown took its place. "No. I'm not here for a visit. I live here now."

Thea stopped breathing. What had he said? "You...you live...?" She pursed her lips, trying to think. If Quint lived here... "Where's Aunt Maudie?" she asked in a frightened whisper.

Quint's frown deepened and his blue eyes darkened. "Don't you know? I thought that was why you were here. She's in a nursing home."

Aunt Maudie in a nursing home? And Quint Richards living in her house? Thea felt suddenly, violently ill. Where would she and her sons go? What was she to do? She blinked once, twice; Quint's face swam in and out of focus.

"Thea?"

His anxious voice seemed to be coming from far away. She reached out her hand to steady herself, but touched only air. A black cloud swirled around her and the world disappeared.

"WHAT'S WRONG with her?" Alan asked.

"Is she gonna die?" Max whispered in a quavering voice.

"No, she's not going to die!" Quint said much more sharply than he'd intended, the harshness in his voice startling even himself. "She's going to be all right," he added in a softer tone, lowering Thea's limp body to the sofa in the living room.

"But what happened to her?" Alan persisted.

"She fainted, that's all. She'll be coming around soon."

"What made her faint?" Alan asked, continuing to probe.

"Probably the heat," Quint answered patiently. "Plus the shock of hearing that her aunt's in a nursing home." *And my stupidity,* he added to himself. Damn him, anyway! Why had he blurted out the news like that? Why couldn't he have told her in a kinder, gentler way?

From the corner of his eye Quint saw both Alan and Max move closer to the sofa, but neither of them attempted to touch their mother. They were afraid of her, and of the strange and frightening thing that had happened to her. He'd seen the same reaction in his own kids, when their mother was dying.

Snap out of it, he told himself. Thea wasn't dying. She was white as a new sheet, though, and the small hand he picked up and gently started massaging was cold to the touch. He sat down on the sofa beside her.

"Alan, take your brother with you to the kitchen and bring back a wet towel and a glass of water," Quint said briskly. "The kitchen's at the end of the hall, and there should be plenty of clean towels around. The glasses are..." He paused, trying to remember, but drew a blank. "They're in one of the cabinets. You'll just have to search for them. Okay?"

"Yessir," Alan replied, hurrying for the door with Max right at his heels. A smile touched Quint's lips as he watched them leave. They were nice boys. Handsome little rascals, too. They looked like their mother.

He shifted his gaze back to her. She was beautiful! She'd been pretty at sixteen. More than pretty. So much more that he'd felt at a disadvantage around her, awkward and inept, in spite of being five years older. Because of his feelings, he'd kept his distance and pretended indifference. But he had noticed her, all right. How he had noticed!

He sighed. If she had been pretty at sixteen, she was almost heartbreakingly beautiful now, lying motionless on Miss Maudie's sofa, her warm chestnut hair forming a halo around her face, her long black lashes resting on soft, smooth cheeks.

He looked at the graceful, feminine hand he held in his own. She was fragile. He'd noticed it immediately when he'd caught her on the porch. Then, lifting her into his arms to bring her inside the house, he'd felt as if he were carrying a precious, delicate flower.

He reached out to brush her cheek with the backs of his fingers. Her eyelids fluttered, then opened. "Hi," he said softly.

She closed her eyes and immediately opened them again. "Did I faint?"

"I think so."

"I've never done that before."

Another wave of guilt washed over Quint. "I'm sorry. It was my fault, springing the bad news about Miss Maudie on you like that."

"What's wrong with her? Is it serious?"

"It could be worse. Could be better, too. She fell and broke her hip about a month ago, and they had to replace the joint."

"Oh, no!"

"The doctor says she's coming along fine, though, especially for somebody her age. How old is she, anyway?"

Thea gave a shaky laugh. "She has to be at least in her mid-eighties, but nobody knows exactly except her, and she won't tell."

"Hmm. Well, the doctor thinks she's doing great. They moved her from the hospital to the nursing home this week. If the physical therapy works the way they believe it will, she should be coming home in another month or two."

"Another month! That's an awfully long time."

Quint heard the disappointment in Thea's voice. "Not for what happened to her and at her age. The doctors say it's a miracle she's doing as well as she is."

"Oh." She compressed her lips while she appeared to digest the information. "Uh, you said you were living here in Aunt Maudie's house now?"

He nodded. "For almost a year. I've lived here with Miss Maudie and my two kids."

Thea's eyes widened, and Quint laughed at the expression on her face. "Like I told you before, it's been a long time since we've seen each other. Now you're a mommy and I'm a poppy."

"But...uh, your uh..."

He knew she was struggling for the right words to ask the questions that were on her mind, and he decided to tell her everything.

"Look," he said, "the whole town knows my situation, and if you stay around here for any length of time, you'll find out about it, too. It's no big secret." He hesitated for a fraction of a second. "My wife died a little more than a year ago."

"Oh, Quint! I'm so sorry!"

Looking down, he saw that he was still holding Thea's hand, squeezing it, actually, and abruptly released it. "Those things happen, even though we hope and pray they never will." He swung his hand in a dismissive motion. "But they happen, anyway. The problem afterward is trying to deal with the leftover mess. In my case, it was a lot of debts.

"I'd been in private law practice. I sort of neglected it— hell, I practically abandoned it during my wife's long illness."

"What—?" she began, but stopped.

He answered anyway. "Ovarian cancer. Her...death... took a long time. And it was very painful for everybody, most of all for her. After it finally happened, I didn't know what to do with myself. There I was with two kids, a mountain of bills, and no will or way to deal with any of them.''

Quint rubbed the back of his neck. "Miss Maudie saved my life. Three lives, really. She took me firmly in hand and told me exactly what I had to do—sell my house, apply the money to the outstanding debts, and make arrangements with the bank to pay off the others gradually—and move in with her.''

He shook his head, remembering. "My law practice was already down the tubes, so she even offered to loan me some money. I didn't take it, of course, and soon found another job, but I'll never forget it. She's a great human being, Thea.''

"I know.''

Looking at her, Quint saw Thea's eyes fill with tears and was embarrassed. "Hey, I wasn't looking for sympathy. I just wanted you to know the truth about—''

"I understand. Really.''

This time she was the one who reached out. The completely natural way she took his hand and the look she gave him afterward told him that she more than understood; she cared. Quint felt a tightness in his throat. Theodora Anne Patricia Cameron had grown up to be a very special lady, just like her aunt.

THEA HAD NEVER KNOWN the pain of having someone really close to her die. Judging by the suffering she'd seen in Quint's eyes while he tried to talk unemotionally about his wife, it had been a long, excruciating death. That the pain was still raw after more than a year said a lot about the loving relationship they must have had. She envied him that but she also felt the agony he carried with him and tried to hide from other people. The handsome young man she'd adored at sixteen had matured into a strong, caring human being any woman would be proud to love.

"Where are the boys?" she asked, releasing his hand and pushing herself to a sitting position.

"What?" Quint asked blankly.

Thea pressed her fingers against her temples. She still felt a little giddy, probably because she'd had almost nothing to eat for two days. "My boys, Alan and Max. Where are they?"

"I sent them to the kitchen for water a little while ago. Maybe I should go check—"

"Look what I caught!"

Thea let out a startled gasp, and Quint jumped to his feet. They both gaped. Her two sons were being herded into the room by a towheaded, forty-pound vigilante in a cowboy hat, plaid flannel shirt and baggy jeans, which were tucked inside muddy, calf-high boots.

Bound together back-to-back by the rope that encircled them, Max and Alan were walking sideways.

"I found these crooks messing around the kitchen," announced their captor as he pulled the other end of the rope, his bright blue eyes sparkling with animation. "I tied and lassoed 'em for you, Pa."

The boy looked so ferocious that Thea had to clasp one hand over her mouth to keep from laughing out loud.

"J.R.!" Quint didn't seem to find the situation amusing. "Let go of that rope immediately!"

"But, Pa—"

"You heard me. Turn those boys loose. Now."

J.R. reluctantly dropped the rope, leaving Alan and Max to wriggle free on their own. "Aren't you going to take 'em to jail?"

"I certainly am not."

"Aren't you even gonna arrest 'em? I caught 'em in the kitchen—"

"I sent them to the kitchen on an errand, J.R. They're guests. This is their mother, Thea...." Quint turned back to her with an apologetic half smile. "I forgot to ask your married name."

"It's Cameron," she replied quickly. "I'm divorced, and I took back my maiden name."

"Oh."

Thea saw a flicker of something in his eyes. Curiosity? Interest? Whatever it was was gone so quickly that she wasn't even sure whether she'd seen it or not.

"This is Mrs. Cameron, Miss Maudie's niece," Quint told the vigilante, who had poked out his bottom lip in a determined sulk. "And these are her sons, Alan and Max." He walked over to touch J.R. on the shoulder. "And Thea, I'm forced to admit this scamp is my son, Joshua Richards."

"How do you do, Joshua," Thea murmured.

Two bright blue eyes stared back at her. "Why are you here?"

Thea didn't know how to answer, but didn't have to, because J.R. abruptly wheeled and bolted for the door. "I don't want them here!" he shouted over his shoulder.

Everyone else in the room stared in stunned silence at the door through which he'd disappeared. Nobody spoke.

Finally Quint cleared his throat. "I apologize. J.R., uh...has had a hard time dealing with Miss Maudie's accident." His blue eyes, so much like his son's, focused on Thea. "He doesn't believe she's coming back from the nursing home."

Because of what happened to his mother. Thea's heart ached for the little boy and for his father. "I understand," she said in a choked whisper.

Chapter Two

Thea sat perfectly still, listening to the ticking of the grandfather clock in the corner, the only sound in the large, shadowed room. At last Max broke the silence. "Are we going to stay here, Mom?"

She had a hysterical impulse to laugh. How typical of Max to shatter an awkward silence with an even more awkward question. Not that the question wasn't one she'd been wondering about herself.

"Max, you shouldn't—" she began.

"Of course you're going to stay here," Quint interjected. Then, seeing Thea's expression, he added, "Aren't you? I mean... aren't you going to visit in Planters' Junction for a while?"

So many unexpected things had happened so quickly, she wasn't sure about anything anymore. She shrugged.

Quint narrowed his eyes. "What *are* your plans?" he asked.

Fear threatened to suffocate Thea. How much could she safely tell him? Or anybody, for that matter. She had to be so careful about everything she said.

"I don't know," she answered truthfully. "Aunt Maudie wasn't expecting us. This...this was sort of a surprise visit. And now..."

"It'll be a wonderful surprise for her. Better than medicine."

"You think so?"

"I know so. She talks about you all the time, in spite of all the years you haven't seen each other."

Thea felt guilty again; she'd become so caught up in her own concerns that she hadn't kept in closer touch with Aunt Maudie.

"It wouldn't be fair to her if you went away before the two of you had a chance to get reacquainted," Quint continued.

"Well..."

"And naturally you'll stay here with us while you're visiting Miss Maudie. Where else would you stay in Planters' Junction except at your own aunt's home?" he said, finishing his little speech in a rush and with a conspiratorial grin on his face.

Thea swallowed, deeply touched by the way he was trying to put her at ease. "It's your home now, too," she said. "I wouldn't want to—"

"I know you wouldn't. But you know how big the house is. There's plenty of room for everybody."

"And there's J.R.—"

"Don't worry about J.R. I know my son. He's probably already forgotten what he said to you by now." The grin on Quint's face changed, softened, she thought, as he continued watching her. "Any other objections?"

Now she had to smile. "I can't think of any more at the moment."

"Good. It's settled, then. I'll go get your bags, while you decide which bedrooms you and your boys want." He hesitated. "I've been using the room at the left front upstairs."

That was her old room, the one she'd always used when she visited Aunt Maudie. Thea wondered whether Quint knew he was sleeping in the bed she used to sleep in, the one in which she used to dream about him late at night.

She pushed the thought aside and tried to concentrate on more immediate concerns. Did the car contain any evidence that they'd been living in it? She couldn't remember any, and was thankful that she had washed it and disposed of their accumulated trash at the service station. Still, she might have missed something, and it was far safer for them if nobody knew they'd been using the car for a motel.

"Any rooms are fine with us," she said. "And it's not necessary for you to get our things. The boys and I can bring in what we need for the night."

"The night? I thought we agreed—"

"We agreed that we'd stay here and visit Aunt Maudie, Quint," she said, lifting her chin. "I don't recall any mention of how long we'd visit."

He studied her for a long moment. "I don't remember your being so stubborn years ago."

She felt her cheeks grow warm. "People change," she said. *Sometimes they have no choice,* she thought, but didn't say it. *They have to change in order to survive.* "Back then I was just a little pleasing machine, always trying to make everybody happy."

"I remember," he said. "Johnny Eason used to tease you by calling you the cheerleader."

She made a face.

"It was a compliment! He meant you were nice, really nice. I agreed with him."

In spite of herself, Thea felt a quick surge of pleasure at the backhanded compliment—and the need to deny herself that pleasure. "Being too nice, too docile, can be destructive."

"To yourself?"

"And to others, as well." She was the one who'd brought up this subject, but wished now she hadn't. It was making her increasingly uncomfortable.

"How is that?" Quint asked.

"They can come to depend on you too much, to make more demands on you than you can handle...." Damn! Why had she said that? She looked away, but felt his eyes on her, watching her, looking into her soul. "At least, that's what I've read," she finished lamely.

Quint took a deep breath. "I think half the guys in Planters' Junction were in love with you when you visited here. You were the prettiest girl they'd ever seen, and the nicest. I'm sorry you've been hurt—"

"I wasn't talking about myself! I—" She stopped once again when she glanced at him and saw he didn't believe her. His eyes were filled with compassion. *Damn him!* She didn't want his sympathy.

She forced a smile. "Besides, I'm surprised you noticed anything about me. You were so...so enthralled with that blonde who was always hanging all over you. What was her name? And whatever became of her?"

The expression in Quint's eyes changed, and he looked at her steadily before he answered. "Her name was Sally, and I married her."

"Oh, no!" She rose quickly from the sofa and almost bumped into him. The sudden movement made her slightly dizzy again.

"Thea, are you all right?"

She stared at the broad male chest in front of her, so close that she could feel his body heat through the knit fabric of his polo shirt.

"Thea?" he asked again.

She lifted her head. It was a mistake. Probing blue eyes gazed at her, causing all sorts of crazy notions to flash through her mind. How long had it been since anyone—any adult male—had expressed such genuine concern for her? She blinked. "I'm fine." Was that her voice sounding so thin?

"Are you sure?"

"Yes. Oh, Quint. I'm so sorry. What a terrible, witchy thing that was for me to say...."

"You couldn't have known."

"It was awful."

"No, it wasn't."

"Don't be so nice to me."

"Okay, I won't. It was a terrible thing for you to say. Feel better now?"

"Not much, but thank you for trying."

He smiled, and Thea watched the laugh lines deepen at the corners of his mouth. She saw the smoothness of his firm lips. Were they as soft as they looked? When his tongue suddenly darted out to moisten his lips, she caught her breath.

"Thea."

She forced herself to look into his eyes. They weren't angry, upset or even judgmental, only understanding.

"It really is okay," he said.

She wished he wouldn't be kind. She was a sucker for kindness; it made her weak, when she needed to be strong. She nodded, not trusting herself to speak.

"Well, uh..." he began, "are you sure you don't want any help with your bags?"

She shook her head.

"I guess I'd better go find J.R. He should have cooled off by now."

She wanted to look away, but couldn't.

He didn't look away, either. His eyes continued gazing at her with an expression she hadn't seen in a man's eyes in . . . how long? She wished she wasn't seeing it now, but at the same time reveled in his look, exulted in it; she felt it wrap around her like a smooth, satin sheet. Her mouth felt dry, and her fingers tingled with the desire to touch him.

"Mom . . ." Max said, breaking the spell.

Thea blinked. "I guess I'd better . . ."

Quint took a deep breath. "Yeah. Me, too. I'll see you later."

She watched his long legs carry him swiftly out of the room, leaving her with the impression that he was almost running. Running from her?

She sighed and turned toward her son. "What was it you wanted, Maxie?"

"I need to use the bathroom."

At the sound of Max's familiar voice expressing his primary concern of the moment, Thea felt all tension drain from her body. As was usual with Max, it related to a basic body function. She grinned and gave him directions.

"Are we really going to stay here, Mom?" Alan asked as soon as his brother left the room.

She looked at the boy. That was a question she'd been asking herself—almost from the moment they'd arrived at Aunt Maudie's house to find her gone and Quint Richards here—very much here. His strong, masculine presence still seemed to linger in the living room.

She remembered the intensity in Quint's gaze when they had first met again a little while ago. She had felt that those eyes could see all the way into her soul, that they might see things they had no business seeing, and discover secrets she had to keep hidden.

There was his family, too. Two children. Aunt Maudie's house was big, but was it big enough to hold Quint and herself and four children without absolute chaos? And possibly all-out war?

Since they arrived here she had considered all those things and more. But she knew she was deluding herself, because none of them really mattered in the long run. What everything finally came back to was one simple fact—for the time being, she and her two boys *had* to stay here in Aunt Maudie's house, Quint Richards or no Quint Richards. They had no other choice. They had no money and nowhere else to go.

Thea forced a smile and tried to inject confidence into her voice as she answered Alan's question. "Of course we're going to stay here, at least for a while."

"How long is that?" Alan asked, his tone edged with suspicion.

"I'm not sure. We'll see how things work out."

"I don't want to go back to California," he said, his bottom lip trembling.

Thea clenched her fists, wanting to cry herself. She wrapped her arms around Alan and pulled him close, kissing the top of his head. "Don't worry, darling. We're not going back there…ever. And whether we decide to stay here or go someplace else, the three of us will be together. Remember that."

"Is Alan crying again?" Max asked, strolling back into the room.

"No, he's not crying," Thea said quickly, answering for the older boy in order to give him time to compose himself. She knew how much he hated Max's teasing. "Not that there's anything wrong with crying. Everybody does it occasionally."

"Not me," Max vowed.

"Ha!" Alan scoffed.

"When did I ever—?"

"Boys," Thea interrupted, "why don't you go outside and look around while I get our things out of the car?

There's a wonderful carriage house out back, with a couple of antique buggies inside. And there's a barn—''

"And horses?" Max wanted to know.

"Not anymore," Thea admitted regretfully. "Aunt Maudie got rid of the last of them a few years ago. She probably still keeps some chickens, though, and there's always the lake."

They were off at a run.

Thea smiled, remembering how eager she'd always been to explore the place as soon as she arrived every summer. The first thing she'd do was take off her shoes in order to get full enjoyment from the soft carpet of crimson clover under her feet as she ran to the barn. Wonderful horses had been housed in the barn in those days—proud, magnificent animals, but none of them more so than Candida, her favorite.

After renewing her acquaintance with the horses, Thea would rush to the backyard to climb her favorite chinaberry tree, then to the gardens to inspect Aunt Maudie's flowers and vegetables, then to the lake to check on it and also on the status of the two giant live oaks guarding it, their limbs draped dramatically and majestically with Spanish moss.

She would always save the best until last—exploring the house itself. The house was white-framed, built in the nineteen-twenties by Aunt Maudie's first husband, a cotton broker and textile mill owner, who had amassed a tidy fortune before his death at a relatively young age.

To Thea it was the most wonderful house in the world, with its ornate Victorian architecture, gables and turrets everywhere...and gleaming lightning rods perched atop every single one of them! Counting the root cellar and attic, it had four stories, each one a gold mine begging to be discovered—and thoroughly investigated—by her.

Aunt Maudie's second husband had had both old money and a passion for travel. Before his death, he and Aunt Maudie had traveled all around the world and brought back souvenirs from every place they'd visited. Aunt Maudie never threw anything away; she merely rearranged things to make room for new acquisitions, so the house was filled from top to bottom with priceless antiques, fascinating bric-a-brac—and plain junk.

Thea glanced around the big, high-ceilinged living room. She'd spent some of the happiest times of her life in this house. Now perhaps her children would, too, if only for a short while...but only if things worked out. So many things could go wrong.

She sighed and headed for the front door to get some clothes from the car. After that, she desperately wanted a bath. The blower on the car's heater and air conditioner had conked out about halfway across Texas, and since she hadn't had the money to have it repaired, they'd alternately shivered and sweated the rest of the way to Georgia. She planned to soak in a big tub of water for hours, maybe days.

Halfway down the hall she changed her mind and detoured to the kitchen. Quint hadn't mentioned anything about dinner, but it was almost five o'clock now and her kids—and his, too, probably—would be getting hungry soon. Maybe he'd let her cook. It seemed like years since she'd been in a kitchen, and she'd missed it.

The big, old-fashioned room looked much the same as she remembered it, except for some gleaming, new appliances she hadn't seen before. Thea crossed the linoleum floor to the refrigerator. Opening the door, she looked inside and almost fainted again.

Food! Not stamped-out, assembly-line food like she and the boys had been eating, but the real thing. Milk. Cheese.

Eggs. The remains of a yummy-looking roast. Butter. Fresh corn. Ripe strawberries, for heaven's sake!

She closed her eyes. Then, realizing she was holding her breath, she let out a long sigh. Were they going to eat tonight!

WALKING ACROSS THE MEADOW in search of his son, Quint cursed himself for acting like a total, absolute idiot. What kind of fool would bolt out of his own house like that, almost running, merely because a woman looked at him! Granted, she was the most gorgeous creature he'd probably ever seen; and she had stood so close that he'd almost been able to feel her breath on his face. What's more, it had been forever since he'd been with a woman, but *still!*

Damn! Why did Theodora Anne Patricia Cameron bring out the worst in him? She always had, even when he was younger and considered himself God's gift to women. Other women, that was; not Thea. Never Thea. In his eyes she'd always been different, special. And because he'd always wanted to impress her, he'd always ended up disgracing himself instead. He'd done it again now.

He took several deep breaths, trying to calm down. So Thea was back in town, divorced, with two kids. She also had a chip on her shoulder the size of a small oak tree. He wondered what had caused the change. The Thea he knew had been open, fun-loving, even a little wild and reckless. He'd often compared her to the flower children of the sixties and had teased her about it at times. She'd merely laughed.

Now she was . . . different, on edge, and so tightly wound that he had the impression her control could snap at any moment. What had happened to make her so defensive, so desperate? Maybe her ex-husband had treated her badly, and maybe desperate was too strong a word.

Or was it? The look he'd seen in her eyes when he told her Miss Maudie was in a nursing home had been one of sheer panic. Then she had fainted. He'd felt guilty about it at the time, but hadn't she overreacted? Surely she wouldn't be that upset to learn her aunt—an aunt she hadn't seen in thirteen years—was in a nursing home.

He stopped walking. What did he know about Thea—*really* know about her? He'd been so addled by her sudden, dramatic reappearance in his life that he'd forgotten to ask her anything. Where had she come from? Where was she headed? She'd said her aunt didn't expect her, so why had she suddenly decided to bring her boys to Georgia for a visit, after thirteen years?

Her boys. Quint frowned as he thought of something else. It was only the first week in May, so why weren't Thea's boys in school? Was she so irresponsible that she didn't care whether they missed school or not? Or was there some specific and compelling reason she'd decided to bring them here at this particular time?

A lot of questions. Quint decided he'd like some answers.

THEA TILTED HER HEAD against the high-backed rocking chair and looked up at the starry sky. She spotted the Little Dipper immediately. The Big Dipper took a little longer, but she remembered just where to look for it from Aunt Maudie's front porch. There it was!

She relaxed with a sigh and rocked the chair a couple of times. It was strange how much better, brighter, more beautiful the whole world looked after a bath, a meal, and the prospect of a good night's sleep in a real bed.

It's unfortunate that we take such simple pleasures for granted until we don't have them anymore, she thought to herself. *Then we realize how terribly important they are, not only for survival, but also for our sense of self and self-worth.*

"I brought you a crème de menthe over ice," Quint said, stepping out onto the porch. "I would have made a frappé, but the blender wore out last week. Too many milk shakes finally broke its blades," he explained, handing her the frosty glass.

"This looks wonderful," she said with a laugh. "But you're too good to me. You're spoiling me rotten."

"No, I'm not. It's not every day that Miss Maudie's niece comes back to town," he said, repeating the words he'd said earlier in the evening when he insisted on cooking steaks on the grill, rather than letting her prepare dinner in the kitchen. He had allowed her to toss the salad and shuck the corn to roast along with the steak, but had adamantly refused to let her help him clean the kitchen after dinner.

"This is your boys' first night in Miss Maudie's home. You have to show them where everything is and help them get ready for bed," he'd said. "I can manage in here just fine."

Thea took a sip of her crème de menthe. "Mmm, this is delicious, Quint, and so was your steak. Maybe you should have been a chef and missed your calling."

"Could be," he said, settling into the chair beside her and tasting his drink. "We don't always wind up doing the things we were meant to do...or being with the people we should be with," he added.

He'd obviously been happy in his marriage, Thea thought, so he had to be referring to her marriage. She decided to ignore his remark. "Tell me about your daughter."

"Alfie? I thought I already told you. She's spending the night with a friend."

Thea was silent for a moment. "I guess that makes us even. I avoided your reference to my ex-husband, and you avoided my question about your daughter."

"Is that what you thought I was doing?"

"Wasn't it?"

He hesitated. "Yes."

Thea took a deep breath. "I loved my husband when I married him, and for a lot of years after that. But . . . he changed. For a long time I tried to deal with the changes. Maybe too long. I finally realized I wasn't helping him. I was only hurting myself and our children. So I got out."

Quint nodded but didn't speak for a long time. "Alfie's ten years old, a straight-A student," he finally said. "And she's mixed-up as all get-out. She's surly, sarcastic, has no friends except the one she's spending the night with . . . and that girl's almost a basket case herself. As far as I know, Alfie hates almost everybody, but especially me."

They were both silent, then looked at each other across the white wicker table between their two chairs.

"Well," she said, "I guess we got that out of the way."

"I guess," he said, lifting his glass in a silent toast.

"I'm sorry about your daughter."

"Thanks. I'm sorry about your marriage."

"Thanks." She sighed. "Maybe we should stick with safe topics of conversation from now on."

"Maybe we should," Quint agreed. "Tell me about your trip. Max said you drove all the way from California. . . ."

Thea's muscles tensed again. This wasn't a safe topic of conversation; it was about as unsafe as it could be, but now she was trapped. "There's not much to tell. We left the West Coast about two weeks ago—"

"That long ago?"

This was getting worse by the moment. Anything she admitted was potentially dangerous. "We took the scenic route . . . you know, the usual tourist attractions."

"Sounds great. Sally and I always planned to take the kids on a trip out west. Did you see the Grand Canyon?"

"I'm not sure. . . ."

"You're not sure whether you saw the Grand Canyon? It's not that easy to miss. . . ."

"Yes, we saw it! But it's just that we've been on the road so long and everything starts to look the same after a while. And I'm tired, and you're bombarding me with all these questions. . . ."

"Thea, I'm sorry," Quint said, rising from his chair. "I forgot how tired you must be. You even fainted this afternoon and I . . . Please forgive me."

"Of course I do," she said, placing her glass on the table and getting to her feet. "And I overreacted, too."

"No, you didn't. I was stupid and inconsiderate. I suppose I ask so many questions because I'm used to doing it in my job and it carries over . . . like a bad habit."

"It's okay, Quint. Really." He was so contrite that she smiled to reassure him. "What is your job, by the way?"

"I'm the district attorney."

She stood very still, trying desperately to keep her panic under control.

"I thought I told you before, but I guess I didn't."

She shook her head, hoping that would suffice as a comment. It was all she could manage.

"The old D.A. finally decided to retire, right after Sally died. I'd neglected my law practice so much during her illness that almost nothing was left of it, and I needed a new source of income fast. To make a long story short, I called on the governor. He liked my credentials and appointed me to fill the post of interim D.A. until the next general election."

He was looking at her, waiting for her to say something. What could she say? "That . . . that's nice."

"I've been thinking of running for the job next November. I have a little time left to decide. It's almost six months until the election and—" He stopped abruptly. "Hey, you're not interested in all that, and I'm keeping you up."

"I am tired. . . ."

"Can I get you anything?"

"No, thanks."

"You're sure?"

"Positive. I'm fine. Good night, Quint," she said. Walking up the stairs to her bedroom, though, Thea knew she'd lied. She wasn't fine at all. Her insides were twisted into a hard knot, and her heart was pounding about ninety miles a minute. She'd been so sure that Aunt Maudie's home would provide a haven for her children and herself. And even after she'd learned that Quint Richards was living there, she'd still been sure she could make do with the situation. Now she wasn't sure at all.

Quint was the local district attorney. Being D.A. meant he was a legal official. A cop of sorts. That was bad. Terrible. It was as bad as it could possibly be for her.

Because she was a criminal on the run.

Chapter Three

She was a kidnapper.

True, she had kidnapped her own kids, but that didn't make her actions any less illegal. A California court had awarded joint custody of the boys to Thea and her ex-husband. Instead of complying with the order, she'd taken the boys and run...all the way across the country.

Her ex-husband and the police in several states—maybe all fifty—were probably looking for her by now. And Quint, as an officer of the court, had a sworn duty to turn her in, to prosecute her, to send her to jail.

If he knew.

What a mess.

Thea rolled over in bed, wide-awake. She'd been trying to sleep for what seemed like hours. She knew she needed the rest; she'd only slept in short snatches for days. She hadn't allowed herself more than that, because she was on guard in the rest areas or on the dirt roads where they'd parked for the night.

She didn't know which of the two was worse. The rest areas had bathrooms and were better lighted, but that also meant they were more public. Perfect strangers would come up to their car at three or four o'clock in the morning to peer inside to see what was going on. Once a security guard had rapped on the car window and flashed a light into Thea's eyes in the middle of the night.

"Didn't you read the sign that says No Overnight Parking?" he had asked. "This is a rest area. We don't allow vagrants."

Thea had been so embarrassed that she'd cranked up the car and driven nonstop until the middle of the morning.

The deserted side roads she'd started resorting to after that were both better...and worse. They were quiet, private and dark, which helped the boys sleep better. But they were also so quiet, so private, and especially so dark that she found herself barely able to sleep at all. She kept the doors locked, of course, and the windows rolled up as high as she dared—after all, she didn't want to suffocate them—but still...

In her imagination, all sorts of dangers were lurking just outside. Wild animals, raging floods and escaped criminals were the primary dangers she envisioned the moment she closed her eyes. The criminals weren't your ordinary, run-of-the-mill thieves and robbers, either. They were panting rapists, wild-eyed child molesters, and deranged lunatics armed with chain saws.

Thinking about it now in the soft comfort of the feather bed in Aunt Maudie's house, her fears on the road seemed slightly ludicrous. Maybe the fears she had now would seem ludicrous in time, too, but she doubted it.

What was she going to do? What could she do? What were her options, her last-ditch desperation measures?

She still had an expensive watch and several pieces of jewelry she could pawn to provide them with a little cash. They could drive to another town, rent a small apartment, and she could look for a job.

That was the point where she always hit a dead end. What kind of jobs were available where she wouldn't need a reference, or social security identification at the very least? None, as far as she knew, and she didn't dare use her real identity.

If she had enough money she could start her own business, but that was wishful thinking. What kind of business did she know, anyway? She had marketing experience, but it was at the managerial level, working for big companies.

She sat up in bed and reached over to switch on the bedside lamp. She wished she hadn't thought about her marketing experience, because it reminded her of Alan—Alan Kirkland, Sr., her ex-husband and the father of her sons. The thought of him reminded her in turn of the things that had led up to the terrible trouble she was in now.

THEA WAS A SENIOR and a marketing major at UCLA, when she had landed an internship at the independent TV production company. It was the high point of her life up to that moment. She met Alan her very first day on the job. One of the rising young stars of the company, he was a brilliant producer on his way to the top.

Spotting her at lunch, he pursued her with the intense purpose and determination that was so characteristic of him in those days. She didn't resist at all; she was just as enthralled by him as he was by her. Soon they were seeing each other every day and sleeping together every night. They married the day after she graduated.

After graduation she worked for an ad agency until a few weeks before Alan, Junior's birth. She took a leave of absence, planning to return to work after a few months. But Alan was making so much money by then, and the baby was such a joy to be with that she never went back. She'd never been happier in her life.

Sometime after Max's birth a couple of years later Thea began to notice a change in her husband. He'd always been intense and volatile, but now at times he was so hyper that it bordered on the manic. At other times he was deeply depressed and only wanted to sleep. Thea insisted he see a doctor and he promised he would, but never did.

One night, watching a TV special about the Hollywood drug scene and the growing use of addictive drugs by affluent young professionals, Thea knew what was wrong with her husband. They could have been describing Alan.

She confronted him with her suspicion. He denied it at first, then broke down and confessed. After they'd argued all night, he finally agreed to enroll as an outpatient in a drug treatment program.

Things improved considerably for a while, then gradually deteriorated again. Alan started staying late at the studio, and was so keyed up that he couldn't sleep when he finally did come home. Thea was almost sure he was back on drugs. He denied it, saying his problems stemmed from trouble at work, along with his withdrawal symptoms, and she should try to be more understanding.

Thea wanted to believe him, tried to believe him, tried to trust him, but she knew he was getting worse. He was jittery, irritable, easily excited. He'd fly into a rage at the slightest provocation, then apologize profusely. Thea was near the breaking point herself, walking on eggs around Alan, trying to keep the boys away from him when he was at his worst, wondering what was going to become of her family.

She went out to dinner one night when her college roommate was passing through town, and left the kids with Alan, who was working at home. Returning later than she'd expected, Thea found Maxie screaming hysterically and Alan, Junior, frantically trying to revive his father, who had passed out in the middle of the living-room floor. Thea thought at first that he was dead. He almost was.

Thea stayed with him throughout his emergency treatment at the hospital and nursed him when he came home. All the time she was thinking about their situation. At last she reached a painful conclusion: Alan's drug abuse not only was destroying him but the whole family. And she was letting it happen.

As soon as he was well enough, she told him she planned to file for divorce. Alan said he didn't blame her, suggesting an uncontested, no-fault divorce and promising to give her sole custody of the boys. Thea wanted no alimony, but Alan insisted on paying child support.

The divorce whizzed through with no problems. Thea found another job in marketing and a small apartment with a school and day-care center nearby. Things were finally settling down again for the boys and herself.

About a year after the divorce, the phone calls started. At first the phone would ring, Thea would answer it, and the person at the other end would hang up immediately. She thought it was a crank caller, a weirdo, and had her phone number changed to an unlisted one as a precaution. After only a few days the calls began again, even worse than before. The caller began staying on the line longer, breathing into the phone, and she became frightened.

She was even more frightened when the man started making obscene comments and threats. She'd hang up almost immediately, but not quickly enough to avoid hearing a few words—enough to convince her that the caller was someone who knew her!

"Your breasts looked *real* fine in that green dress," he'd say in his low, scary voice. Or: "I thought about slitting your throat at the supermarket today...."

One night she stayed on the line a little longer than usual, and the caller made the mistake of laughing. It was Alan! She'd thought about the possibility that he was the one making the calls, but dismissed it. Now she was sure. He might be able to disguise his voice, but not his laugh. She'd know it anywhere.

The next time he called, she interrupted him. "Alan, I know it's you, and if you don't stop these calls *now*, I'm going to the police."

He beat her to it and took her to court almost immediately, suing for joint custody of Max and Alan, Junior.

In court she was surprised by his appearance. Given the nature of his phone calls, she'd expected him to look like a crazy person, unkempt and desperate, but he was as handsome as ever, immaculately tailored, self-assured.

Thea stole furtive glances at him across the aisle that separated their two tables. She finally saw his hand begin to shake, then grab a pencil and clutch it so tightly that it broke. She lifted her gaze and saw his clenched jaw and the veins standing out in his neck.

It was suddenly perfectly clear to her that he was using every ounce of self-control he possessed to keep up the appearance of being normal.

She had to give him credit; his facade was convincing. She'd have been taken in by it herself if she hadn't known better. More credit went to Alan's expensive, smoothly persuasive lawyer. He paraded witness after witness through the courtroom on his client's behalf—counselors at the drug treatment center who testified that Alan had been drug-free for more than a year; people with whom Alan worked, many of them minor and not-so-minor celebrities; and friends of Alan's who vowed he was genuinely remorseful and desperately wanted to reestablish a relationship with his sons.

Hearing the glowing words being said about her ex-husband, Thea began to doubt her own judgment. Had she imagined Alan's distress at the beginning of the hearing?

Could she have been wrong about him? Could it have been someone else calling her? Was she being paranoid not to trust him again? Was it fair of her to try to deny a father the right to be a part of his sons' lives?

By the time the proceedings ended, Thea was so confused that it was almost a relief to hear the judge grant Alan joint custody. Surely an experienced judge could discern the truth and make an impartial ruling; she must have been mistaken about Alan. She got up from her chair to speak to him, but he turned away and hurried out of the room before she could reach him.

When he called several days later, she apologized and agreed to have their sons ready to visit him the following weekend.

Alan arrived at her apartment exactly on time Friday night. As soon as she saw him looking tanned and relaxed in casual clothes, Thea breathed a sigh of relief. Everything was going to be all right.

She kept telling herself that whenever she had moments of misgiving during the weekend. Nevertheless, she felt a great weight lift from her mind when it was finally time for her to pick up the boys at Alan's house on Sunday.

When nobody answered Alan's door, all her old fears came back in a great rush. She ran the bell repeatedly and knocked with an increasing sense of panic. Finally she tried the knob and the door silently swung open. She stepped inside the foyer. "Alan?"

Only silence answered her. She took a few more steps. "Alan, Junior? Max?" The only sound she heard was that of her own rapid breathing, and her heart felt as if it were going to explode.

Almost frantic, she looked around. The door to the living room was open, so she headed for it. "Is anybody—?" She stopped and gasped. Alan was seated in a chair facing the door, looking straight at her. There was insanity in his eyes and evil in the small, triumphant smile that touched his lips. His expression was unsettling, but what made her heart stop beating was what he held in his hand—a huge kitchen knife. Thea covered her mouth with one hand.

"I see you're right on time," Alan said. His voice was calm, but Thea could see the wildness in his eyes. He was high on something. Dangerously high.

"The...the boys," she managed to whisper. "Where are they?"

Alan's manic laugh was the most frightening thing she'd ever heard.

"Alan! *Where are my children?*"

His laugh ended abruptly. "*Our* children. Remember? I have joint custody now."

"Yes," she said, trying to appease him and hold on to her sanity at the same time. "Yes, of course you do. But where are they?"

"You tried to keep them away from me. You threatened to take me to court...."

"So it *was* you making all those phone calls."

Alan wagged his index finger. "No, no. You're not going to trap me into saying that."

"I'm not trying to trap you—"

"Don't lie to me!" he shouted, jumping to his feet and waving the knife in a slashing motion.

"I swear!"

"You scheming liar! You've been out to get me for years!"

"No—"

"But I showed you, didn't I? I showed everybody!"

He crouched and walked toward her with the knife pointed directly at her midsection. Thea wanted to run, to scream, but didn't dare. That might send him over the edge, and she had to find out where the boys were. She had to save them, if it wasn't already too late. *No!* It wasn't too late! It couldn't be too late.

She took a deep breath and stood still, keeping her voice steady as she asked, "Alan, where are the kids?"

Instead of answering, Alan gave a brief, harsh laugh and grabbed her hair. He pulled back her head, holding her in a painful, viselike grip. "Ask me no questions and I'll tell you no lies."

"Alan, please..."

He jerked her head farther back, and she felt the tip of the knife touch her throat. She flinched involuntarily.

"How does it feel to be on the receiving end for a change, Thea?"

She closed her eyes. *Please, Lord, let my children be all right. Take care of them.*

"I asked you a question!" he shouted. "How does it feel?"

"Not good," she managed to whisper. "Awful."

"Now you know how I felt!"

No, she didn't know. Never in a million years would she know the warped workings of his drugged mind. "Yes," she whispered.

She stood very still, keeping her eyes tightly closed, listening to the labored sounds of his breathing, wondering what he would do next, wondering....

Abruptly he released her and pushed her away. She opened her eyes. Alan crouched again, still breathing heavily.

"Remember that," he said in a low voice. "And don't you dare ever threaten me again. Understand?"

She nodded.

"Say it!"

"I...I understand." Thea held her breath while she watched his mood undergo another sudden, dramatic shift. He stood up, ran his fingers through his hair and smiled! Then he walked to an end table and casually placed the knife on it.

"The boys are out back, swimming in the pool," he said calmly, as if nothing unusual had happened. "I already packed their bags, so they're ready to leave when you are. I think they had a good time. I know I did. I'm looking forward to their next visit."

Thea stared at him, speechless.

Alan started toward the door, but suddenly stopped and turned back to her. "One other thing, Thea. Like the judge said, growing boys need two parents, so I expect the two of us to be working closely together from now on. After all, we wouldn't want anything bad to happen to *our* sons, would we?"

The implied threat in his words was reinforced by the direct threat in his voice, and Thea felt cold all over.

This Alan wasn't the man she'd married; he wasn't even the man she'd divorced. This Alan was a dangerous drug addict, capable of anything. And, as he'd just reminded her, he now had joint custody of their children!

As soon as Alan left the room, Thea rushed out to the swimming pool. Max seemed fine, but Alan, Junior, started crying in the car on the way back to the apartment. Thea immediately pulled to the curb.

She was almost afraid to ask what was wrong. "Did...did your father do anything to you or Max?"

"No," Alan said. "But I think he's sick again, Mom. Worse than ever."

Thea's heart broke for her older son. He'd always been sensitive and much older than his years. And unlike Max, he remembered the way his father used to be—teasing, playful, sympathetic. Wonderful. The kind of father his friends envied. The father he loved so much.

She knew how much it hurt Alan to see his father as he was now. It hurt her the same way.

"Mom, I don't want to go back there," Alan said, his eyes filling with tears again. "He scared me."

He scared me, too, honey. Thea hugged her son to her breast, pushing back his hair from his forehead, loving him with all her being. "It's okay," she said, choking back her tears. "Everything's going to be okay."

"Is Dad going to be okay, too?" Max asked, joining the conversation from the back seat. Thea was sure he didn't know everything that was going on, probably not even half of it, but Maxie—sweet, loving Maxie—always wanted to be in on everything.

"I hope so," she said, meaning it from the bottom of her soul.

"But do we have to go back and visit him again?" Alan asked.

Thea hesitated as her heart hammered against her chest. Did her sons have to go back to visit their father again? The judge had said they did. What could she do?

She could take Alan back to court and try to regain sole custody, but could she *win*? Alan would be so furious that he'd pull out all the stops, and she had no concrete, provable evidence against him. Even Alan, Junior, had said he hadn't done anything to harm them, so it was her word against his. She might win, but what if she tried and lost? There was even the remote possibility that she could lose her rights to the boys. That idea was unbearable.

So what course of action was available to her? Did she dare do what she was thinking?

"Mom?" Alan asked again.

"No," she said, making her decision. "You don't have to go back," she said more forcefully. "In fact, I've been thinking that the three of us should go on a trip."

"Really?" Max asked. "To where?"

"I dunno. But it'll be a long trip."

"When do we leave?" Max asked, jumping up and down in the back seat.

"Right away," Thea said. "Tonight."

"No kidding?" Alan asked. "What about school?"

"There are only a few weeks left until the end of the term," Thea pointed out. "You can skip school."

"You mean it, Mom?" Max exclaimed, leaning over to wrap his chubby arms around her neck. "You really mean it?"

"Sure. We'll all run away from home!"

Both Alan and Max collapsed into fits of giggles.

Thea had made it seem like a grand adventure to the boys, but she knew how deadly serious her scheme was. She'd never have had the courage to attempt it if she hadn't been desperate, terrified for the safety of her children.

That same night, as soon as she, Alan, Junior, and Max got home, she packed the barest necessities for the three of them, hurried the tired, sleepy, but excited boys into the car, and left town.

THEA LOOKED DOWN and saw that her hands were trembling as they clutched the coverlet on the bed in Aunt Maudie's home, the one place in the country where she'd thought she and her sons could find refuge. Instead they'd found the local district attorney living under the same roof!

What irony! Thea would have laughed if she hadn't felt so much like crying. Why couldn't things ever work out the way they were supposed to? It wasn't fair.

It also wasn't like her to be so full of self-pity, she told herself sternly. Okay, so the situation wasn't exactly what she'd envisioned, and they hadn't received quite the warm welcome she'd been hoping for. At least they had a roof other than the one on the car over their heads tonight.

And even if Quint was a law official, he was still a friend; he'd already proven that by being so kind to the boys and herself. He was no more a threat to their safety than anyone else. Anybody who knew what she'd done would be obligated to turn her in. If they didn't, that would make them accessories to a criminal act.

Thinking about that, Thea felt better, and knew she'd feel even better tomorrow. She'd talk to Aunt Maudie; that always gave her a lift. Then she'd look for a pawnshop.... No, she couldn't do that tomorrow, because it was Sunday and they'd be closed. But she'd do it first thing Monday morning. She had to have money, in case they needed to leave town in a hurry.

Thea reached over to turn out the bedside lamp, then grinned as a sudden thought occurred to her. Living in the same house with a lawman for a couple of days might work to her advantage. It would put her above suspicion.

Who'd ever think to look for a criminal in the local D.A.'s home?

Chapter Four

The car had Missouri license plates.

Quint wondered why he hadn't noticed them yesterday. Curious, and slightly winded from his morning run, he slowed to a walk and approached the Ford. He tried first one door, then another. All four were locked.

There wasn't anything really unusual about that; most people locked their car doors, even in a remote little South Georgia town like Planters' Junction. What was unusual was that Thea and her sons supposedly had come here from California, yet their car had license plates from another state.

Quint sighed. Her affairs were none of his business. Thea had made it perfectly clear last night, when he had innocently quizzed her about her trip. "You keep bombarding me with all these questions!" she had said, almost shouting. *So let it be,* he told himself. He had enough problems of his own without prying into anyone else's.

His son J.R. was one of them, although Quint felt relatively sure that the boy would be all right as soon as Miss Maudie came home and he saw that not everybody who was sick or injured would automatically die, as his mother had.

Alfie was another matter altogether. She was breaking Quint's heart. He loved her, yet seemed unable to get through to her, never mind establish a friendly relationship with her.

Part of the problem was her age. Alfie was ten now, on the brink of puberty, but had been only seven when her mother first became ill. A child. A very frightened child. Her mother hadn't helped things any. As soon as Sally learned she was going to die, she had retreated into her own private hell, pretending her children didn't even exist.

Quint didn't blame Sally; not everyone faced death gallantly. He only wished she had tried to make her fatal illness a little less traumatic for their child. He had tried to nurture Alfie as much as he could, but the increasing demands Sally made on his time and attention had eroded the tenuous relationship he had had with his daughter.

She had ended up hating him, feeling he was somehow responsible, not only for her mother's death, but for the breakup of their home and family. The memory of Alfie's accusing eyes at her mother's funeral was burned into his mind for eternity.

Yes, he had enough problems with his own family without meddling in Thea Cameron's affairs. Quint turned from the car and started toward the house. Thea would be gone soon enough and he'd probably never see her again. He'd steer clear of her as much as possible and let her keep her precious privacy and her secrets until then.

Still, he couldn't quite forget the desperate look he'd seen in her frightened brown eyes, and he couldn't help wondering about the Missouri license plates.

THEA'S EYES FLEW OPEN. Her heart pounded wildly and the cotton T-shirt and briefs she used for a nightgown were wet with sweat. She had been dreaming, an awful nightmare about a terrible man who'd come to take away her children.

Her children! Thea threw back the covers and bolted out of bed, racing for the door in blind panic. Flinging it open, she raced into the hall. Whump! She felt as if she'd collided with a stone wall. Then she noticed the stone wall had muscled arms and strong hands that were holding her shoulders in a firm grasp.

"In a bit of a rush, are you?" Quint said.

Thea looked into the handsome masculine face only inches from her now. "I . . . I had a nightmare. I was going to check on the boys."

Quint nodded, releasing his grip on her shoulders and gesturing toward Alan and Max's bedroom.

Feeling a little foolish, but still wanting to reassure herself, she hurried across the hall and opened their bedroom door. Bright sunlight streaming through the window caused her to blink, but seemed to have no effect on the boys. They were both still asleep. Alan was curled on his side in his favorite fetal position; Max was on his stomach with his rump in the air, a habit that had been carried over from babyhood.

Thea gave a sigh of relief, closed the door and turned back to Quint.

His expression was guarded. She didn't understand it until she suddenly remembered what she was wearing—a thin T-shirt, a wet one at that, and the skimpiest of bikini briefs.

Should she ignore his look and pretend she didn't know what he was seeing? What she really wanted to do was clasp her arms across her chest. It took every ounce of willpower she had not to do it.

She forced herself to remember she wasn't a shy young innocent; it wasn't as if a man had never seen her before. She lifted her chin and stared back at him. It wasn't her fault that he'd been coming down the hall at the same time she'd come out to check on her sons.

And what about the way *he* was dressed? A cotton T-shirt even wetter than her own, and brief running shorts that hugged his slim hips and accentuated... She quickly shifted her gaze back to his face.

"Why is your T-shirt wet?" she asked. She was as surprised by her sudden question as he seemed to be.

"I've been running," he answered, making a rapid recovery. "I do it almost every morning."

"Oh."

"And as long as we're asking personal questions..."

She braced herself for a comment about her own wet T-shirt, but he surprised her.

"Why does your car have Missouri license plates?"

The question caught her completely unprepared. What could she say? Contrary to what she'd told him the night before, she and her sons hadn't spent two weeks on the road visiting tourist attractions. They had been busy covering their trail; selling the Mercedes her ex-husband had given her while they were still married—one he would surely be able to trace in no time—taking a bus to another state before buying the used Ford; then slowly weaving their way to Georgia, keeping to less-traveled roads and frequently backtracking.

She remembered hearing somewhere that when you tell a lie, you should stick as close to the truth as possible to make the lie more plausible. "It's a used car," she said. "I bought it just before we left, and didn't have time to get new plates."

Quint nodded his head, accepting her explanation.

Thea didn't want to press her luck. She needed to get away before he could ask any more questions, questions she wasn't prepared to answer in her present state of mind. "If you'll excuse me now, I'd like to get showered and dressed. Then I'll go down and start breakfast."

"You don't have to do that."

"I'd like to. I make great pancakes, if I do say so myself."

"Sounds good."

She rushed back to her room, trying not to think about the gleam she'd seen in Quint's eyes. She needed the protection of proper clothes before she faced him again. She refused to think about the fleeting suspicion that she also wanted to escape the sight of him in those revealing shorts.

Later, dressed in her last fresh shirt and clean jeans, Thea made her way to the kitchen. She was relieved to find it empty, but Quint had obviously been there sometime before her. A fresh pot of coffee sat on the counter. She closed her eyes and inhaled deeply, savoring the pungent aroma for a long moment.

Then she got busy with breakfast. She knew exactly what she was going to fix—fresh strawberries and cream for starters, followed by her own special recipe for pancakes—and crisp bacon. Lots of it. Maybe sausage, too. Why not?

The bacon was fried, the strawberries were cleaned, cored, and draining in the colander, and the pancake batter was ready to be poured when Thea suddenly felt the back of her neck prickle. Somebody was in the room, watching her. She whirled around.

A young girl stood in the doorway. Tall. Too thin in too-short jeans. Long, raven-black hair. Eyes the color of a midnight sky.

"You must be Alfie," Thea said, smiling and wiping her hands on a towel as she headed toward the girl.

"Who the hell are you?"

Thea halted in her tracks, her smile dying a quick death as the memory of J.R. uttering those same words—almost the same—flashed through her mind.

"I'm Thea Cameron," she said. "Miss Maudie's niece. My two sons and I are here for a visit. A very short visit, you understand. We'll be gone in no time." Realizing she was babbling, she stopped.

The girl said nothing.

"You *are* Alfie Richards, aren't you?" Thea finally prompted.

The girl gave one quick, sullen nod.

"I'm making breakfast. Would you like some?"

"I'm not hungry."

"It's pancakes," Thea persisted. "The griddle's already hot, and it'll only take about thirty seconds to cook you a batch."

Seeing Alfie hesitate, Thea pressed the point. "You can have some fresh strawberries while the pancakes are cooking."

Alfie still didn't speak, and didn't take her blue eyes off Thea, but she did walk over to the table, pull out a chair and sit down. Thea supposed it was a victory of sorts. Without pausing to savor it, she rushed to serve the strawberries.

While the pancakes were cooking, Thea glanced over her shoulder at Alfie. The girl was eating strawberries as fast as she could. Smiling, Thea flipped the pancakes, then cleared her throat to get Alfie's attention. "I understand you're ten years old. What grade are you in?"

"Fourth."

"I remember fourth grade. I loved it. Do you like school?"

Alfie shrugged and turned her attention back to the strawberries.

Well, so much for that scintillating conversation, Thea thought. She picked up the pancakes and started to butter them, then thought better of it. Instead, she brought the butter to the table, along with Alfie's plate of pancakes.

"Breakfast is now served," she said. "Bacon, sausage and syrup are on the table."

Alfie looked at her plate, then back to Thea. "The pancakes aren't buttered."

"No, they aren't. I thought you'd want to butter them yourself, so you can have them the way you like them. My son Alan insists on buttering his own, but I'll do yours if you want me to."

Thea reached for Alfie's plate, but the girl held up her hand. "No! I'll do it."

"Okay. Would you like me to get you some milk?"

"Yes," Alfie mumbled, picking up a knife to cut the butter.

"Yes what?"

Alfie looked up with a puzzled expression on her face.

"Aunt Maudie always gave me holy hell if I didn't say please and thank you," Thea explained. "Doesn't she do that to you?"

One corner of Alfie's mouth twitched. "Sometimes."

"Right. So would you like me to bring you some milk?"

"Yes, please."

Thea winked. "Gotcha."

She poured Alfie's milk and a cup of coffee for herself, and brought them to the table. "Here's your milk."

"Thank you," Alfie said very formally.

Thea was delighted to see a mischievous twinkle in the girl's beautiful blue eyes. "You're welcome. Do you mind if I sit with you for a minute? The pancakes are better when they're hot, and I don't want to cook any more until somebody else comes down to eat. Okay?"

Alfie hesitated briefly. "Okay."

Thea sipped her coffee in silence while the girl buttered her pancakes with extreme care, spreading the butter evenly over the entire surface. Finally, after she had the pancakes buttered and syruped to her satisfaction, she took a bite. Thea was surprised to find herself holding her breath.

"These are good," Alfie said.

Thea released her breath. "Thank you. They're my specialty."

The girl took another bite. "They're really good."

"I'll teach you how to make them if you'd like."

Alfie frowned and Thea knew she'd gone too far. "I mean, if there's time enough before we leave."

"When are you leaving?"

"I'm not sure. I haven't seen Aunt Maudie in quite a few years. I wanted her to get to know my sons...." Thea wondered why she was feeling so guilty talking to Alfie like this; she wasn't lying this time.

Then she knew. She wasn't lying, but she wasn't telling the whole truth either, and Alfie didn't deserve to be deceived, not even a little bit. "A lot of other things are involved, too, but that wasn't your question, was it? We might be here for a few days, maybe as long as a week or two. Would you mind?"

"Me?"

"Yes."

"Why are you asking me?"

"Because you live here, and I don't want to make you unhappy," Thea said. "Would you mind if my sons and I stayed here with you and your family in Aunt Maudie's house for a while?"

"How old are your sons?"

Thea grinned. "You're pretty smart. That's a good question. Alan is seven and Max is five."

Alfie made a face.

"What?" Thea asked.

"I have a little brother. He's five, too, and he's a real brat."

"We've already met J.R. He tied and lassoed Alan and Max as soon as we arrived yesterday afternoon."

"Really?"

Thea crossed her heart with her finger. "Word of honor."

"Were they mad?"

"Furious."

"I told you J.R. was a terror," Alfie said with a certain amount of pride.

"I am not a terrier!" exclaimed J.R.

Thea and Alfie looked around, to see Quint shooing three fresh-faced boys into the room. "The guys and I got a whiff of all those good breakfast smells coming from down here," Quint began. He stopped when Alfie sprang from her chair and pushed it back so hard that it toppled over.

"Alfie..." Quint said as the girl started for the door.

"Don't you want to finish your breakfast?" Thea shouted.

"I'm not hungry!"

Thea watched Quint's face crumble. The incredible sorrow in his blue eyes was like nothing she'd ever seen before; she hoped never to see it again. She could tell he was terribly hurt, and was grateful that he turned away before she had to. He walked to the counter and poured himself a mug of coffee. His hand shook.

Blinking rapidly to push back tears that threatened to overflow, she went to the stove to cook more pancakes.

QUINT DIPPED THE BRUSH into the can of white paint, then slapped it against the weathered siding of the house, spreading the paint in long strokes. Repeating the movements again and again, he worked steadily, even relentlessly, ignoring the sweat that dripped from his brow and formed a trail down his cheeks and neck. At times like this he didn't stop for anything. He was exorcising his demons.

He didn't know why Alfie's attitude still upset him so much after all this time. He should be used to it by now. And he was, but it still bothered him, bothered the hell out of him. He'd never felt so helpless in his life, loving her, wanting to help her, yet being totally unable to penetrate her armor. Damn! What would it take for him to get through to her?

Thea had broken through the barrier. From the easy, relaxed way the two of them had been talking to each other this morning before Alfie noticed *he* came into the room, he knew that Thea had already established a rapport with his daughter. How had she done it? And so quickly, too.

Maybe he should ask her advice.

And maybe snow would start falling out of the sky some May morning.

Suddenly an image of Thea unexpectedly flashed through his mind—Thea as he'd first seen her this morning—her lips soft and pink and her face flushed from sleep. He remembered her tousled hair and bare legs, the latter long, slim and tanned golden. And he remembered his body's instant reaction to the sight of her breasts, clearly outlined and almost visible through her sweat-soaked T-shirt.

Unfortunately he remembered her response to his body's reaction, as well. She had boldly challenged him at first, staring him straight in the eye, and he had admired her for that. But then she had practically knocked him over in her haste to run away. Did she think he was going to jump her in the hall, right outside the bedroom where her sons were sleeping? Did she think he was some sort of perverted monster?

Probably.

He sighed. Sharing a house with a healthy, attractive woman was becoming more of a strain than he'd suspected when he insisted Thea move in with them during her visit.

It was just as well that she'd be leaving soon. After she was gone, he could put the whole thing behind him and get on with his life, such as it was.

"Quint?"

He looked down and saw Thea standing at the bottom of the ladder, her hand lifted to shade her eyes from the sun. Or maybe she was trying to block him from her view. "Hi," he said.

"We're almost ready to visit Aunt Maudie now, and I need directions on how to get to the nursing home."

"I'll be right down."

"You needn't—" she began, but he'd already placed the brush on top of the paint can and started down the ladder.

"You're a really fast painter," Thea said when Quint reached the ground. "I'm amazed at how much you've covered in such a short time."

He looked up to the second story, following the direction of her gaze, and was surprised himself. He must have been painting even more furiously than he'd thought. He was surprised, too, to find himself pleased that she'd paid attention to his activities.

He had been acutely aware of what she had been doing, of course. Earlier he'd seen her go to her car, unlock the trunk, pull out a bundle of clothes and carry them into the house. Later he'd seen her return the clothes—clean, pressed and neatly folded—to that same trunk.

"It's easier to paint fast when you're that high up," he said. "It's so far away from the ground that people can't see the spots you've missed."

She laughed; it was a light, feminine sound that floated through the spring sunshine. Glancing at her, Quint thought she looked a bit like spring herself in a soft green dress that enhanced her tan and clung to her graceful, slim figure. Nobody—especially someone who was as prickly and secretive as Thea Cameron was these days—had a right to look and sound so appealing.

"If you'll give me a couple of minutes to wash up, I'll drive you to the nursing home," Quint said. He hadn't forgotten his resolve to steer clear of her as much as possible, but thought he owed it to Aunt Maudie to make the offer.

"That's not necessary, unless you want to visit her, too."

"I'll see her tomorrow. She already knows I was planning to paint today."

Thea nodded. "What about J.R.? Would he like to come along?" she asked, carefully avoiding the subject of Alfie, who'd been holed up in her room since breakfast.

"No, thanks."

"I thought that since Alan and Max would be going—"

"J.R. doesn't visit her in the nursing home, period. I forced him to go once, against his will. He screamed the entire time and upset Miss Maudie so much she—" Quint paused. "I promised her I'd never make him go back there again."

"Oh."

"Besides, you and your sons need some time to visit alone with her."

Thea listened quietly while Quint gave her directions.

EVEN THOUGH THEA WANTED to see Aunt Maudie, she dreaded facing her. She loved her aunt, but knew just how formidable Maude Hazzard Arnold Brewster could be, and how hard she was to deceive. Thea had never been able to hide anything from her as a child; she could only hope that her aunt would accept her children and herself without too many questions now. If not, she and the boys might be off again even sooner than she'd thought.

Thea stopped outside the door to Aunt Maudie's room and looked down at her sons, freshly scrubbed and dressed in the clean clothes she'd washed that morning. "Boys, why don't you wait out here while I go in first and say hello?"

Alan looked worried, and even fearless Maxie seemed a little skeptical about the plan. Both of them were intimidated by the bustle and antiseptic air of the nursing home. Thea didn't blame them; she was a little intimidated by the place herself. She was also nervous about the prospect of facing her aunt.

"It'll be okay," she reassured them. "I'll be back out to get you in no time." Squaring her shoulders, she took a deep breath, pushed the door open and stepped inside her aunt's room.

The tiny woman sat in a wheelchair beside the casement window, watching a squirrel that was perched on the ledge outside. The squirrel watched her, too; in fact the fascination seemed to be mutual. Neither moved, and since both were oblivious to Thea's presence, she took the opportunity to study her aunt.

Surprisingly, in spite of her recent accident, Aunt Maudie looked much the same as she had thirteen years ago— sharp nose, high cheekbones, dark, flashing eyes. She had a few more wrinkles, but on her they added even more character to a well-worn face that already had plenty. Barely five feet tall, and seeming smaller than that in her wheelchair, Aunt Maudie still commanded attention. And she still colored her hair the same ghastly orange-red shade she always had, Thea noticed with a grin.

She cleared her throat. "Aunt Maudie?"

The older woman turned from the window with an impatient frown on her face at the interruption. The frown slowly faded and was replaced first by surprise, then by incredulity. "Theodora?"

Thea took a hesitant step toward her. "Yes."

"It's really you?"

"Oh, yes!" She ran the rest of the way and flung her arms around Aunt Maudie's neck. "It's really me."

"I can't believe it!"

"It's so good to see you again!"

"Oh, my dear, you don't know how good it is to... Oh, dear."

They held on to each other for a long time.

At last her aunt pushed her away, but not far, and still held Thea's hand, grasping it with her small, bony fingers. "I can't believe it," Aunt Maudie repeated.

"And I can't believe you look so great. I didn't know what to expect after your terrible accident."

"Did you come because of the accident? And why didn't you let me know you were coming?"

"I didn't know I was coming myself until the last minute. It was a spur-of-the-moment thing." Thea hesitated. "And I didn't know about the accident until I got here," she admitted. "Quint told me about it when we arrived yesterday."

Aunt Maudie brightened at the mention of Quint's name. "Ah, that darlin' young man. He's been so good to me."

Thea stiffened. She was wrong, she knew—it was selfish—but she couldn't help feeling a little resentful because that darlin' young man, the district attorney, no less, was living in Aunt Maudie's house. If it weren't for him, her sons might be in a safe home now for a long, long time.

"From what Quint told me, you've been good to him, too, taking him and his family in the way you did."

"It wasn't anything anyone else wouldn't have done," Aunt Maudie insisted, waving her hand in dismissal. "But did you say 'we' arrived? Did someone else come with you?"

Thea smiled. "Alan, Junior, and Max are here."

Aunt Maudie clasped one hand to her throat. "You brought your sons?"

"I certainly did. They're waiting right outside. I'll go get—" Thea began, starting for the door.

"No!"

Thea stopped in midstride.

"I can't let them see me like this the first time we meet," Aunt Maudie declared. "Bring me my comb and mirror so I can make myself presentable."

A few minutes later Thea escorted Alan and Max into the room and presented them to her aunt.

"So," Aunt Maudie said as soon as they'd been introduced, "did your mother ever tell you about the time she was swinging from a rope in the barn and fell and broke her arm?"

"Our mom?" Alan asked in disbelief.

"No kidding?" Max said.

Aunt Maudie launched into the story, embellishing the details outrageously. She was a born storyteller, following the tale of Thea breaking her arm with another long story, then another. Her audience was enthralled. Alan and Max both protested when she finally said, "Now I want to talk to your mother alone for a bit."

They capitulated when she gave them change for the snack machines in the lobby.

"Well," Aunt Maudie said when the boys were out of the room, "you've done a fine job, Thea. They're marvelous children."

"You're just saying that because they liked your stories."

"It shows they have good taste. They're a lot like their mother," Aunt Maudie continued. "You always enjoyed my tall tales, too, as I remember."

"I adored them! And you, too," she added quietly.

Aunt Maudie made a production of rearranging the afghan covering her legs. "Yes, well... Tell me what else Quint told you yesterday."

The command caught Thea by surprise. "Not too much, really. He said he was left with a lot of debts after his wife died, and you invited him to move in with you."

"I didn't invite. I insisted."

Thea grinned. "I can imagine."

"And I'll tell you a secret, Thea. Quint Richards has done more for me—much more—than I'll ever be able to do for him."

Thea didn't know what to say.

"When you get to be my age, with no children and with your closest relatives living hundreds of miles away... Well, let's just say Quint has been like a son to me. He has shared himself and his family with me, shown me kindness and love...." The older woman's voice broke.

Thea was ashamed of the selfish resentment she'd felt toward Quint earlier. "He...he seems to be a fine man."

"You're darn right he is!" Aunt Maudie said, recovering her composure. "He's made all sorts of repairs around that old house of mine, too. I hadn't realized the place was so run-down."

Thea nodded, relieved to be in less emotionally threatening territory. "He was painting when I left this afternoon."

"Did you know he pays all the household expenses, too?" Another surprise. "No."

"He wouldn't move in unless I agreed to it." Aunt Maudie shook her head, and Thea saw a loving expression on her face. "That man can be almost as stubborn as I am. He even insists on paying my housekeeper."

"Housekeeper? I didn't see her."

"Betsy has Saturday afternoons and Sundays off."

Thea's eyes widened. "It's not the same Betsy who used to work for you years ago...!"

"It certainly is. She thinks the house would fall apart without her to run it, and she's probably right."

"I hope I get to see her."

"Of course you'll get to see her. She'll be there tomorrow...." Aunt Maudie stopped and frowned. "Aren't you staying at my house?"

"We stayed there last night, but—"

"You're not planning to leave right away, are you? You just got here."

"Well...we were on our way to Florida. Of course I wanted to stop by and visit you, but..."

"But what?"

"I don't know how long we can stay."

"You'll have to stay at least a few weeks. I insist."

"I don't think so, Aunt Maudie. What with Quint and his family living there, too..."

"What does that have to do with anything? Surely you're not worried about gossip?"

"Not really." That was true in a sense, but Thea didn't want to broadcast her presence in Planters' Junction by having the whole town talking about her, either.

"Then what's the problem?" When Thea didn't answer, Aunt Maudie frowned again, then broke into a broad, wicked grin. "It's Quint! You're attracted to him!"

"No!"

"I don't blame you. I'd be attracted to him myself, if I were your age. Or even twice your age."

"I'm not—"

"There's nothing wrong with it, you know. He's a widower now and you're divorced, so..."

"I am not attracted to him, Aunt Maudie," Thea said evenly.

"You're not still eating your heart out over that fancy Alan Kirkland you married, are you?"

"Absolutely not."

"In that case, Quint would be perfect for you. He's kind, loving, and he's as bright as you. Did you know he graduated with honors from Harvard Law?"

"Please, Aunt Maudie!" Thea said. "I am not in the market for a man."

"And Quint is so—"

"*Any* man. Even your precious Quint Richards," she insisted. In spite of her protesting, an unwanted image of Quint in his shiny running shorts flashed into her mind. There was no denying that he was physically attractive. More than that. He was downright sexy. Vibrantly, gloriously male. Outrageously appealing. Dangerous.

She cleared her throat and got up to leave. "I'd better find my boys and take them home now. They're probably getting antsy."

"Will you come again tomorrow?"

"Yes, if you'll promise to stop matchmaking for me."

"If you insist. But perhaps you're not as bright as I always thought you were."

"Probably not," Thea agreed. "Is there any message you want me to give Quint and his family?"

"Just tell them hello for me."

"What about J.R? Any special message for him?"

Thea was dismayed to see sudden tears well up in her aunt's eyes at the mention of J.R.'s name. She realized almost as suddenly that Aunt Maudie loved J.R. as much as he loved her. They were both being torn apart by the pain of their separation.

The older woman ducked her head. "No special message," she whispered.

Thea nodded and swallowed a lump in her throat. She could almost feel her aunt's anguish. It was that strong. She wished she could do something to help ease it, but she couldn't.

She'd already made her choices. There were only two people in her life who mattered now—Alan and Max—and she'd committed everything she had to them. She would protect them at any cost, with her own life, if necessary.

She had nothing to offer anyone else. Nothing.

Chapter Five

A late-model Oldsmobile was parked in the driveway at Aunt Maudie's house when Thea and her sons returned from the nursing home. She briefly considered turning her car around and driving away until whoever it was had gone.

The thought came too late. A tall, auburn-haired woman was already getting out of the Olds and waving to her. Thea reluctantly killed her engine and got out, too.

"Hi, there. You must be Thea Cameron," the woman said.

Thea's first reaction was alarm. How did this person know her name? Was she a policewoman? She calmed down as soon as she got a better look at the woman. Police didn't come to arrest you wearing expensive silk dresses and three-inch heels. And they didn't smile at you and hold out their hands the way this woman was.

"I'm Liz Bartlett, a friend of Quint's."

Thea extended her own sweaty palm to accept the proffered handshake. "How do you do?"

"Quint has told me so much about you."

"Really?" Thea knew Liz Bartlett was lying. Quint didn't know all that much about her; she'd made sure of that. And even if he had known, she felt instinctively that he wouldn't have blabbed it around. "These are my sons," she said.

After the introductions, Alan looked at Thea. "Mom, is it okay if we go to the barn to play?"

"I suppose so. But change out of your good clothes first." The boys were off at a run.

"Nice kids," Liz said.

"Thanks."

"I understand you're from California."

"That's right. Uh, do you live here in Planters' Junction?"

"In Deadsville, you mean?" Liz said, lifting a perfectly arched brow and rolling her expressive green eyes. "I'm afraid so, for the time being at least. I moved back after my divorce last year."

Liz was extraordinarily attractive. Thea wondered briefly just how good a friend of Quint's she was. "The town is that bad?"

"Worse. This place is so dull it makes Mr. Rogers's neighborhood seem hedonistic by comparison." Liz lowered her voice and spoke in a confidential whisper. "But I have zis plan, you zee. I'm making my getaway zoon."

Thea laughed.

"I've been trying to convince Quint he should get out of here, too."

"And?"

"He's being his usual stoic, cautious self so far. He keeps spouting off about how much his kids need a stable environment and all that kind of rubbish."

"There is something to be said for it."

"It's a cop-out. What he's really doing is staying around this dump because of some misguided sense of loyalty toward Sally. He doesn't realize he doesn't owe her anything. He's already more than paid his dues."

"I don't understand," Thea said. "I thought they were so happy together."

"Don't get me wrong." Liz held up her hand. "They were happy at one time. And Sally was my friend when we were growing up, too. But you wouldn't believe all the grief and the guilt trips she piled on him while she was dying. She made that man's life a living hell for more than two years."

If Sally had done that to Quint, perhaps she was the cause of some of Alfie's problems, too, Thea thought, looking at the situation in a new light.

"But enough about that depressing subject," Liz said, linking her arm with Thea's and pulling her toward her car. "Come help me carry the goodies I brought into the house. Then after we raid Miss Maudie's refrigerator and throw together a potluck supper, I'll start practicing my feminine wiles on Quint again."

Sudden anxiety swept through Thea. She had resigned herself to facing Quint, at least at mealtimes, but the idea of fending off questions both from him and from someone as intuitive as Liz was too much.

She saw Liz glance at her and stop abruptly. What had she seen? Thea tried again to hide her feelings, but it was too late.

"What is it?" Liz asked.

"Nothing. I just wasn't prepared for... I mean I wasn't expecting..."

"Company?" She saw Liz look at her shrewdly, obviously assessing the situation. "Or competition? Are you interested in Quint for yourself?"

"No!"

"That was a pretty violent reaction. What's the old saying about protesting too much?"

"No, I really mean it." For the second time that afternoon, Thea found herself denying any romantic interest in Quint Richards. "I'm not interested in him or any other man."

"Why not?"

What could she tell Liz? The truth was, she had nothing against men in general. In fact, the idea of being in love again, of sharing her life with another human being, was enormously appealing. But she didn't dare allow herself to get close enough to a man to become interested in him. It was too dangerous.

Thea hated having to lie, yet now she was constantly caught up in telling one falsehood after another. "I was divorced not too long ago...and things got pretty messy."

"So now you're man-shy, huh?"

"Something like that."

"I'm sorry."

"Thanks."

"But I'm glad, too."

"What?"

"I'm glad because it means we're not after the same man. And *that* means we can be friends, right?"

Thea had to laugh at Liz's candor. "Right."

"So c'mon, buddy. Help me get this stuff out of the car."

They were at the front door, their arms loaded with food, when Quint suddenly appeared. "Alan told me you were... Good grief! What did you bring, Liz, the entire menu from the Main Street Café?"

"I'll have you know I cooked all this wonderfully nutritious, delicious food myself. Here, grab this pie before I drop it."

He laughed, a rumbling male sound that came from deep in his chest. Thea had never heard that kind of relaxed response from Quint, and felt a little envious of the easy camaraderie between him and Liz. They were obviously right for each other. So why didn't that make her happier?

Quint took a casserole from Thea's arms, too, and the three of them made their way to the kitchen. Once there,

Quint took a seat at the kitchen table and Liz, obviously familiar with the place, set about serving supper.

Thea felt like a fifth wheel, definitely in the way, but didn't know how to make a graceful exit. She finally offered to slice the leftover roast beef she'd seen in the refrigerator.

"That's a wonderful idea," Liz said.

Feeling like a puppy who'd just been rewarded with a pat on the head, Thea went to the refrigerator and got the roast. She selected a sharp knife from the rack on the wall and started carving.

"I brought a bottle of wine," Liz said. "Why don't you make yourself useful and pour us a glass, Quint?"

"Sure thing."

Thea didn't turn around, but could hear the sound of his chair being pushed back, and could feel the slight vibration of the floor as he moved across it. Or was that her imagination? It must have been, because suddenly he was standing right beside her.

He must have showered and shaved after he finished painting, she realized. His cheeks were smooth, and she caught a faint whiff of cologne. He held out a glass, and his blue eyes pinned her to the spot with their intensity.

"Wine, Thea?"

His voice was like deep velvet. She swallowed. "Thank you."

"My pleasure."

Their fingers brushed when she took the wineglass. Thea turned her head suddenly and saw Liz watching them with narrowed eyes. Damn! Liz would be sure to think she'd lied to her about not being interested in Quint.

"A toast!" Liz said after a moment.

Thea watched the other woman raise her glass in Quint's direction. "To old friends," Liz said, gazing at him with a look that could have coaxed a bee into surrendering his entire year's supply of honey.

"And to new friends," Liz continued, turning toward Thea. She still wore a smile, but somehow it didn't seem as open and friendly as it had earlier.

After the toast, Thea put her glass onto the counter and was about to start carving again when J.R. suddenly burst into the kitchen. His face was flushed and his eyes were big. Scared.

"Dad! Come quick! There's been an accident!"

Thea's heart stopped beating.

"Where?" Quint asked, starting for the door.

"In the barn. Maxie's hurt bad!"

"No!" Thea exclaimed, pushing past Liz and J.R. and racing out the door right behind Quint. By the time she reached the bottom of the steps, he was already yards ahead of her, his long legs carrying him at full speed toward the barn.

Thea cursed herself for not changing shoes as soon as she got back from the nursing home. Her medium heels weren't meant for running and she stumbled several times, almost falling. But she didn't slow down and she didn't dare let herself think about what might be waiting for them inside the old building.

She was panting for breath by the time she finally reached the barn, and didn't know whether the terrible pain in her chest was from running or from fear. She didn't care. Nothing mattered now except her baby.

She saw him as soon as she stepped inside the door, lying on the floor. Not moving. She raced to his side. Quint was already there, kneeling beside him, exploring his sturdy little body with gentle hands.

Her heart caught in her throat when she got her first glimpse of Max's face. He was pale—she'd never seen anyone so pale—almost blue. But he was alive. *Thank you, God,* she thought as she dropped to her knees beside him and reached out a shaky hand to touch his forehead. It was cold and clammy.

"I hurt myself, Mom," Max whispered. He hadn't been crying before, but now a single big tear welled into one eye and rolled down his dirty cheek.

"I know, darling, but we'll take care of you." She picked up his grimy, pudgy hand and brought it to her lips.

"I was a bad boy."

She could hardly see him through her own tears, but shook her head emphatically. "We won't talk about that now."

"I love you, Mom."

"And I love you, always and always." She leaned over to kiss his cheek, his lips, then his other cheek. "And you'll be okay. I promise." She glanced at Quint for confirmation and saw him motion with his head toward Max's right leg.

She looked at it and felt sick. Twisted at a funny angle below the knee, it was already beginning to swell. She wiped away her tears with the back of her hand to see it better, then glanced at Quint again.

"Broken?" She mouthed the word so as not to frighten Max any more than he already was. Quint nodded his head.

"Anything else?" she whispered.

"I can't be sure, but I don't think so."

"Good Lord, look at that leg!"

Thea and Quint turned around simultaneously to see Liz, who had just walked in with J.R.

"Be quiet, Liz," Quint commanded in a steely voice.

"But the leg's obviously broken."

"I told you to—"

"Am I gonna die?" Max asked, his voice quivering.

"Of course not!" Thea stated emphatically.

"People get broken bones all the time," Quint said. "Miss Maudie broke her hip, and you saw how—"

"I don't wanna hear this!" J.R. shouted and bolted for the barn door.

"Oh, dear," Thea said. "I'm sorry that happened."

Quint sighed. "It couldn't be helped. I guess." He flashed Liz an angry look, then turned back to Max. "I'll tell you exactly what's going to happen, sport. We're going to take you to the emergency room at the hospital. The doctors will set your leg and put it in a big white plaster cast, about yea big." Quint made a big circle with both hands. "After that, we'll bring you back home and put you to bed. And tomorrow we'll all write our names and draw funny pictures on your cast."

"Will it hurt?"

"It'll hurt some."

"It already hurts."

"The doctors will give you something to make it feel better."

"A shot?"

Quint nodded. "It's possible."

"I hate shots!"

"So do I, but they only sting for a little bit, right?"

"I guess so."

"And don't you always feel better afterward?"

Thea watched Quint with admiration. He was talking to her son quietly, honestly, matter-of-factly...reassuring him without raising false hopes and expectations. She felt enormous gratitude toward this strong, gentle, caring man.

What would she have done if the accident had happened somewhere else, someplace where there wasn't a Quint around? What if it had happened when she and her sons had been alone? She shuddered.

Quint finally got to his feet. "Okay, here's the plan, gang." He winked at Max. "I'll go to the house and get some blankets and pillows and then drive my station wagon as close to the barn as possible. I'm sure Thea will want to go with Max and me to the hospital, so would you mind feeding and taking care of the other kids until we get back, Liz?"

"Of course not."

"Alan goes with me," Thea said.

Quint and Liz both looked at her, but neither protested. They probably knew it wouldn't have done any good if they had. There was no way on this earth that she was going to be separated from either of her sons tonight.

"IT WAS ALL MY FAULT, Mom," Alan said quietly.

Quint took a quick glance at the boy sitting in the passenger seat beside him. Alan stared straight ahead, his face grave; it was much too grave and weary for a seven-year-old kid.

Thea didn't respond immediately. Then Quint heard her warm, rich voice coming from the back of the station wagon, where she was crouched on the blankets they'd spread out so Max could lie flat. "How do you figure that?"

"I was the one who strung up the rope we were swinging on."

Another pause. Then, "I see."

Alan swiveled around as much as he could while strapped inside the shoulder harness of the seat belt. "We got the idea from Aunt Maudie, when she was telling us about how you used to swing on a rope in the barn."

"Did you also remember her telling you how I fell and broke my arm?"

"I guess we forgot."

"I guess."

Alan turned back and lowered his head. "I'm sorry, Mom."

"Tell me, Alan. Did the rope come loose? Is that how Max fell?"

"No, ma'am! I swung from it first and it held just fine."

"Did you force Max to swing on the rope?"

"No! He begged me to let him do it! J.R. wanted to swing next, but I figured I'd be nice to Maxie, since he was my brother and all."

Quint compressed his lips to hold back his comments...and his snicker.

"Well, Alan," Thea said, "obviously no more swinging from ropes in the barn will be allowed. But since the rope held, and since it was Max's own decision to swing from it, I don't see how we could hold you responsible. We'll put this incident behind us. Everybody's been punished enough."

Quint heard Alan release a long sigh of relief. He reached over to pat the boy's bony leg and saw Alan's sheepish, lopsided grin outlined by the glare from the dashboard.

When they reached the hospital, Quint left the others in the car while he went inside to get a stretcher for Max. He didn't think there were internal injuries, but it was always better to be cautious. Two emergency room technicians came back with him to load Maxie onto the stretcher.

Quint offered to fill out the emergency room admission forms, but Thea insisted on doing it. "You stay with Max. Please. He trusts you."

Quint started to protest that her son trusted her, too, and might be more at ease with his mother, but stopped himself when he saw the doelike pleading in her brown eyes. There was no way he could deliberately hurt Bambi.

He shrugged and accompanied Max into the treatment room, taking Alan with them. Quint held one of Max's hands, and Alan held the other, while a young doctor examined the broken leg, then probed thoroughly for other injuries.

Thea rushed into the room only moments later, frantic and close to hysteria. "They want to know how I'm going to pay for Maxie's treatment!"

"That's no problem," Quint said, dropping Max's hand and heading toward her.

"But don't you see? I don't have any money!"

He grabbed her shoulders and squeezed hard. "Stop it, Thea."

"You have to understand. I—"

"I said it was no problem. My insurance will take care of everything."

"I can't—" She stopped and blinked rapidly. "What did you say?"

"I said my homeowner's insurance will cover it."

"Are you sure?"

"Thea, I'm a lawyer, remember? I know about these things."

"And your insurance will . . ."

"Pay all expenses. I told you that you should have let me handle the admission. Stay here with Max while I go straighten this out."

She seemed to deflate like a punctured balloon, and grabbed the side of Max's stretcher for support. Quint looked at her and frowned. "Will you be okay if I leave you alone with the boys?"

She nodded and kept on nodding. She was still nodding when he reached the door and looked back. He debated with himself for a moment, then rushed out to deal with the admissions clerk.

Max had already been given a painkiller by the time he returned. Thea, although a trifle pale, seemed to be in control of herself again.

"I'm sorry I panicked a while ago," she apologized.

"It's okay. I understand."

"It was just that they were saying they couldn't treat Max without . . . And I didn't have the money." She stopped and blinked. "I do have money, you understand. I just didn't bring any with me."

Quint nodded, unsure whether to believe her. This was no time to argue about it, though. She needed all his support, and he was prepared to provide it. Poor Thea. What it must have been like for her! First, seeing her son looking like death warmed-over after his accident, then rushing to the hospital, only to be told they wouldn't treat Max unless she proved she could pay for it!

He had read about hospitals setting up rules like that, but hadn't known that it happened in Planters' Junction. It was immoral, if not illegal, and he planned to look into it as soon as he got the chance. In the meantime he needed to take care of Thea. He wanted to be there for her if she needed him.

He was ashamed of how he'd maligned her by thinking she was irresponsible because she took her sons out of school to come to Georgia. Seeing her tonight, no one could doubt her total devotion to them. Her children were more important to her than anything else. "Alan goes with me!" she had said, the earth mother speaking, guarding her off-spring like a lioness, defending them from any outside forces that threatened. Now Quint knew without doubt that Thea Cameron would protect her sons at all costs, with her own life if necessary.

He had seen the powerful, unbreakable bond of love be-tween her and both her sons tonight, too. He had almost been able to feel it, touch it, taste it. Maybe someday, some way, he could have that same bond with Alfie. Miracles did happen.

A technician came to take Max to X ray, and Thea went with them while Quint stayed behind with Alan. The boy was still entirely too subdued. "Are you okay, Alan?"

"Yessir."

"But you feel bad about your brother?"

Alan nodded.

"Don't worry too much. Your mother already said she didn't hold you responsible for the accident, and the doctors will fix Max up just fine."

"He looked so terrible! All sweaty and pale . . ."

"I know. He was in shock. But I'll bet that by later tonight he'll be laughing and bragging about the whole thing."

"You think so?"

"I sure do."

"Max likes to brag."

"Well, he'll certainly have an opportunity to do it now. And he'll have an audience. And attention! You wouldn't believe all the attention he's going to get. Betsy—that's our housekeeper—will cluck over him like a mother hen. And your mother will probably read to him and tell him stories and feed him ice cream."

Alan nodded. "Yeah. She does that when we're sick."

"So you see, you shouldn't be feeling too bad about Max. You should be feeling sorry for yourself."

"Huh?"

"With all the attention Max is going to get, you'll be feeling neglected within a couple of days."

Alan frowned.

"Tell you what," Quint continued. "I'll probably be feeling neglected, too, so why don't we take off and go fishing together? I might ask J.R. to come along, too, if that's okay with you."

"That's okay, but . . ."

"What?"

"I don't know how to fish."

"You mean nobody ever took you fishing before?"

"My mom would have, except she was working," Alan said defensively. "And my dad..." The boy hesitated. "He was sick."

Sick? Thea had told him her ex-husband had changed, but she hadn't said anything about him being sick. Nothing at all.

"Well, that's no problem," he said to Alan. "I can teach a smart seven-year-old like you how to fish in no time. If you'd like to learn, that is. Would you?"

"Sure."

"It's a deal, then." Quint looked at his watch. "In the meantime, why don't we check out what they have to eat in the snack bar? We'll probably be here for another hour or two and I'll bet you're hungry."

"A little."

"Me, too. Let's go."

It was well past ten o'clock by the time the doctors had finally finished with Max and the four of them were loaded in the station wagon for the drive home. Thea looked bone-tired and Alan could barely keep his eyes open. Quint knew how they felt; he was sagging himself.

Not so Max. He was pumped sky-high with adrenaline and painkillers. "It was neat, Alan! I could hear the bone go pop when they set my leg. And then they kept piling on all this gooey white stuff, and the doctor kept talking about what a brave boy I was."

"What did I tell you?" Quint whispered to Alan in the front seat.

Alan grinned.

Liz was waiting for them at home. "The kids had dinner, and now they're sound asleep. At least, I assume Alfie's asleep. Her door's locked."

"Thanks, Liz. I really appreciate it," Quint said, heading up the stairs with a still wide-awake Maxie in his arms. Thea, Liz and Alan followed him and watched when he started to lower the patient onto one of the twin beds in the boys' room.

"No!" Max bellowed. "I want to sleep with Mom!"

Quint turned to her. "Thea?"

She hesitated, then capitulated. "I suppose it's okay. But it's only for tonight, Max."

Quint carried the boy across the hall to Thea's room. She quickly swished back the covers and fluffed a pillow.

"There," Quint said as he placed Max in her bed. "Are you comfortable now?"

"I could use another pillow."

"I'll go and—" Quint began.

"I'll take care of him now, Quint," Thea interrupted, attempting a smile. "Thank you so much. For everything."

Her sad little smile made his heart turn over... and also made him want to wring her neck. Why did she insist on being so stubbornly independent at a time like this? She was obviously exhausted, dead on her feet. There were dark smudges under her eyes, and a dollop of white plaster from Max's cast was stuck on her cheek.

Yet she insisted she could handle things by herself. Didn't she know he wanted to help? He almost felt the *need* to help, although for the life of him he couldn't figure out why.

He shrugged and followed Liz downstairs.

THEA LOOKED AT MAX. It had taken her forever to get him calmed down, but he was finally asleep in her bed, his broken leg elevated on a pillow.

She wouldn't cry. She had the definite suspicion that if she ever started, she'd never be able to stop. Ever since she had decided to kidnap her children two weeks ago, she had tried to block thoughts of the future out of her mind. *Don't think about it,* she had kept telling herself over and over like a broken record.

After what had happened to Max tonight, though, she was forced to think about the future. And it was bleak, terrifying. If it hadn't been for Quint, she wouldn't even have been able to have her son's broken leg treated!

What would happen the next time one of her children had an accident or became ill? And what about school? She had blithely withdrawn them for the remainder of this year's term, but what about next year? And the next?

She closed her eyes and pressed the heels of her hands against her throbbing temples. What was going to become of her children? How was she going to take care of them, protect them? *Think. Think.*

It was no use. She was too tired. She was utterly exhausted, mentally, physically and emotionally. But she was too nervous to sleep—and too scared.

A glass of milk might help her relax, but should she risk going downstairs? She didn't want to interrupt a panting love scene between Quint and Liz.

The house had been quiet for ages. Did that mean Liz was gone and Quint was in bed, or were things so quiet for another reason? She finally decided to go downstairs, no matter whom or what she interrupted.

She hastily pulled on a light cotton robe she'd borrowed from Aunt Maudie's closet. Too narrow in the shoulders and only reaching to midcalf, the flowered robe at least covered more of her than her T-shirt. She'd learned her lesson about *that* this morning.

Thea opened the bedroom door and peeked out. The hallway was quiet, illuminated by a single night-light at one end. She tiptoed to the stairs and started down. The first step gave a loud squeak as soon as her foot touched it. Listening, she waited a moment, and heard only silence.

She continued down the stairs, holding onto the banister as the dim glow from the night-light gradually faded. By the time she reached the downstairs hall, she was in complete darkness. She thought about turning on a light, but decided against it; she'd wait until she got to the kitchen, so she wouldn't disturb anyone. She moved slowly, trailing her hand along one wall to feel her way.

Once inside the kitchen, she couldn't remember where the light switch was. Groping along the wall without success, she finally decided to cross the room to the refrigerator. She would open the door and use its light to help her find the switch.

She'd taken only a couple of steps when she collided with something hard. She felt a sharp pain shoot through her shin. "Ouch!"

The room was suddenly flooded with bright light. Thea whirled around and saw Quint standing inside the door with his hand on the light switch she hadn't been able to find.

He was barefoot, the same as she was, and wore only a pair of chinos and an undershirt. His hair was tousled, as if he'd just gotten out of bed. He was looking at her with a puzzled expression in his blue eyes.

"I heard a noise," he said. "What were you doing down here in the dark, Thea?"

She burst into tears.

Chapter Six

Before she knew what had happened, he had crossed the room and gathered her into his arms, holding her against his broad, warm chest.

She burrowed her face into the soft fabric of his cotton T-shirt, as if trying to hide. When he tightened his arms around her to bring her closer, the dam inside her burst, as she'd known it would.

Quint didn't speak, didn't try to comfort her with words that would have been incomprehensible to her now. He did something infinitely more meaningful; he simply held her.

Her convulsive shudders gave way to deep sobs, then to a steady stream of tears, tears that gradually eased the fear she'd felt for weeks, the tension she'd felt for months. They even helped erase some of the anxiety that had been with her for years.

And still she cried—for her children, for herself, for Quint, a beautiful man who didn't deserve the cruel blows life had dealt him. She cried for Alfie, who was hurting so much that she tried to hurt everyone else, too. She cried for Sally, the lovely young woman who'd died, kicking and screaming all the way to her grave.

She cried for Aunt Maudie, miserable in the nursing home, not because she was facing her own mortality but because she missed a little boy. And she cried for J.R., terrified of illness because of what had happened to his mother. She even cried for Alan, the man she'd once loved, a man who'd had so much and wasted it all.

Finally the tears diminished. She supposed it was because she'd used them all up. She hiccuped. Quint loosened his arms and she lifted her head from his chest. Their eyes met. He still didn't speak, but his eyes sent her a million words.

She tried to say something, something about gratitude and embarrassment, but her voice didn't work. Then his eyes and his face came closer. He was going to kiss her. She knew she should move away, say something, stop this from happening. But she stood motionless, waiting.

His lips touched hers so lightly that they caressed her almost like a summer breeze. But his eyes burned all the way into her soul, warming her with their fire. Then his lips were back, claiming hers more firmly this time.

She closed her eyes and was immediately swept back to thirteen years ago. She was sixteen again, aglow with love and innocence. And Quint Richards was kissing her. The man she'd dreamed about for years was kissing her the way she'd wanted him to forever. It was as good as she'd always dreamed it would be.

She brought up her arms and wound them around his neck, drawing him closer. She felt the hardness of his body beneath the soft clothes he wore, and almost cried aloud with the sweet pleasure that surged through her.

Time was suspended and the outside world ceased to exist. There were only Quint and herself, their bodies pressed together, their mouths clinging, their breath mingling, their tongues caressing.

She didn't know how long they kissed. Seconds? Minutes? It seemed a long time before a semblance of sanity returned and she remembered that after all she wasn't sixteen, and Quint wasn't a boy anymore. He was a man—very much so, judging by the feel of his body in intimate contact with hers.

She shouldn't be doing this, not with Quint, not with anyone, but she didn't want to stop. It wasn't only the sensual contact she wanted, although she'd almost forgotten until now how pleasurable it was, and how much she'd missed it. She also wanted the comfort of strong male arms around her, making her feel warm and safe. She could be strong. She *was* strong most of the time, but not always. And not now. Now she felt completely vulnerable, in need of protection.

She sensed that Quint was vulnerable, too, and lonely. His mouth was as hungry as her own; their arms clutched each other almost in desperation. At this moment they needed each other. She strained toward him. His hand found her breast, and she heard the little sound of pleasure that came involuntarily from her.

She had to stop this. *Think,* she told herself. *Think. Remember who he is. Remember who you are and what you've done. Remember your children.* Thea opened her eyes and unwound her arms from his neck. She placed her hands between them and pushed against his chest, turning her head to tear her mouth away from his.

"We can't do this," she said, her voice cracking.

He relaxed his hold on her but didn't let go completely, his hands still on her waist. "I know."

"Let me go."

He dropped his hands.

"That shouldn't have happened," she said breathlessly, as much to herself as to him.

He compressed his lips, the lips which, she couldn't help remembering, had so recently been intimately claiming hers.

"If it's any consolation, I didn't intend it to happen," he said.

For some strange reason that admission hurt her. "It can never happen again. Ever."

She felt herself growing warm again as his gaze slowly traveled down her body and up again. "I can't see that any permanent damage has been done," he said finally.

"You needn't be sarcastic."

"And you needn't overreact. After all, it was only a simple kiss."

Their eyes met, and she saw he didn't believe what he'd said any more than she did. There had been nothing simple about their kiss. "Even so," she began, "you have to—"

"Whatever you say," he interrupted, watching her, and suddenly narrowing his eyes. "What on earth is that you're wearing?"

She'd forgotten about the too-small robe and drew it tighter around her, trying to make it meet in front. "It's a robe of Aunt Maudie's I borrowed."

"I see."

She saw a flicker of amusement in his eyes and might have laughed herself, if she hadn't been so upset. "Where's Liz?" she asked, changing the subject.

"She went home ages ago."

"Oh."

"Are you going to tell me why you were down here in the middle of the night, fumbling around in the dark?"

"I came down to get a glass of milk. I didn't turn on the light because I didn't want to disturb anyone."

"And why did you cry as soon as you saw me?"

"It wasn't seeing you that did it! It was...a combination of everything. All that happened."

"I can understand that." He hesitated. "You handled the whole thing very well, Thea . . . the accident and all. I was proud of you."

Why did that make her want to cry all over again? "I'm sorry we spoiled your evening," she said quickly.

"There'll be other evenings."

"All that wonderful food Liz brought over went to waste and . . . I'm sorry."

"Yeah. It was pretty rotten of you to go to the extent of having your son break his leg in order to spoil my evening."

"There you go with the sarcasm again. I was only trying to thank you."

"Is that what you were doing? I thought you were apologizing for being here, for existing."

"You knew what I meant."

He shook his head. "What is it with you anyway, Thea? I didn't do anything I didn't want to do, anything I wouldn't have done for—" He stopped. "For anybody who needed help. And as far as I could tell, you sure needed some help."

"You know I did."

"Then what's the problem?"

The problem was that the idea of depending on him too much, leaning on him and drawing from his strength, was too tempting. It was an insidious trap. If she succumbed to the temptation, it would be pure weakness—selfishness—on her part, and it could place her sons in jeopardy. She would never knowingly do that.

"I don't like involving anyone else in my troubles," she said.

"Even if they want to be involved?"

His words could be taken innocently enough; he could be talking about friends helping friends. On the other hand, he could be talking about something else entirely. "Especially if they want to be involved. I prefer doing things for myself. I don't want to owe anyone.''

Was that anger that appeared briefly in his eyes? It was gone so quickly that she couldn't be sure. ''I do appreciate what you did for us tonight, though, Quint. You were a good friend. Thank you.''

He stared at her for a long time before he answered. ''You're welcome.'' He continued looking at her, his eyes assessing. ''Aren't you going to get your milk?''

''Oh.'' She'd completely forgotten her reason for coming downstairs. ''Yes.'' She walked over to the cabinet for a glass. ''Would you like some?''

''No, thanks. I have to get to bed soon. I have to be in court early tomorrow morning.''

Her hand stopped in midair. For a while tonight, she'd forgotten he was the district attorney, a serious lapse on her part. She got the glass and went to the refrigerator for her milk.

''I'm sorry my midnight prowling disturbed your sleep. I'll try not to do it again...and the boys and I will be gone soon.'' She turned to him with a bright, false smile.

He frowned. ''Not too soon, I hope.''

''What?''

''Surely you're not in such a hurry to get away from me that you're planning to leave right away. Max is in no shape to go anywhere. He'd be absolutely miserable being jostled about in an automobile while he's still in a cast.''

Thea was aghast. Quint was right, and now she had one more reason to worry. She was trapped here for at least...how long? ''What I meant was, we'll leave as soon as Max is able to travel, of course.''

''Of course.''

THEA WAS AWAKENED by angry shouts and the sound of pounding on a door. She blinked groggily and glanced at Max in the bed beside her. He was still asleep. The pounding wasn't on her door, either, so she turned over, figuring the war going on outside wasn't her problem. Then she recognized Alan's voice.

Sighing, she threw back the cover and got out of bed. Remembering her nearly naked encounter with Quint the day before, she quickly pulled on shorts and a blouse before racing out to see what the trouble was.

J.R. and Alan, both in pajamas, were pounding furiously on the door to one of the upstairs bathrooms.

"What's going on?" she asked.

"Alfie's locked herself in the bathroom again," J.R. said.

"She won't let us in," Alan fumed, "and I need to use the bathroom."

"Dad said I had to take a bath because I didn't do it last night, and now she's gonna make me miss the school bus," J.R. added.

"Why don't you two go to the other bathroom?" Thea asked reasonably.

"Dad's taking a shower in it," J.R. said. "He overslept and he's in a big rush to get to work."

Thea felt her cheeks grow warm. She not only remembered that the reason Quint had overslept was because he'd been up late with her, but what they'd been doing. "I'm sure Alfie will be out soon."

"Mom, I *need* to use the bathroom," Alan repeated in a low, urgent voice.

"Oh," she said, suddenly understanding. She knocked on the door. "Alfie, will you be much longer?"

"Go away!" came the surly reply from inside the bathroom.

Thea thought for a moment. "I guess your best bet is sharing the bath off Aunt Maudie's room downstairs."

"Mom! I can't share the bathroom with J.R."

"Why not? You and Max share one all the time."

"But J.R.'s a stranger!"

"He's still a boy. You two have the same equipment. Almost," she added when she saw the expression of indignation on Alan's face at being compared to a kid who was two years younger.

"I'm not gonna use *her* bathroom!" J.R. stated emphatically.

Thea rolled her eyes. "Suit yourselves. Alan, you can go outside if you prefer, and J.R., I can give you a bath in the kitchen sink."

Alan and J.R. grudgingly went downstairs to share Aunt Maudie's bathroom.

By the time Thea returned to her bedroom, Max was wide-awake and demanding room service. By the time she had him pacified, the housekeeper had arrived, and Thea had to spend a few minutes talking about old times with her. That put Betsy behind schedule and caused breakfast to be late, even though Thea helped as much as she could.

Quint rushed in, dressed in a smart-looking business suit, but didn't notice Thea, at least as far as she knew. She couldn't be certain, because she turned away as soon as he came into the room. He told Betsy he'd pass on breakfast, so that he could get to court on time. To complete the morning, Alfie and J.R. missed the school bus.

"What happens now?" Betsy asked, looking at Thea.

"I guess we'll have to skip school," J.R. suggested.

"No way, mister," Thea said. "Either Betsy or I will drive you."

She glanced at Betsy, who shook her head. "I can't drive. Never learned how."

"I'll drive them," Thea said. "Do you mind keeping an eye on my boys while I'm gone?"

Betsy grinned. "I've been itching to find out what your kids are like. Do they get into as much mischief as their mama used to?"

"More."

"Then we'll get along just fine."

Thea had a hard time rushing J.R. and Alfie along, but finally the three of them were in the car. "You'll have to give me directions," she said to Alfie, who was seated in the front beside her. "Should we drop J.R. off at kindergarten first?"

"It's in the same building as my school," Alfie said, looking straight ahead.

"How nice!"

Alfie didn't respond.

"I mean . . . it certainly makes driving easier for me."

Alfie still didn't say anything. J.R. gave Thea directions to the school and jabbered constantly along the way. Thea listened, thinking about how much he reminded her of Maxie. Rough. Tough. And so sweet that she wanted to squeeze him tight and never let go.

When they reached the school, Alfie got out of the car and started down the walkway to the red brick building. Except for that one sentence, she hadn't said a word during the entire drive.

"Thanks, Thea," J.R. said, scrambling across the back seat and getting out in his turn.

"Thank *you*, J.R., for the wonderful company."

"You're welcome," he replied solemnly, then gave her a big, proud smile.

Smiling too, Thea watched him skip down the walkway. Then her gaze moved ahead to Alfie and her smile faded. The girl's back was straight, and her narrow shoulders were squared with determination. She walked as if she were going to face a firing squad. And her clean, faded jeans were at least an inch and a half too short.

Surely Quint Richards wasn't still so strapped for money that he couldn't afford something better than that for his only daughter! On the drive back to Aunt Maudie's house, she thought about ways to bring up the subject of his daughter's wardrobe with Quint.

Betsy was waiting for her in the kitchen. Max, sitting in one chair with his broken leg propped on another, and Alan were eating breakfast. "How did you manage to get Max down the stairs?" Thea asked, thinking that the housekeeper was much too old to attempt something so strenuous. "You could have hurt yourself, Betsy."

"Alan helped me and we did just fine. Didn't we, babies?"

Thea caught her breath. Both her sons absolutely detested being referred to as "baby." By anyone. Anytime. Anywhere.

"You bet," Alan said.

"Sure," Max agreed.

Thea got herself a cup of coffee and sank onto a chair at the table. She was already exhausted, and the day had barely begun.

SHE SPOTTED THE SIGN she was looking for almost immediately, but drove around the block three times and then parked two blocks away, in the parking lot of the First Baptist Church. Her palms were so wet that they slipped on the steering wheel.

She knew she had to do it, but she didn't have the foggiest idea of how to go about it. How on earth would she ever muster enough courage to go inside the pawnshop? And—

supposing by some miracle she *was* able to find the courage—what would she say once she was inside?

"Hello. I need some money."

"Doesn't everyone?"

"I have some expensive jewelry to offer in return."

"Doesn't everyone?"

"But I have two children, you see. I really need *the money."*

"Doesn't everyone?"

She couldn't do it.

Don't be silly, she told herself. Of course she could do it. She'd done tougher things. She'd kidnapped her children, and then hauled them all the way across the country. If she could do that, then a simple thing like visiting a pawnshop for the first time should be a cup of tea.

She got out of the car and locked it. At least Betsy had offered to take care of her sons, so she didn't have them to worry about while she was selling everything valuable she owned. She squared her shoulders and marched down the street.

A bell tinkled over the door when she pushed it open and stepped inside. She stopped in her tracks, completely unprepared for what she saw—other customers. Three of them. She thought briefly about leaving and coming back another day.

"Hi," said the man behind the counter. "Just make yourself at home. Look around and see if there's anything you'd like to buy."

Buy? Of course! She could just as easily be in here to buy something as to sell! Why hadn't she thought of that? She relaxed a little.

Pretending to browse, Thea stole furtive glances at the man behind the counter. The owner? Probably. This was a small shop in a small town and couldn't possibly yield enough income to hire an employee to run the business.

She relaxed a little more. The owner appeared to be a nice man, somewhere around sixty she'd guess, judging from his white hair and the wrinkles on his face. That was good. She'd always been able to get along well with older people.

Two people left, and the owner turned to Thea before attending to his other remaining customer. "See anything you like?" he asked with a friendly smile.

"Lots."

"I'll be with you in a minute."

"No hurry."

The last customer finally left and the owner walked over to Thea. "Now. What can I do for you?"

The moment of truth. "I'd like to talk to you about—"

The bell over the door rang and another person came inside.

"About . . . ?" the owner prompted.

"I'd like to think about it some more. Why don't you go help that customer and then come back to me?"

The man shrugged and walked away. Thea mentally lashed herself for being so jelly-legged. As soon as that customer left, she would make her move, even if Prince Charles himself walked in.

The owner finished with the other customer and came back to her. "I have some things I'd like to pawn," she said quickly, before he could speak—and before she lost her nerve.

"That's what I'm here for. What kind of things do you have?"

That was all there was to it? She wondered why she'd been so embarrassed and frightened. She reached into her purse and extracted a small velvet bag. "A watch and some jewelry," she said, emptying the contents onto the top of the glass case. "It's expensive stuff. Mostly things my husband gave me," she said, wondering why she was babbling. "We're divorced and—"

"Where did you get this?" He was holding up a delicate silver lavaliere. The pendant was a lacy filigree with a small diamond set in the center of the intricate design. It was her favorite, the one piece of jewelry she'd hoped to keep.

"It's an antique. From my grandmother," she replied stiffly. What did he think? That she'd stolen it? She was immediately on her guard again.

"Nice," he said, still holding the lavaliere.

"This necklace and earring set is worth much more," she pointed out, pushing the objects in his direction. "There's a matching bracelet, too. See?"

He examined the set and then nodded his head.

She had to ask the question sometime. "How...how much will they bring?"

"A few hundred."

Thea gasped. "That's all? Only a few hundred for the whole set?"

"For the whole works," the man said, gesturing toward the array of jewelry spread on the counter. "Except for the watch and this," he added, holding up the lavaliere he still had in his hand.

Thea shook her head in disbelief. "You have to be kidding."

"I'm not in business to kid about business."

"But Al— But my husband paid thousands and thousands for this jewelry when he bought it."

"It'd cost him a bundle at a fancy jewelry store today, too," the man said. "That's where he bought it, isn't it? At a fancy jewelry store?"

Thea nodded.

"In case you hadn't noticed, my place isn't a fancy jewelry store, and my customers can't afford fancy jewelry. I know my market and I pay what they can pay. To them, ten bucks is a lot for a pair of earrings."

She swallowed. "The watch. What about the watch?"

The sweet little white-haired man examined the watch with a practiced eye, and then negotiated with consummate skill, Thea noted. "Hmm. Five hundred?"

"Five hundred!"

"I might be able to go as high as seven-fifty."

"But it's worth more than ten times that amount! It's a Rolex! With diamonds!"

"And I'll give you another three hundred for this," he said, holding up the lavaliere he still held clutched in his greedy little hand.

She narrowed her eyes. "Why are you willing to pay so much for that? Three hundred is *almost* what the piece is worth."

"I'm hoping you won't redeem it within thirty days. My wife has a birthday coming up and she'd really love it."

Thea pressed her fingers to her eyes, trying to think. "Are there any other pawnshops around?"

"There's one over at the county seat, and a bunch of them down in Albany. You might be able to do better there, but I doubt it."

Thea lifted her hands away from her eyes and took a deep breath. "So. What's the best you can do? What's your final offer?"

The man rubbed his chin, apparently considering. "Let's see. Seven-fifty for the watch...three hundred for the necklace...and three-fifty for the rest of the stuff. How does that sound?"

"Awful. But I'll take it."

"That comes to..."

"Fourteen hundred. I can count, too."

"You're a smart lady."

"I doubt that."

"I'll write up the agreement."

Thea paced the floor of the cluttered pawnshop while the man first wrote, then pushed the paper toward her. "Better read it to make sure everything's hunky-dory before you sign."

She glanced at the paper, which basically stated that the articles she pawned belonged to her. She signed with a false name.

"I'll get your money now," the man said.

"I'd like it in cash,' she said, trying to sound stern and forceful.

"Doesn't everyone?"

He went to the safe and was back in a few seconds with a stack of bills and her pawn ticket. "Better count it," he said.

She counted. "You gave me too much. There's fifteen hundred here instead of fourteen."

"I know. I was testing you."

"Why, you—!" she exclaimed, ready to explode.

"And I want you to keep the extra hundred for being so honest. I'll play fair with you if you play fair with me. That's my motto. What do you think?"

She didn't know what to think. She shook her head, crammed the money into her purse, and headed for the exit as fast as she could. By the time she reached the car she was shaking.

She wasn't a dreamer. She hadn't expected the moon and the stars when she went to the pawnshop, but she hadn't thought that five thousand dollars was an unrealistic figure, either.

Fifteen hundred! That would be gone before she could blink her eyes, what with the cost of food and the most modest lodging these days. But it was money, she reminded herself. Cash, just what everyone wanted—and it was safely stashed in her purse.

She started the engine and drove to a service station, where she filled up her gas tank. She intended to keep it full from now on, so they'd be ready to leave in case of an emergency. The station was the same one where she'd stopped on the way to Aunt Maudie's house two days ago, and the same attendant was on duty. Both she and the attendant pretended they'd never seen each other before.

She drove to the nursing home to visit Aunt Maudie, then stopped at a ten-cent store before returning home. She wanted to get a few toys and games, some inexpensive things to keep Max entertained while he was immobile. She selected a couple of jigsaw puzzles, one for Max and a more difficult one for Alan, because she didn't want him to feel left out.

Playing cards and board games were always fun, so she chose an Old Maid Board, a deck of crazy eights, and a regular deck for playing go fish. Reconsidering, she put back the deck of crazy eights; the boys could play the same game with the regular deck. Most of the other games were expensive, as were most of the toys. She completed her purchases with a sketch pad and a box of colored pencils, plus a can of pickup sticks.

On the way back to her car, she spotted a sign outside a clothing store. The sign announced a special—a twenty-five percent discount on all jeans. She stopped, thinking about Alfie and her too-short jeans.

The girl was ten now, at an age where everyone wanted to look like everyone else…and no one would be caught dead in a pair of jeans that were too short. "Floods" was the word used by some of her sons' friends—the ridicule even filtered down to their age-group—and floods were almost as bad as wearing jeans that were obviously new.

She really had to conserve her money, but the thought of Alfie being ridiculed by her classmates was too painful to ignore. Besides, she rationalized, she could take Alfie's old jeans and save them for Alan to grow into. She went inside the store.

Even at twenty-five percent off, the jeans weren't cheap, especially the prewashed ones that were so popular. Thea debated, then decided on an unwashed pair. She'd save all that money; and with Aunt Maudie's washing machine and a bottle of bleach she could do a dandy job of aging the jeans herself.

Leaving the store, Thea looked at her wrist for the watch that wasn't there anymore and walked a little faster. She'd told the housekeeper she'd be home by five, the time when Betsy said her nephew usually came to drive her home.

Betsy had been kind to her children and herself, and Thea didn't want to take advantage of her in any way. That was why she'd insisted on helping her with the housework that morning over Betsy's protests, and why she wouldn't be late now if she could help it. She didn't *think* she was late, but without a watch she couldn't be sure.

Not wanting to run the risk of getting a speeding ticket, she drove as fast as she dared on the way back to Aunt Maudie's house. To save time, she decided to drive around to the back of the house, where three steps would take her directly into the kitchen.

She was surprised to find Quint's station wagon parked there, as well. What was he doing home at this time of the afternoon? Then she noticed the other car parked along-side Quint's—and stopped breathing.

Nobody was inside the car now, and the light mounted on the roof wasn't flashing, but bold, six-inch letters painted on the sides announced its owner.

It was the sheriff's car.

Chapter Seven

Thea stared at the official car. This was like a bad dream, the worst of her nightmares come true.

She didn't consider running away; there was no point in that. She was trying to protect her children, not herself, and obviously she'd done a terrible job of it.

She turned off the engine and clutched the steering wheel with both hands, squeezing as hard as she could. She wanted to cry, to wail at the injustice of it all, but had no emotion left. She felt dry, drained of all feeling except one of heavy, overwhelming defeat. And she was tired.

She leaned forward and rested her head against the steering wheel. Was this how it ended? After all the running, the fear and the worry, had it all come down to this? If so, it was a sorry ending. She could have written a better scenario. Much better.

She finally lifted her head, took a deep breath and got out of the car. She half expected Quint and the sheriff to be waiting for her in the kitchen, pistols drawn and handcuffs at the ready, but there was only Betsy setting the table for dinner.

She frowned when she saw Thea. "My goodness! What's wrong with you?"

Thea didn't bother answering her. "I saw Quint's car outside." She was a little surprised to find that her voice still worked.

Betsy nodded. "Court adjourned early. He's gone fishing."

Fishing! "Fishing?" she repeated.

"That's right. Alan and J.R. went with him."

That meant Alan hadn't been taken into custody, at least not yet. "Where's Max?"

"He and Alfie are playing in the living room." Betsy's frown deepened. "What is it, Thea? You're white as a ghost."

"I'm all right." She dreaded asking the next question. "Is . . . is the sheriff here?"

"Oh, sure. He went fishing with Quint and the boys."

Thea blinked.

"Sheriff Potts never misses a chance to go fishing with Quint," Betsy continued. "The two of them are always trying to outdo each other by catching the biggest fish."

Thea grabbed the back of a chair, suddenly so weak that she couldn't stand up anymore. The sheriff hadn't come to arrest her, after all. He'd come to go fishing with Quint!

Starting to shake, she lowered herself onto the chair and heard small sounds coming from the back of her throat. She wasn't exactly laughing or crying. She was just making strange little sounds.

Alarmed, Betsy raced toward her. "Thea! What's the matter?"

Thea shook her head, trying to indicate that she was all right. She couldn't speak, and couldn't seem to stop making the sounds.

Betsy picked up one of her cold, almost lifeless hands and started massaging it. "Talk to me!"

"I'm all right," she finally managed to say.

"No, you're not. Any fool could see you're not."

"I am. I promise." That wasn't entirely true, but she was certainly a lot better than she'd been a few moments ago, even if she was still shaking all over and felt as weak as dishwater. "I've been rushing around this afternoon. I was worried about being late and making you miss your ride."

Betsy shook her head in disbelief. "There was no need for you to worry about that." She gestured toward the kitchen clock over the sink while she continued massaging Thea's hand. "It's only four-thirty."

"So it is." Thea took several deep breaths, and the shaking finally subsided. "I'm feeling better now. Really."

"I'll get you a glass of water."

"Thank you," Thea said when Betsy handed her the glass. She thought for a moment. "I wonder why Quint took my son fishing."

"He said something about promising Alan he would."

"Oh." Alan didn't even know how to fish. When had Quint promised to take him? And why hadn't Alan said anything to her about it?

Another disturbing thought occurred to her—her son was off fishing with both the local sheriff and the district attorney! What if he let something slip, said something he wasn't supposed to say?

She'd carefully rehearsed both Alan and Max, as much as she dared without confusing or frightening them. She had made them promise to avoid talking to anybody who got too nosy. They were supposed to make excuses and send them to her. But Alan was only seven years old. At that age it was so easy to forget precautions, especially if you were having fun fishing for the first time in your young life.

There was nothing she could do about it now. The situation was beyond her control. She could only pray that Alan wouldn't say the wrong thing.

Thea looked at Betsy, who was still watching her with an anxious expression. "I'm fine now. Honest," she said. "Did you say that Max is in the living room?"

"Yep. Alfie's teaching him how to play that old game you and Miss Maude used to play."

Thea frowned. "What game was that?"

"You know. The one where you flick those little round wooden discs across the board with your finger. The two of you used to play it for hours."

"Caroms!" Thea exclaimed.

"That's it."

Thea raised her eyebrows. "And Alfie's teaching Max?"

"I know," Betsy said. "Sometimes she surprises me, too. Just when you think there's no hope for that girl, she ups and does something like that."

"It was really nice. I'll go thank her."

She heard the sound of Max's delighted laughter when she was halfway down the hall. That sound never failed to give her a lift. She wished there were some way she could capture it, bottle it and preserve it to bring out at the bad times.

Max was sitting sideways on the sofa, his injured leg stretched out in front of him. Both he and Alfie were leaning over the carom board.

Max's face lighted up as soon as he saw her. "Mom! You should have seen the shot I just made!"

"Was it good?"

"Fan-tastic! Alfie showed me how."

"You must be good at caroms, Alfie."

"She's the best!" Max answered for her. "She even beat Aunt Maudie one time."

Thea whistled. "That's really something."

"I only did it once," Alfie said.

"That's still more than anybody else ever did. I was never able to come close."

"You wanna play with us, Mom?"

Noticing the guarded look that fell over Alfie's face, Thea immediately decided against it. "I have to help Betsy with dinner now. We'll do it another time."

"Later tonight?" Max pressed.

Thea looked at the girl. "Alfie?"

"I have homework to do later."

"One game?"

"I guess so."

"It's a date." She left the room quickly before Alfie could change her mind.

Returning to the kitchen, she found Betsy had dinner already prepared. The housekeeper's nephew came to pick her up a couple of minutes later, and Thea was left sitting alone at the kitchen table with nothing to do but worry until Quint and Alan returned.

"I've LIVED HERE all my life," Sheriff Calvin Potts said. "I can't understand why I never met you before. I know I'd remember it if I had," he added, flashing a boyish smile.

Quint looked at Thea, seated at the opposite end of the table from him, and waited for her to comment. She didn't speak and he wasn't surprised. She'd barely said two words during the entire meal. The only person at the table who'd talked less was Alfie.

"Thea stopped visiting Miss Maudie after she and her mother moved to California," he explained to Cal. "I think you were in the army the last couple of times she came here."

Quint glanced at her again. She was concentrating on cutting her meat now, seemingly absorbed in the task. Something was troubling her. That much was obvious. What he couldn't figure out was what it was. He could think of several possibilities, but none of them seemed to fit.

One possibility was that she was angry because he'd taken Alan fishing. She'd made a lot of ooh's and ah's when Alan showed her the fish he'd caught, but her exclamations had seemed to him a little phony—forced? True, it wasn't much of a fish, barely a keeper, but Alan was so proud of it! He'd felt a tightness in his own throat as he watched Alan show off his fish, and he wasn't even the boy's father! Why hadn't Thea been more enthusiastic?

"Can I have some more potatoes, Mom?" Max asked.

"May I," she corrected automatically as she filled his plate.

"Me, too," J.R. said, holding out his plate.

"I agree with the boys," Cal said. "These potatoes are delicious. Did you make them, Thea?"

She didn't look at him. "No. Betsy did before she left."

Quint studied her surreptitiously. Could she be upset because he'd invited Cal to stay for dinner after they returned from fishing? That didn't make sense. Betsy had already prepared dinner, and there was plenty for everyone. Thea's problem had to be something else. But what?

Could she be jealous of Alan and him? The boy had followed him around like a puppy dog all evening and had immediately rushed to grab the seat next to his when they came in to dinner, but surely Thea wouldn't object to her son having a mild case of hero worship. Would she?

Perhaps she didn't object to Alan's admiring a man per se, but to the fact that *he* was the man in question. She was secretive about most things, but not about her feelings toward him. She'd made them quite clear, lashing out at him for kissing her last night and then pretending he didn't exist this morning.

Even so, and even though she obviously wished it weren't true, she wasn't immune to him. Much as she might fight it, she was a loving, giving, passionate woman. She'd proved that in his arms last night, kissing him back with a desperate intensity that had matched his own.

Thinking about their kiss, he remembered the almost frightening sensations he'd experienced the moment they touched each other—the surprise, then the fierce surge of passion, a passion so strong that it had left him dazed. She had still been crying then, and he'd felt like a lecher, having such feelings at a time when he was supposed to be comforting her. Had Thea known how very much he wanted her last night? He hoped not.

He had no intention—then, now or ever—of doing anything about that almost desperate wanting. This morning he'd promised himself never to touch her again. It was too dangerous. His self-control could only be stretched so far; after that it could crumble, and that wouldn't do at all. It would be the height of folly—and of male conceit—for him to go around tempting fate. She had her secrets; he had his responsibilities and his own secrets. He didn't want to judge her and didn't intend to. It didn't matter.

He had already decided he wasn't meant for marriage. Knowing that, he also knew that nothing else was possible between Thea and himself. If he ever surrendered to the temptation to make love to her, he'd not only be betraying her and himself, he'd also be betraying Miss Maudie. That was something he'd never do. What kind of jerk would he be if, purely for his own gratification, he went to bed with the niece of the woman who'd been more like a mother to him than his own mother!

Whether Thea Cameron knew it or not, she was completely safe from him.

"How long will you and your sons be staying in Planters' Junction, Thea?" Cal asked.

"I'm not sure," she mumbled, looking first at Quint, then at her plate.

"A few days? A week?" Cal persisted.

"Possibly."

Quint watched the exchange with interest. Thea wasn't only secretive around him; she was that way with everybody. Then he noticed her expression. She wasn't merely being secretive this time but was genuinely disturbed. About what? He felt sad, wondering what had happened to the open, fun-loving girl he used to know.

"I'd be happy to play tourist guide for you while you're here," Cal said.

Cal had been coming on to her all during dinner. Quint had ignored it, but now remembered he'd caught her glancing at the sheriff a couple of times, too, when she thought no one was looking. Was she attracted to him? Was that why she'd been so edgy? It wouldn't be the first time a woman had succumbed to the slow drawl and lanky, Gary Cooperish good looks of the local sheriff. At one time or another, almost every available woman in Planters' Junction had made a play for Cal.

Quint wanted to warn Thea. She was safe from him, but she wasn't safe from Calvin Potts. What she didn't know was that Cal had a knack for avoiding any entanglements that might possibly lead to a commitment. In his late thirties, Cal was a confirmed bachelor, and was perfectly happy in the role. If Thea fell for his boyish charm and big, ultrasincere gray eyes, she could be hurt.

"Thanks, but I don't need a guide," Thea said.

"I could show you—" Cal began.

"I already know my way to the nursing home and back here," she interrupted. "Those are the only places that interest me."

On second thought, Quint decided, Thea was perfectly capable of taking care of herself.

Still, he felt a certain responsibility toward her because of her aunt. After dinner was over and Cal had left to make his nightly patrol, Quint decided to bring up the subject of the sheriff. He waited until he and Thea were cleaning the kitchen alone, while the kids watched TV in the parlor that had been converted into a playroom.

"I think Cal liked you," he said.

Thea dropped a plate into the dishwasher. There was a loud noise that might mean the plate was broken. She wheeled around. "What?"

"I said I thought Cal liked you."

"I heard what you said. What did you mean?"

"Nothing."

"Don't give me that, Quint Richards. You have a reason—usually two or three reasons—for everything you say."

"I meant Cal was on his best behavior tonight, and that made me think he liked you. That's all. I swear."

"Are you playing matchmaker for me, too?"

"Too? Has someone else been doing it?"

Thea turned back to the dishwasher and flung in another plate. "Never mind."

"No, I want to know. Who else has been playing matchmaker for you?"

"Aunt Maudie, if you must know," she replied, keeping her back to him.

"Who was she trying to match you up with?"

Thea's back stiffened perceptibly. She still didn't turn around.

"Who?" he insisted.

"You," Thea mumbled, quickly reaching for more plates.

"Me?"

"I told her it was ridiculous."

Quint let out a long breath. "I'll say."

Thea turned around to face him, her cheeks pink and her eyes flashing with anger. "You find me that unattractive? You didn't seem to last night."

"No, I don't find you unattractive!" He took two long strides and grabbed her shoulders with both hands. "I didn't then and I don't now!"

She turned her head away.

"Look at me!"

She looked at him and his anger evaporated immediately, replaced by fierce, almost painful desire.

She must have been able to read it in his eyes. "Don't you dare kiss me again," she said a little breathlessly.

He wanted to kiss her. Oh, how he wanted to kiss her! He wanted to kiss her until her lips were swollen from being possessed by his, and until he was swollen with the need for more of her. Maybe he wanted to punish her, or himself.

He remembered the feel of her lips under his, remembered how receptive she could be to his touch, remembered how much he'd wanted her last night. And how much he wanted her now. He dropped his hands and stepped back quickly, as if he'd been seared by fire.

They stared at each other.

"You should never dare me," he said. "I might take you up on it."

"A gentleman wouldn't."

"I never claimed to be a gentleman. I'm not even a very nice person."

"That's not true. You—"

"Believe me. There are things about me you don't know, Thea." He immediately wished he hadn't said that. It was as if he were inviting her to contradict him, and she was responding the way he'd known she would, by shaking her head.

"At any rate, I agree with you that we should resist Miss Maudie's matchmaking attempts," he said. "But not because I find you unattractive. Understand?"

She nodded.

"I'd like us to be friends."

Her tentative smile was shy, like that of a young girl, and it made him want to take her in his arms again.

"I'd like that, too," she said.

"It's settled then," he said, feeling like a hypocrite because he knew what he really wanted, and it wasn't friendship. He turned away quickly and went to the table to gather the rest of the dinner dishes. She didn't look at him when he brought them back and placed them on the counter beside her.

"Thank you for taking Alan fishing today."

"I think I enjoyed it as much as he did."

"He's never been fishing before."

"I know. He told me."

She turned to look at him then. "He did? Was that why you invited him?"

"Not really. I thought it would give us a chance to talk . . . to get better acquainted."

"And did you? Talk, I mean."

Quint wondered what Thea was getting at. "We talked a little. Mostly about fishing."

"That's all?"

He decided he'd had enough. "Look, Thea. If you're jealous of your son spending time with me, why don't you come right out and say so?"

"What?"

"Isn't that what this is all about? You're jealous."

"No!"

"Then what?"

"I...I don't want to be a bother to you, and I don't want my children to be a bother."

"That's the most stupid thing I've ever heard!"

"I told you I don't like to owe people!"

"And I told you I don't do anything I don't want to do. You don't owe me a damn thing. Okay?"

"Okay!"

A sudden, awkward silence fell over the room. Quint heard the sound of his own rapid breathing and waited a moment to calm down. "That still doesn't ex—" he began.

"One other thing—" Thea said at the same time.

They both stopped. "You go first," he said.

"No, you go."

"I started to say that still doesn't explain why you were so quiet during dinner. You barely said three words. Were you upset because I invited Cal to eat with us?"

"No!"

"Was it because you felt awkward being around me, after what happened last night?"

"No, that wasn't it."

"Then . . . ?"

"Has it occurred to you that the explanation could be as simple as the fact that I was tired?"

He narrowed his eyes. "That's all?"

"Isn't it enough? Haven't you ever come home from work too tired to be a vivacious dinner companion?"

She could be as sarcastic as he could. "Certainly."

"It's as simple as that."

It was too simple, and Quint wasn't sure he believed her. "What were you going to say before?"

"The same thing I just said. I was going to explain to you why I was so quiet during dinner. I got up early this morning, rushed around all day, and I was tired. T-i-r-e-d."

Quint decided to make one last try before dropping the subject. "Then you have no objection if I take Alan fishing again?"

She tried to hide it, but he saw the quick flicker of something, he wasn't sure what, flash in her eyes before she answered. "Of course not, since you insist it's what you really want to do."

He wasn't sure what he'd seen, but it was enough to convince him there was something she wasn't telling him. Damn her and damn her secrets! It wasn't as if he was trying to learn everything there was to know about her, but couldn't she at least trust him enough as a friend not to lie to him?

STUPID. STUPID. STUPID. Thea chastised herself while she and Quint finished cleaning the kitchen. She'd really made a mess of everything tonight. Everything. But the worst was trying to quiz Quint to find out if Alan had told him anything he shouldn't this afternoon. She realized now that if Alan *had* made a mistake, Quint would have questioned her about it. Since he hadn't, the best thing she could do was ignore the whole matter.

But no. Overanxious little Thea had to go and try to question him. It had made him suspicious, and rightfully so. She could tell he hadn't believed her lie about being tired at dinner, either. No wonder. It was so flimsy that only an idiot would be taken in by it.

She hoped Quint didn't realize how close he'd come to the reason for her silence when he brought up the subject of Cal Potts. He *had* been the reason she'd been so quiet. She'd been nervous—scared to death—at being seated at the same table with the local sheriff.

She really hated this, all of it—the lies, the cat-and-mouse games, and most of all the constant fear of discovery. As soon as Max was well enough to travel, she was taking her sons and getting away from here. They'd go somewhere, anywhere, maybe to a deserted island where no one would ever come around to threaten them again, ever! They'd throw up a tent, play in the sun, and live off fish they'd catch in the surf.

She knew the idea was impossible, but it did have a certain appeal. At least they would be faraway from innocent-looking sheriffs and dangerous district attorneys.

She chanced a quick look at Quint. His back was to her, and she saw the muscles move in his shoulders as he wiped the table with a damp sponge. Her glance dropped lower, to his low-slung jeans and narrow hips. Sexy hips. Everything about him was sexy. That, as much as the fact that he was a law official, was what made him so dangerous.

She was vulnerable, susceptible to a man's look, a man's touch, a man's kiss. Until he kissed her, she hadn't realized how vulnerable she was. Now that she did know, she was also aware that she had to be constantly on guard. She couldn't, wouldn't jeopardize her sons' safety by trading soul-stirring kisses with the district attorney.

She finished loading the dishwasher, and Quint finished cleaning the table at the same time. They looked at each other.

"Well," he said, "since you're so tired, I suppose you'll want to get ready for bed soon."

Was he being sarcastic again? She decided to ignore it. "As a matter of fact, I promised Max that I'd play a game of caroms with him and Alfie." A sudden idea occurred to her. "Why don't you play, too? We'll make it a foursome."

He shook his head. "I don't think Alfie would like that."

"You'll never know unless you take a chance. Besides, we won't give her a choice. She's already promised to play, and I'll pretend I don't know what's going on between you two."

"You're pretty good at pretending, aren't you?"

Thea felt a surge of embarrassment that was quickly replaced by anger. "I'm trying to do you a favor. Yes or no?"

He shrugged. "Like you said, I'll take a chance."

The game started out surprisingly well. Alfie didn't say a word of protest when Thea announced that the two of them would be partners against Max and Quint, although a startled look crossed her face.

Alfie and her father were much better players than Max and his mother, Thea thought. She also thought the two teams were pretty evenly matched, just as she'd hoped when she suggested the pairings. She gradually relaxed as everyone got into the spirit of the game.

"Good shot, Alfie!" Quint exclaimed after the girl made a particularly difficult shot. Thea wanted to applaud him, and herself for having this idea, when she saw the pleased look on Alfie's face.

The game went to the wire, with Quint making a shot, Alfie making another, and both Max and Thea usually missing theirs. They were finally down to the last piece left on the board, and it was Quint's turn to shoot. If he made the shot, he and Max would win the game; if not, Alfie would have a chance to win for their team.

Three pairs of eyes watched intently as Quint lined up his playing piece, hesitated, then flicked it across the board with his finger. The carom skidded straight into the pocket.

"We won!" Max exclaimed.

"Congratulations," Thea added.

Quint didn't say anything as he looked at his daughter.

"I'll bet you really enjoy beating a little ten-year-old kid, don't you?" Alfie said in a flat voice. Then she got up and headed for the door.

Thea rose to go after her, but Quint's hand on her wrist stopped her. "Don't," he said.

"You—" she began. She had meant to say, "You can't let her get away with that," but paused when she saw Max watching with interest.

She nodded. "It's time we got you ready for bed now, Max. You, too, Alan," she called across the room to her other son, who was working a jigsaw puzzle with J.R.

"I'll carry Max up the stairs," Quint said.

She started to protest that she was perfectly capable of taking care of her own son, then saw the challenge in Quint's eyes. "Thank you," she said instead.

"That's better." He scooped Max into his two strong arms. "Come on, J.R. It's time for your bath."

"Aaaw, Dad."

"Don't 'Aaaw, Dad,' me. We don't want another scene in the morning like the one we had today. Betsy told me about your missing the bus and Thea's having to drive you to school." He looked over his shoulder at Thea, who was following him. "I meant to thank you."

"It was no problem," she said, but her mind was on other things. She was thinking about the way Quint was so forceful with J.R., but allowed Alfie to get away with anything. Maybe things would be better between them if he tried to deal with her the same way he dealt with J.R. It was really none of her business, and Quint would probably tell her exactly that, but she decided to express her opinion.

"May I talk to you later?" she asked him after he'd deposited Max in his room.

He nodded. "I'll be downstairs after I get J.R. in bed."

Thea ran water into the tub for Alan's bath and sponged down Max. Alan talked constantly about his fishing trip. She was sorry she'd been so distracted by the sheriff's presence that she hadn't been able to respond with proper enthusiasm earlier, but tried to make up for it now, listening intently and shushing Max when he tried to interrupt.

Alan was still prattling on when Thea tucked the two boys into bed. She couldn't remember the last time she'd seen him so excited about anything, certainly not in ages. And his brandy-colored eyes, as she leaned over to kiss him good-night, were clear, with no trace of the haunted look she'd seen in them so often lately.

"I had a good time today," he announced.

She swallowed the lump in her throat. "I'm glad, darling. I'm really glad."

"Do you think Quint will take me fishing again?"

"I'm sure of it."

He closed his eyes, a satisfied smile lighting his thin face and turning up his pink lips at the corners.

Chapter Eight

Quint sat in a chair in the living room, reading papers she assumed were legal files. The district attorney was at work. Somehow his occupation didn't upset her the way it once had; she was probably getting used to it. She watched him from the doorway for a moment, then cleared her throat to alert him to her presence.

As he started to get up, she waved him back with her hand. "No, please." She walked over and sat down at one end of the sofa.

"Did you get your boys settled in for the night?" he asked.

"It took Alan forever to finish telling us about the fishing trip. I can't remember when I've seen him so excited. Thank you for taking him, Quint."

He shrugged. "I enjoyed it. He's a nice kid."

"I think I should warn you. He's developed a huge case of hero worship on you. Do you mind?"

"Not me. I'm flattered. Do you mind?"

"Of course not. Why should I?"

"I don't know. You tell me."

"Quint, I told you earlier tonight. I am not jealous of you and Alan. I think it's wonderful that he has someone like you to look up to and to admire." She hesitated. "The only problem I have is that I worry about his missing you and being unhappy after we leave. But that can't be helped."

He frowned. Obviously that thought hadn't occurred to him. "I see your point, and I don't want to hurt him. Would you rather I tried to ignore him?"

"Oh, no! Please don't. That would be even worse. It would break his heart. He's already making plans for the next time you take him fishing. I mean…if you want to take him again."

"Certainly I do. I'm sorry about the other. Is that what you wanted to talk to me about?"

"Alan was part of it." She took a deep breath. "Alfie's the other part."

"I don't think there's much more to be said on that subject."

"But there is! You saw how her face lighted up when you complimented her on that shot tonight."

"And you heard her accuse me of enjoying beating a ten-year-old kid later."

"That was—"

"That's the way it always is with Alfie and me. One step forward and two steps back."

"But it doesn't have to be that way! She's hurting!"

"You don't think I'm hurting, too?" He jumped out of his chair and paced the floor. "It kills me that things are the way they are between us. I've tried everything."

"Maybe you've tried too hard."

He stopped pacing and looked at her. "What do you mean?"

"I've seen the way you are with J.R., fair but firm. You're not the same way with Alfie. You don't stand up to her the way you to do J.R."

"She's a girl."

"I can't believe you said that. She's a human being and she's a child."

"She's also my daughter, not yours."

"So why don't you treat her like a daughter?"

"What are you suggesting?"

"Maybe you should stop trying so hard to please her and be firm with her instead. Get tough."

"And destroy every last shred of love between us?"

"I can't see that there's much left to be destroyed!" She clamped one hand over her mouth, wishing she'd never said that, wishing she could call back her words, wishing she'd never interfered in the first place.

Quint glared at her with something close to hatred in his eyes. "What makes you qualified to judge me, Thea? Are you such a model mother?"

"I'm not perfect, but I'm pretty damn good!" she shot back angrily.

He had to agree with her on that. "How about being a wife? Were you pretty damn good at that, too?"

"What do you mean?"

"You're divorced. You told me you left your husband because he changed, but Alan told me his father was *sick*."

"He . . . he told you that?"

"Yes! So which is it, Thea? Did you walk away from your marriage—and your husband—because you didn't like the fact that he was sick? Did you?"

"No! That isn't true!"

"Then why did you leave him?"

"Because he was a drug addict! He still is!"

Quint stood completely still, stunned. Never in his wildest imagining had he envisioned anything like that. Not that it didn't happen. He read about drug busts and drug addiction all the time in the papers. He'd encountered addicts and dealers in court, too. But they weren't people he personally knew. They weren't...

"Thea, I'm so sorry," he said, sitting down beside her. "I didn't know. I never imagined." He took her hand. It was small, smooth and cold.

"I told the boys he was sick. I didn't know any other way to explain why he acted...the way he did."

"I understand."

"It was the only thing I could think of to say."

"It was close enough to the truth. You did the right thing."

"I don't need you to justify what I did! I mean...people get divorced all the time, and for a lot less reason."

"I know they do. And I owe you an apology for even suggesting you had less than sufficient cause for yours." He squeezed her hand. "My only excuse is that I was angry at what you said about Alfie, and I wanted to hurt you back. I'm sorry."

She had been looking at their hands, but now raised her eyes to meet his. "I'm sorry, too. I had no right to say what I did, either."

"You were trying to be a friend."

"I guess I'm a little rusty at it."

Quint looked at her. "I'm not prying, Thea. And if you don't want to do it, then don't. But...would you like to talk about your ex-husband?"

Yes, she would, she realized with surprise. She hadn't meant to tell Quint that Alan was an addict. The only other people who knew were her mother and stepfather. She couldn't see any harm in telling him, though, and it was such a relief to share at least a small part of her troubles with someone else.

"From all I've read and heard," she said hesitantly, "ours wasn't an unusual story."

"Unless it happens to you. Then it's unique."

She nodded. "At least, we think it is."

"I was thinking a little while ago that I've dealt with addicts in court. I've felt sorry for them. I've been angry at them. But . . . I was never *personally* involved. To have that happen to someone you love must be . . . devastating?"

"Yes! Oh, yes. He was talented, too, Quint. Brilliant. He had so much to offer. Do you understand what I'm saying?" She clutched his hands with both of hers, squeezing hard, trying to make him understand.

"I think I do. It's horribly sad when someone has so much, and then throws it all away. It's such a terrible waste."

She nodded. He *did* understand.

"When did he start using drugs?"

"I think it was sometime after Max was born. I'm not sure. He was—is—pretty clever at hiding his addiction."

"Did he ever get treatment?"

"Once. It was an outpatient program and it helped for a while. Then he got worse again."

"That's when you divorced him."

"Not then. Later. I thought it might help if I enrolled in a therapy program myself—one for families of addicts."

"And did it?"

"Not much. I did learn a little about myself, and I learned that you don't help addicts by giving in to them. You have to be strong enough to give tough love."

Quint gazed at her for a long time. "That's what you were trying to tell me about the way I handle Alfie."

"Something like that."

"Do you think it might work?"

"I honestly don't know, Quint. It didn't help in my case. I don't even know who I think I am to be giving advice."

"I value your opinion."

"I can't imagine why you would."

"Because you're intelligent. You're caring. And you're my friend." He gave her a crooked smile. "At least, I hope you still are."

She smiled back. "I hope so, too."

They sat on the sofa, holding hands and looking at each other. Quint had the strange sensation they were absorbing each other, drawing from each other's strengths, healing each other's hurts. Neither of them moved or spoke for a long time.

"Thea," he said at last, "would you tell me some more about tough love?"

"Do you really want to know?"

"Yes. Please."

She thought a moment. "It's doing what you know in your heart is right, no matter what."

"Being true to yourself."

"Yes, but there's more to it than that. If the other person does something wrong, you don't let them get away with it. You call them on it, every single time."

"Even if they hate you for being so tough?" he asked quietly.

"I'm afraid so. You have to be strong."

Quint lifted his hand to touch her cheek. "Strong Thea. Tough Thea." She looked anything but strong and tough, and he hated her ex-husband for putting her through hell.

She shook her head. "I told you it didn't work in my case."

"But you think it might with me and Alfie?"

"There are no guarantees, and I'm not sure of anything anymore."

"But there's a chance?"

"I think so."

"Alfie went through a terrible experience when her mother died," Quint said. "I think she still hasn't recovered from the shock of that."

"She was at the age when it would hurt the most, too," Thea added.

"Yes."

"A lot of kids have some of her problems to a lesser degree. I can remember how I was always pushing my mother to let me do things when I was about Alfie's age. Most of them were things I didn't really want to do, or was afraid of doing, but they were things everybody else was doing.

"I think I wanted to assert myself as much as anything, and expected her to turn me down, which she did. It's a sort of power struggle. You want to be grown-up, but you want to be protected at the same time. You're struggling for independence, but you're afraid of it. You want your parents to take care of you by being firm. It's one way they show you they love you."

She looked at Quint. "Does that make any sense?"

"It makes a lot of sense. And I'll think about it. Okay?"

"Fair enough." She sighed. "I guess I might as well tell you now what else I did to interfere in your affairs today. I bought Alfie a new pair of jeans."

"You did what?"

"I bought Alfie a new pair of jeans."

"She already has tons of jeans."

"They're too short. I noticed—"

"No. I mean she has a whole drawer full of new jeans that I've bought her. She just won't wear them. I suppose it's because I was the one who bought them."

Thea thought about that, digesting the information. "I can see her trying to hurt you, but not if she's hurting herself even more. She's a smart kid. She knows the other kids in her class must be making fun of her for—" She stopped;

another thought occurred to her. "What kind of jeans did you buy?"

"Jean jeans. Blue denim. What other kind is there?"

"Dark blue?"

"Yes."

"Not prewashed or distressed or acid-washed or anything like that?"

"What on earth are you talking about?"

"I have an idea. Would you mind if I washed some of her new jeans tomorrow?"

"It's okay by me." He shrugged. "It's too late to return them, anyway. But what's the point?"

"All the kids today want their jeans to look old. They even tear them at the knees."

"In that case, her old jeans should be right in style."

"Nope. They're too short."

"I don't see the difference."

"Having your jeans look old is fine; it's desirable. But having them too short is an absolute no-no."

Quint rubbed the back of his neck. "I thought all that stuff didn't start until kids were teenagers."

"Sorry to be the bearer of bad news, but it starts earlier every year."

"Even at age ten?"

"Even at seven. Alan is already becoming fashion conscious."

Quint sighed. "How did we get from drug addiction and alienated daughters to teen fashions?"

Thea laughed. "Beats me."

He became serious again. "I appreciate what you're trying to do."

"It's not much."

"It is to me. Thank you, Thea."

THEA WAS FEELING very pleased with herself as she headed down the nursing-home corridor toward Aunt Maudie's room the following afternoon. The jeans she'd washed in bleach several times that morning had turned out even better than she'd hoped. She was sure Alfie would like them, too.

More important than her success with the jeans, however, was the fact that Quint had said he would think about her suggestion that he treat Alfie with firmness. He hadn't promised he would do it, but thinking about it was a beginning.

She stopped walking as a disturbing thought occurred to her. Why had she become so caught up in Quint's problems? She should have been avoiding him and his children as much as possible. She certainly didn't want to become attached to any of them. So why had she done it?

Gratitude, she told herself. He had been so kind to her family, taking charge the night of Max's accident, and taking Alan fishing later. It was only fair that she should try to repay him in some slight way. After that she would again avoid him.

She continued to her aunt's room and entered.

"Hello, Thea," Aunt Maudie said. Instead of smiling as she usually did, she frowned.

"Is something wrong?" Thea asked.

"I think perhaps there is."

"You're not worse?" Thea began.

"No, I'm fine. It's not me." Aunt Maudie reached into the pocket of her robe. "I think you're the one who has some kind of problem," she continued, opening her hand to reveal the object she had pulled from her pocket.

It was the antique lavaliere Thea had pawned. She stared at it as if it were some horrible alien monster about to attack her.

"A man brought this to me this morning," Aunt Maudie said. "Is there something you want to tell me?"

Thea shook her head. She couldn't talk. She could barely breathe.

"The man's name is Dan Bridges. He owns a pawnshop in the nearest town east of here." Aunt Maudie looked at Thea, waiting for her to say something, but she didn't speak.

"Dan said a young woman came into his shop yesterday wanting to pawn some jewelry. This was one of the pieces."

"But..." Thea said, finally finding her voice. "But why would he bring it to you?"

"He thought it belonged to me. He thought I might have given it to the young woman who pawned it...or that she might have stolen it from me."

"What?"

"I explained to him that there are two identical lavalieres. Mine, and the one that belonged to my sister, your grandmother. I told him Papa gave them to us when she was seventeen and I was sixteen. I told him that mine is still in my possession." Aunt Maudie paused to reach inside the collar of her gown and pull out a lavaliere that was identical to the one she held in her hand.

"He finally agreed with me that the necklace the young woman pawned must be the one your grandmother gave you before she died."

Thea's mind raced furiously, and her heartbeat kept pace with it. "I...I still don't understand why he brought the necklace to you."

"Dan and his wife have been in my bridge club for years. They've seen me wear my necklace many times. Dan recognized the design immediately."

"I see."

"So, Thea, why did you pawn the necklace your grandmother gave you?"

"I didn't!" she lied, feeling desperate, like a trapped animal. "I . . . I lost it."

"Don't lie to me!"

"It's the truth!"

Aunt Maudie shook her head. "No. Dan gave me a very good description of the young woman who pawned this necklace. It was you. That's why I wouldn't let him report it to the police."

Police! Thea suddenly felt sick and sagged in defeat. "Okay, it was me. I pawned it."

"Why?"

"I . . . I needed money."

"So much that you were willing to part with this?"

"I didn't want to! But I felt that I didn't have any other choice."

Aunt Maudie narrowed her eyes. "Why did you really come to Planters' Junction, Thea?"

This was the moment she'd dreaded. She couldn't tell her aunt the whole truth, but had to tell her something. The question was what and how much. "I . . . I wanted to get away from Alan. He's been causing problems."

"Your ex-husband? You told me the divorce was friendly. Why would he cause problems after all this time?"

"He's sick, Aunt Maudie. He's . . . on drugs."

"Prescription or the other kind?"

"The other kind."

Aunt Maudie leaned forward in her wheelchair, fury flashing in her dark eyes. "Has he hurt you? Or your precious children?"

"No."

"Then he's threatened to hurt you!"

"No. I mean, not exactly."

"What exactly?"

"I'm afraid of him! And the boys are afraid of him!"

Thea lowered her head, but felt the older woman's eyes on her, studying her, assessing the situation.

"So you ran away from him and came here to hide," Aunt Maudie said after a long moment.

"I didn't say that!" Thea declared, looking defiantly at her aunt.

"You did the right thing," her aunt said, nodding her head. "It's what I would have done myself under the circumstances. Tell me all about it."

"I'm sorry, Aunt Maudie. I can't tell you much more than I already have."

"Can't or won't?"

Thea swallowed the knot in her throat. Much as she wanted to seek comfort from her aunt, she absolutely would not tell her the whole truth. If she did, she would incriminate Aunt Maudie by making her an accessory to the kidnapping.

"A little of both," she said. "Please trust me when I say it's better if you don't know."

"It's that serious?"

Aunt Maudie was watching her intently, and Thea once more had to force herself to look her straight in the eye. This was another moment she'd been dreading. "Yes," she stated emphatically. "It's that serious."

She held her breath and waited, hoping her aunt would accept the situation without asking further questions. If not...

"In that case," Aunt Maudie finally said, "you're right to be careful what you tell me. My memory's not as good as it used to be, and I might forget and say something I shouldn't."

Thea closed her eyes with relief.

She opened them again when she heard her aunt's chuckle. "You were smart to think of Planters' Junction. Who'd ever think to look for you in this old town?"

Thea smiled weakly.

"Here, this belongs to you," Aunt Maudie said, holding out the necklace. "Consider it a gift from me this time."

"I can't let you do that," Thea protested. "I'll pay you back what—"

"You'll do no such thing. Would you like me to call Dan and redeem the rest of your jewelry?"

"No!"

"You could consider it a loan, if you prefer."

"No, really. I don't want it."

Aunt Maudie narrowed her eyes. "Besides, you'd rather have the money than the jewelry."

"That, too," Thea admitted.

"What we really must do is find you a job so you can earn some money."

Thea nodded, wishing it were possible. Without even a social security number, what kind of job could she get? She was a nameless, homeless nonperson.

"There aren't many jobs available around here," Aunt Maudie continued, thinking out loud.

"I suppose not."

"You might find something in Albany, but that's pretty far to commute."

"Mmm."

They fell silent.

"I have it!" Aunt Maudie suddenly exclaimed. "I don't know why I didn't think of it sooner!"

"What?"

"You'll work for me!"

"I don't understand."

"You'll be my driver! My chauffeur," the older woman added with a laugh.

"You've lost me. Where would I drive you? And when and why?"

"You'll drive me to and from my therapy sessions as soon as I get out of this place!"

"Oh."

"Don't you see? I'll be able to go home right away."

Thea knew how desperately her aunt wanted to go home. "You think the doctors would let you leave?"

"I don't see why not. The main reason I'm here is for the therapy, and with you to drive me every day, I can live at home. Will you do it . . . if I pay you?"

Her aunt was as excited as a young child on Christmas morning. "I'll be happy to drive you while I'm here, Aunt Maudie. If your doctor says it's okay for you to go home," she added. "But I certainly won't accept any money for it."

"Don't be silly. Of course you'll accept money. Do you know how much it costs me to stay in this . . . this *place*?" Her aunt made "place" sound like a dirty word.

"If I go home, I'll be able to pay you a nice salary and still come out ahead."

It almost sounded too good to be true. Thea tried to find something wrong with the plan, but couldn't.

"You'll more than earn the money, Thea. You know how demanding I am . . . and I'm a lot of extra trouble these days." She frowned. "I'd forgotten for a moment how much extra trouble I am. Maybe this wasn't such a good idea, after all."

Aunt Maudie looked as if Santa had just taken back all her presents from under the tree. Thea made up her mind.

"It's a *very* good idea," she said. "The boys and I need to stay here until Max is better. And you know I need the money. I accept your job offer!"

"You're sure it won't be too much for you?"

"It'll be a snap. I should be paying you . . . but I won't."

Thea and her aunt smiled at each other.

"Should I tell Quint and…and the others?" Thea asked.

"Not yet. I'd better clear it with my doctor first, to make sure. I don't believe he'll give me any trouble, though."

"Why not?"

"He's afraid of me."

Thea guffawed. "I should have known."

Chapter Nine

It was official. Aunt Maudie was coming home.

Thea told Quint her aunt's doctor wasn't as afraid of her as she'd thought, however. It had taken him more than a week to give her his permission—and her freedom, as she called it.

The doctor had even summoned Thea and Quint into his office to discuss the situation at home. The three of them had finally agreed that it would be better to hire someone to come in at night to sleep in Aunt Maudie's room, in case she needed assistance.

Aunt Maudie opposed the plan. She didn't need a sitter, she argued, so how could she possibly need a sleeper?

Betsy volunteered to handle the job of finding someone suitable to sleep in Miss Maudie's room. She produced a young girl with stringy blond hair. "Jacinda won't finish high school for a few weeks yet, but staying here at night won't interfere with her schooling. I know for a fact she's dependable, and she really needs the money."

Thea couldn't understand why Betsy was so adamant that they hire Jacinda. "Does she need the money for college?"

"No, she's the oldest of nine kids," Betsy explained. "Her whole family needs whatever money she can bring in."

Thea turned to Quint for his opinion. He shrugged. "I guess it's settled, then," she said. "Will you ask Jacinda when she'll be available to start?"

"She's available now," Betsy declared. "I'll go tell her she's hired. You won't be sorry."

After the housekeeper hurried out of the living room, Quint looked at Thea. He couldn't remember when he'd seen her happier or more beautiful. She almost seemed to glow. It was quite a contrast from the tense, anxious woman she'd been when she first arrived. It was even a contrast from the past week, when she'd been polite to him—too polite—but cool and distant. They had encountered each other in the upstairs hall on Thursday, though, and she had actually smiled at him.

It was the intimacy of the week.

Quint didn't know why he felt so disgruntled by her aloofness. Keeping each other at a distance was for the best. It was what he wanted and what he might have done himself, if she hadn't beaten him to it.

"So," he said, "she's finally coming home."

"It looks like it. Have you told J.R. yet?"

"Yes, but I think he's not sure whether he should allow himself to believe it or not."

"Poor little guy."

"He's going to be a mighty happy little guy when he finds out it's true and she's really here. Thank you for making it possible, Thea."

"Don't thank me. It was Aunt Maudie's idea to come home, not mine."

"I know, but—"

"And she's paying me to drive her to therapy."

"She told me that. Still—"

"I am not going to argue with you now and certainly not about this."

He hadn't thought he was arguing, but suddenly decided it might not be a bad idea. "What will you argue with me about?" he asked.

"Why do you want to argue?"

"It's a form of communicating."

"Meaning?"

"You've been avoiding me. Why?"

She looked at him directly for an instant, and he was amazed, excited, delighted—and scared to death—by what he saw in her eyes before she quickly turned away. "I thought it was best," she said in a low voice.

Quint knew he hadn't imagined the look in her eyes, or what it meant. It was raw desire. She wanted him as much as he wanted her. He didn't know what to say—or do.

Neither of them spoke for a long time.

"I've been meaning to ask you something," she finally said.

He caught his breath and watched her averted profile.

"Did you ever hear from your insurance company about Max's hospital bill?"

He almost laughed out loud. Talk about non sequiturs! "Sure," he said. "They paid the whole thing, like I told you they would."

"I'm glad."

"I've been meaning to ask you something, too," he said. He saw her jaw tense automatically. "Did Alfie ever thank you for bleaching her jeans?"

"Yes, she . . ." Thea finally turned to face him. "Why do you ask?"

"I told her to, and I wanted to know if she had."

"You did? That's wonderful, Quint! Not that she thanked me, but that you told her to do something and she did it."

"It's not much."

"It's a beginning."

"I suppose so." He thought for a moment. "Do you think we should celebrate Miss Maudie's homecoming?"

"That's a marvelous idea!" she exclaimed.

"We could have a big party..." he began, but paused when he saw the excitement fade from her expressive face. "Or we can make it a private celebration."

"Let's keep it small," she said.

Quint heard the relief in her voice. "Okay, we can still decorate the house."

"Oh, yes! And we can all dress up, and we'll get Betsy to cook all Aunt Maudie's favorite foods."

Some things don't change, Quint thought as he listened to her make plans for the party. Thea looked happier and acted more at ease some of the time, but she still closely guarded her precious privacy...and her emotions.

That night during dinner, Quint and Thea told the kids about Aunt Maudie's homecoming party.

"Oh, wow!" Max said. "Do you think she'll play caroms with me?" Caroms had become his favorite game of all time. He had improved with practice, too, and had been itching to play with Aunt Maudie since he learned how good she was at the game.

"She might be too tired the first night she's home," Thea said. "But I'm sure she'll play with you later."

"Will we have cake and ice cream?" Max asked.

He was so excited about the party that it made Thea suddenly realize how bored he was and how much he hated being confined by his broken leg. She resolved to try to think of more ways to keep him entertained.

"Will we have to dress up?" Alan asked.

"Certainly!" Quint answered with mock severity. "It's a party, isn't it?"

J.R. was quiet, but Thea noticed he paid close attention to everything that was said.

"What do you plan to wear to the party, Alfie?" she asked.

"I'm not going to be here," the girl said.

Everyone stared at her.

"Why do you say that?" Quint asked.

"I'm spending the night with Denise."

"This is a special occasion," he said. "I would think you'd want to—"

"I *always* stay with Denise on Saturdays."

Thea looked at Quint and saw his jaw tighten. "Not this time, Alfie. Miss Maudie's coming home."

"I don't care!"

"I care," he said quietly. " We should all be here to welcome her."

"You promised me I could stay with Denise!"

"No. I've let you visit her on Saturdays…until now. But I've never promised."

"You can't do this to me!"

Thea saw Quint take a deep breath and saw the sadness in his eyes, but his voice was determined. "I can and I will. I insist that you be here for the party. There'll be plenty of other times for you to—"

"You hate me! You always have!"

"Of course I don't hate you."

"And I hate you, too! I hate all of you!" Alfie pushed away from the table and ran out of the room.

Thea bit her lip; Quint's pain was obvious. He wouldn't look at her. For perhaps the hundredth time since she'd suggested that Quint be firm with Alfie, she wondered if she'd done the right thing. For perhaps the thousandth time, she wished she'd never tried to interfere.

When she went upstairs later to get her boys ready for bed, she heard noises coming from Alfie's room. As usual, the door was closed, but no one could mistake the sound of deep, heartrending sobs.

"Mom?" Alan asked, looking at her anxiously. "Should we go see about Alfie?"

"I don't think we can help her, Alan," she said sadly. She wasn't sure anyone could.

She didn't see any more of Quint that night. The next morning, she walked into the kitchen in time to hear him telling Betsy not to prepare any food for Alfie at Miss Maudie's party because she wouldn't be there. She was spending the night with a friend.

Thea knew he knew she had entered the kitchen. He still wouldn't look at her. Her heart ached, and her body longed for him. She hated it. She especially hated the fact that her own body would betray her at such a critical time in her life. She tried to will him out of her thoughts, out of her bloodstream. So far she hadn't had much success with either.

She had even begun to dream about him. The dreams weren't like the romantic fantasies she'd had about him at sixteen. These dreams were much more erotic. Sensual. Sexual. They seemed realistic, too. In that sense, they weren't as much dreams as possibilities, if she would allow them to happen. And if he would.

She often thanked him silently for being strong enough to resist the powerful attraction that they both knew existed between them. At other times, usually in the dark loneliness of the middle of the night, she silently cursed him for denying them the solace of fulfillment.

THEA STOOD in the middle of the living room, examining it with a critical eye. She finally nodded with satisfaction. The room, along with the rest of the house, was so clean that it almost glistened. It should be. She and Betsy, with Jacinda helping after school, had spent days cleaning from top to bottom.

It was worth it, she thought now. And everything looked so festive! There were brightly colored balloons everywhere, and there was a huge, hand-lettered sign reading Welcome Home! suspended from the ceiling of the living room.

Everyone except Alfie had pitched in to help Max and J.R. blow up the balloons. The sign, on the other hand, was Quint and Alan's special project. The two of them had spread it on the floor and spent hours lying on their stomaches, talking and laughing while they painted the lettering. Thea had never seen her older son happier.

Quint was so good to him—to all of them. He had even brought out an old toy wagon and fixed it up for Max to use as transportation. He had made a backrest by bolting a board to the rear end of the wagon, added pads and pillows, then plopped Max inside. Max fitted perfectly into the wagon, cast and all, and now he was mobile! At least, he was mobile as long as someone was around to pull the wagon, and Max loved it.

Before he left to pick up Aunt Maudie at the nursing home, Quint had pulled Max to the front window and handed him a pair of binoculars. "You're our official lookout," Quint said. "Your job is to keep a sharp watch and let everyone know as soon as I get back with Miss Maudie. Can you handle that?"

"You bet!" Max said, fairly bursting with importance.

Thea sighed. It wasn't fair that Quint was a hero to her sons and not to his own daughter. Sometimes she thought she'd like to throttle the girl. Then, remembering what Alfie had suffered and knowing how much she hurt inside, Thea wanted to hold her in her arms and cry along with her.

The truth was, even though she had decided to remain uninvolved with Quint and his children, she was already involved. She thought about Quint much too much; he was rarely out of her mind. And Alfie was breaking her heart.

Hearing a sound behind her, Thea turned as Betsy entered the room. Though it was Saturday, the housekeeper's day off and the day she usually visited her daughter, she had insisted on being there for Miss Maudie's homecoming party.

"Everything looks wonderful, Betsy," Thea said. "I don't know how we could have done it without Jacinda, though." That was true. The girl had been everywhere—polishing, dusting, seeming to know what needed to be done without being told.

Betsy nodded. "I knew you'd like her."

"I do. I suppose we'll be losing her when she graduates from high school in a few weeks, though."

"Maybe so, maybe not. Jobs aren't too plentiful around here because of the droughts. The whole economy's depressed."

"What about down in Albany? A bright young girl like Jacinda should be able to get a job with a future there."

Betsy thought for a moment. "I'm not too sure. Without any college or special training, she'd be part of the unskilled labor market, and Albany already has plenty of folks who'll work for minimum wage . . . or less."

Thea was outraged. "Nobody should have to work for less than minimum wage today! What about human rights?"

"Some of them don't have any rights, as far as society's concerned. They don't even speak English."

"Are you talking about illegal aliens?"

Betsy nodded. "They've been moving north from Miami, hoping to find something better up here. A few of them do. Most don't."

Thea shook her head, then frowned as a thought occurred to her. "How are they able to work at all? Don't they need a social security card?"

"They simply make up a number."

Thea blinked. "You mean...they make up a number—any number out of the blue—and get away with it?"

"It can't just be *any* number. It has to be a reasonable number, with the right amount of digits and all. I've heard that some people coming into the country even buy the first three digits down in Miami. It's a big business."

Thea crossed her fingers; a whole new world of hope started to open up before her. "What about income taxes? Doesn't someone notice the false numbers on tax returns?"

Betsy chuckled. "The people who use the numbers are long gone by then. They change jobs a lot, move around a lot."

"And...and then they make up a new set of numbers at the new job?"

"That's right." The black woman suddenly frowned. "Why are you so interested in this?"

"I was simply curious, that's all." Curious, all right, but that wasn't all. She was about as excited as a person could be. If she made up reasonable numbers and moved around a lot, she could *work*, earn money and support her children! Thea clenched her fists.

"She's here!" Maxie suddenly shouted from his lookout post by the window.

QUINT LEANED across Miss Maudie to open the front door. He had tried to convince her to let him push her in the wheelchair but she had insisted on using her walker, even though her progress was woefully slow. "Here we are," he said.

Miss Maudie didn't move. "How do I look?"

"Beautiful."

"Quint, you're the worst liar I've ever heard. The most I can hope to look is presentable."

"Haven't you ever heard that beauty is in the eye of the beholder?"

She squinted at him. "Have you been practicing pretty phrases like that on my niece?"

"I told you before. We're just friends." And not even very good ones at that, he thought, remembering how he'd avoided Thea ever since he chickened out and let Alfie go to her friend's house tonight, instead of insisting that she come to the homecoming party.

What else could he have done? Alfie had cried for hours. Listening to her, he had felt like crying himself. She was obviously in pain—pain that he had caused her. Finally, when he couldn't bear it any longer, he had gone to her room and told her that he'd changed his mind. She could spend Saturday night with Denise, as usual.

She hadn't even thanked him. He didn't know what he had expected, but her calm, cold emotionless acceptance of his change of mind hadn't been it. Had he done the right thing? Probably not. Now he felt both guilty about Alfie and guilty around Thea. He was guilty as charged. Guilty of being a lousy husband and father, guilty of desperately wanting a woman he could never have. Guilty, guilty, guilty!

"Shall we go inside?" he asked.

Miss Maudie squared her shoulders and nodded her head.

Quint stepped inside first and held the door open for her to follow him on her own. He watched with admiration as she took faltering steps.

The hallway was quiet, shadowed, deserted. "Well," he said, "how does it look?"

"It looks wonderful," she replied in a voice that was audibly choked with emotion. "It looks like home."

He stood silently by her side, observing her savor her return to the home where she'd lived for more than sixty years, the home she probably had thought she might never see again.

She finally turned to him with a hint of tears glistening at the corners of her eyes. "It's splendid," she said.

He took her hand and squeezed it. "I think some people might be waiting in the living room to see you."

Her answering smile was shy and sad and happy all at the same time. He wished he could capture it on film.

"I certainly hope so," she said.

He squeezed her hand again before releasing it, then moved ahead to open the living-room door.

"Surprise!" came a chorus of voices to greet them. "Welcome home!"

Quint had never seen Miss Maudie at a loss for words, but she was now. Thea and Betsy, both wearing broad smiles, stood closest to the door. Jacinda had pulled Maxie's wagon away from the window, and she and Alan stood beside it. J.R. was a couple of steps behind Alan, and was the only one who wasn't smiling. He simply stared at Miss Maudie.

She nodded to everybody in the room, then her gaze went back to J.R. and lingered there. The rest of them fell silent, watching the two.

"Aren't you going to say hello?" she asked at last.

J.R. opened his mouth to speak, but nothing came out.

"How about a hug, then?" she asked.

The boy hesitated a moment, then ran forward and flung himself at her. Quint moved quickly to catch Miss Maudie, who had released her grip on the walker so that she could bend to embrace his son.

J.R. clutched her around the neck; she wrapped her bony arms around his shoulders and buried her face in his blond hair. Quint held on to both of them to keep them from falling, and felt tears sting his eyes.

He glanced up after a moment and saw Thea regarding him. Tears streamed down her cheeks, too. He shook his head. She nodded, obviously as happy about J.R.'s reunion with Miss Maudie as he was.

After long moments, Miss Maudie lifted her head and looked at J.R. again, oblivious of everyone else in the room. She placed her hands upon his shoulders and pushed him back slightly to get a better look. "I think you must have grown an inch since I've been gone."

J.R. stood up straighter. "Really?"

"At least that much." They both grinned.

Eventually Miss Maudie looked around and sniffed. "Does anyone here have a tissue? I seem to have left mine at that *place*."

With the private reunion over, everyone crowded around Miss Maudie, laughing and talking at the same time.

"Well, look at you!" she exclaimed when she spotted Max and his cast in the wagon. "You're in even worse shape than I was."

"Did they put a cast on you, too?" Max asked.

"No, but they did everything else. You've never seen such poking and prodding. Did they do that to you?"

"Yeah, they sure did!"

Max and Miss Maudie exchanged details of their broken bones. Then she complimented Betsy and Jacinda on the house, Thea on the party, and the rest of them for welcoming her home this way. Through it all, J.R. never left her side, and they touched each other frequently. Quint thought they were each making sure the other was still there, and that this was really happening.

Finally Betsy brought out hors d'oeuvres and Quint served drinks—fruit punch for the boys and Jacinda, a glass of wine for Thea and Betsy, and bourbon with water for Miss Maudie and himself. "To you," he said, raising his glass to her in a toast.

"To *home*," she responded. "It's the place where we're treated the best and grumble the most!"

Alan, Max and J.R. laughed as loudly as the grown-ups. The festive mood continued during dinner, which they ate in the dining room rather than the kitchen. Betsy had cooked Miss Maudie's favorites—baked chicken with dressing, fresh green beans, carrots, creamed asparagus, and peach cobbler topped with homemade ice cream for dessert.

"Come here, old woman," Miss Maudie said when Betsy came in to announce that her nephew had arrived to drive her home.

"Who are you calling old? I'm at least twenty years younger than you are," Betsy replied indignantly. "And don't you go falling down anymore, you hear? We all have better things to do than worrying about a foolish old woman."

Quint glanced across the table and caught Thea's eyes. They both suppressed their laughter as they saw the two old friends embrace and exchange loving insults.

Later, after Betsy had left and Jacinda had cleared away the last of the dinner dishes, Miss Maudie gave a long sigh. "It's been a grand party," she announced.

J.R. uttered a similar sigh. "It sure has."

She reached out and patted his hand. "I think it must be past your bedtime now, though."

"Aw," he started to complain. "Do I have to—?"

She silenced him immediately by lifting one eyebrow.

"I guess so," J.R. said.

She smiled her approval.

He got up, kissed Miss Maudie's cheek, and headed up to bed without another word of protest. Quint watched with amazement. He couldn't remember his son ever doing that before—never in his entire life.

"It *WAS* A GOOD PARTY," Quint said.

Thea glanced around at the sound of his voice. She was finishing up in the kitchen while Jacinda helped Aunt Maudie get ready for bed. Quint had volunteered to tuck in the three boys. "Yes, it was," she agreed. "Did the boys give you any trouble?"

"None at all. Alan and Max were good as gold, and J.R. was better than I've seen him since ... a long time."

She nodded. "He was just dear tonight. Aunt Maudie was, too. They love each other so much...." She looked at him directly then, for the first time since he'd come into the room, and caught her breath at the depth of feeling in his eyes.

"I've been avoiding you the last few days," he said.

"I know," she breathed.

"I felt so damned guilty."

"About Alfie."

"Yes, but about you, too."

"There's no reason for you to feel guilty about me."

"I told you I'd think about what you said."

"But you never promised to follow my suggestion."

"It was implicit," he insisted. "And I let you down."

"Alfie's your daughter, and it was your decision to make."

"Don't be so understanding," he said. "I'm trying to apologize to you."

"You don't owe me anything, including an apology."

"Because you're not involved, right?"

"Right."

"I don't believe you," he said.

He was standing only inches from her. When had he moved so close? Before she knew what had happened, she felt his arms around her waist, pulling her against him. "Don't—" she began, but it was already too late. His mouth closed over hers, muffling her half-hearted protest.

She placed her hands upon his shoulders to push him away. Once more she felt the warmth of his body and the strength of his muscles through the softness of his cotton shirt. Suddenly confused, she hesitated.

Wasn't this what she wanted? Wasn't it what she'd been dreaming about at night, and thinking about much too much? She had wanted this to happen and at the same time, she'd been determined that it wouldn't.

That made no sense at all. Nothing made any sense except his strong arms around her and his soft lips against hers. They made all the sense in the world. Abandoning any pretense of resistance, she moved her arms to encircle his neck and her lips parted of their own volition.

Sometime later—much later—she relaxed her arms and felt Quint do the same. Each moved back slightly and gazed at the other.

His breathing was as rapid as hers was, and he appeared as startled as she felt.

She waited a moment for her heart to slow down. "Why do we keep doing this to each other?"

He still held her around the waist, but raised one of his hands to touch her flushed cheek. "Maybe I want to punish you for being so desirable ... so passionate ... and still denying your own emotions."

She swallowed. "And you? What about you?"

"Maybe you want to punish me—and I want to punish myself—for wanting you too much. For being a bad boy."

Then he smiled and gave her a light kiss. The kiss barely grazed her lips, and his smile was devilish instead of romantic. But together they turned her into complete mush.

The dreams about Quint returned that night, more erotic than ever, more arousing. Thea barely slept at all. The next morning she felt like a zombie, and thought she probably looked like one, too. *Overstimulation will do it to you every time,* she told herself as she went through the motions of making breakfast.

Denise Taylor and her parents dropped off Alfie just as everyone finished eating. Alfie talked with Aunt Maudie for a few seconds and gave her a brief hug, then excused herself and went to her room.

"I see she hasn't changed much while I've been gone," Aunt Maudie said to Thea when they were alone in the kitchen later.

"I'm afraid not," she agreed.

Aunt Maudie sighed. "I wonder what will become of her."

"And of Quint," Thea added.

Her aunt nodded. "I think—" she began, but was interrupted by the sound of the phone ringing.

Thea answered it. It was one of Aunt Maudie's friends, who'd heard she was home again. That first phone call opened a Pandora's box. Aunt Maudie would barely hang up the phone before it would ring once more and Thea would have to run to answer it. Again.

Visitors stopped by after lunch and after church. Thea later decided that everyone in Planters' Junction must have called or come by sometime during the day. At first she tried to avoid the visitors, hiding in her room the way Alfie did. Then Quint asked whether she minded if he took Alan and Max fishing with J.R. and himself, and she couldn't say no.

After they left, she was the only one available to answer the phone and the door, serve refreshments and help Aunt Maudie keep her visitors entertained. The visitors kept coming, and the phone kept ringing.

Late that afternoon, one of the phone calls was from a woman who identified herself as Denise's mother. She wanted to speak to Alfie. Thea called the girl to the phone, then eavesdropped shamelessly while Alfie made a few surly, one-syllable responses. Alfie hung up the phone a few seconds later and went back to her room.

Sighing, Thea returned to the living room to help the queen of Planters' Junction entertain her loyal subjects.

By the time the last visitor had left, she was exhausted, and gratefully accepted Quint's offer to make salad and scrambled eggs for supper. They were just sitting down at the kitchen table when the phone rang yet again. Thea groaned.

"I'll get it," Quint said. "The rest of you go ahead without me."

He was gone a long time. When he finally returned, he didn't come all the way into the kitchen. "May I speak to you a moment, Thea?" he asked from the doorway.

All her old fears came back in a great rush. It must be something important because he was so serious. Had the phone call been about her? Slowly, feeling as if she were going to her doom, she got up and walked into the hall with Quint. He closed the door behind them.

"Is . . . is something wrong?" she asked.

Quint merely looked at her, and she knew immediately that something *was* wrong. Terribly wrong.

Chapter Ten

She was afraid to ask, but had to know. "What is it, Quint?"

"That was Cal on the phone," he said solemnly.

She held her breath.

"Alfie's friend Denise Taylor has disappeared. Cal thinks she may have been kidnapped."

Thea blinked, trying to comprehend what he'd said. He wasn't talking about the kidnapping she had done. This was something entirely different. "Denise?" she repeated blankly.

"Yes. Alfie's friend, the one she stayed with last night. Her parents haven't seen her since early this afternoon. They're afraid something might have happened to her."

"Oh, Quint, how awful!"

"I know. Cal is organizing a search party and I'm going with them. Can you manage things here by yourself?"

"Certainly."

"I don't know how long I'll be gone." He shook his head. "I feel sorry for the Taylors. Having your child kidnapped is the worst thing I can think of. I think I could actually kill someone who did that."

She nodded, unable to speak.

"Don't wait up for me," Quint said, then was gone. She stood motionless in the hall, waiting for her heart to start beating again.

THEA SAT ALONE at the kitchen table staring at the clock over the sink, watching the minutes tick by while she waited for Quint to return. Twelve o'clock and one o'clock came and went, and still there was no sign of him.

She probably should get up and go to bed, she thought dully, but knew she wouldn't sleep. She was much too nervous, so she might as well worry here as in bed.

How ironic it was that Planters' Junction might have a kidnapping only a couple of weeks after she'd arrived here with her own kidnapped kids! She wondered if there had ever been a kidnapping in the town before. Probably not.

She hoped Denise hadn't been abducted. It was a terrible thing. She remembered Quint's face as he'd said, "I could actually kill someone who did that." He had meant it, too, every word of it and she didn't blame him.

Maybe it hadn't happened to Denise. Maybe Quint would come in any moment and tell her that the child had merely wandered off, that she had been found unharmed and had already been returned safely to her parents. Maybe.

If not—if the girl really had been kidnapped—the whole town would be in an uproar by tomorrow. They'd bring in outside law enforcement officers to help, probably the FBI. Oh, yes. And there'd probably be a door-to-door search.

She couldn't be here when they did that. She and her boys had to be gone by then; that meant they had to leave right away, tomorrow or the next day, even if Max's broken leg made it uncomfortable for him to travel. The alternative— being discovered and having Alan and Max returned to the custody of a dangerous drug addict—was too horrible to consider.

They had to leave; there was no other choice. Perhaps they could sneak away in the middle of the night, as they'd done once before. She wouldn't tell anybody they were leaving.... But she had to tell somebody; otherwise their sudden departure would be too suspicious. People might even think that she had something to do with Denise's disappearance!

She would tell Aunt Maudie they were leaving, but not where they were headed. Suppose she told her aunt that her mother had suddenly been taken ill and she had to go to Arizona to see her? That was fine...except for the fact that Aunt Maudie would probably call her mother to check on her. Thea discarded that idea. She had to think of something else. But what?

She heard a noise and looked up to see Quint coming into the room. She got up and started toward him, but stopped when she saw the expression on his face. "Denise?" she asked, knowing the answer in advance.

He shook his head. "No luck."

"You look dead on your feet. Would you like something to eat or drink?"

Again he shook his head. "No, thanks."

"Then come into the living room and sit down." She took his arm and led him down the hall to the living room, where he collapsed onto the sofa.

"They called off the search for tonight because it's so foggy outside," he said wearily. "We'll start again at daybreak."

"Were you able to find anything? Any trace of what happened?"

"Nothing much. The last time her parents saw her was around one o'clock in the afternoon. Denise went to her room right after lunch.... Evidently she's a lot like Alfie in more ways than one.

"Later in the afternoon, her mother went to check on her and she wasn't there. Mrs. Taylor said she phoned Alfie to find out if she knew where Denise was, or if Denise had said anything to her."

"She did phone. I answered it and called Alfie. She didn't talk long."

Quint nodded. "Mrs. Taylor said Alfie told her she didn't know anything. Did you tell her about Denise being missing?"

"No. I told Aunt Maudie in private. I didn't want to alarm the kids unless . . . unless we had to."

"I'm afraid there's a good chance they'll find out about it tomorrow. There's even some talk of closing the school and advising parents to keep their kids at home."

"Oh, dear!"

"There's the other thing I haven't mentioned, Thea." He paused. "Cal had the Taylors check their house to see if anything was missing—you know, clothes and such. So far, they haven't noticed anything missing . . . except Denise's bicycle. We, uh, we found it by the side of the road, about a mile from the Taylor farm."

Thea clamped one hand over her mouth.

"Cal is almost convinced that the girl was abducted."

She felt sick. "How horrible! How . . ."

"I know. I feel the same way."

"You look exhausted," she said, noticing how he rubbed the back of his neck. "You'd better get some rest. I'll turn out the lights if you want to go up to bed now."

"Cal will be by to get me in only a couple of hours, so it's hardly worth the trouble to go to bed." He bent to remove his shoes and stretched out on the sofa. "Besides, I think I'm too tired to climb the stairs. Will you stay here and talk to me for a few minutes?"

"If you'd like."

"I would like," he said with a crooked smile. "Very much." He closed his eyes.

"What would you like to talk about?" she asked softly. He didn't answer. He was already asleep.

Thea walked to the sofa and gazed down at him. Fatigue had deepened the laugh lines around his eyes and mouth. His beard, which he had shaved only that afternoon after he and the boys returned from fishing, already needed shaving again.

His shirt was sweat-stained. His trousers were torn and dirty from trudging through the woods, looking for a lost little girl. How like Quint to exhaust himself in such a search. That was the kind of man he was. Gentle. Compassionate. Caring. She remembered the way his quiet words had calmed Max when he broke his leg—and the way he'd comforted her when she'd cried later.

She felt the desire to touch him, to do something for him. She thought about putting a coverlet over him, but he was already fully dressed and the night was warm, almost balmy. She thought about putting a pillow under his head, then reflected that the movement might wake him. She sighed.

Then she bent and did what she'd been wanting to do for days. For years? She touched his thick, dark hair, pushing it back from his forehead, then combing her fingers through it. It felt so good that it made her shiver. Quickly withdrawing her hand, she left the room and headed upstairs to her lonely bed.

QUINT AWOKE with a start and peered around the room in confusion. He had been having a dream about Thea—another one. This time she had been running her slender fingers through his hair. Then she had kissed him. He ran his tongue over his lips, almost imagining that he could taste her.

He closed his eyes again, trying to remember what had happened next in the dream. She had undressed. She hadn't been coy or teasing; her movements had been completely natural, uninhibited in spite of the fact that he was watching her. He had caught his breath at his first sight of her in all her glorious, naked beauty. Her body was a work of art—firm, high breasts, flat stomach, gently rounded hips, long, slender legs.

Then she had moved closer and leaned over again, offering herself to him. Her ripe red lips had descended toward his. His heart was pounding...pounding so hard that he could hear it.

"Dammit, Quint! Open the door!"

He opened his eyes.

"Did you hear me?" Cal shouted. "Open the damn door!"

"I hear you!" Quint shouted back. "I'll be there in a second."

He heaved himself off the sofa, but didn't straighten immediately. His back was so stiff that he wasn't sure whether he'd ever stand completely straight again. He must have slept in the wrong position. Slowly, painfully, he moved toward the front door.

"Stop shouting," he said as he fumbled with the night latch. "You'll wake the kids." He finally managed to open the door.

"It's about time," Cal grumbled, stepping inside. "Didn't you set your alarm?"

"I forgot," Quint said, too tired to explain that he'd slept on the sofa.

"How about making us some coffee to wake us up?" Cal suggested.

Quint nodded and hobbled toward the kitchen. He tried to keep ahead of Cal so his friend wouldn't see his arousal and tease him about it. Cal had a warped sense of humor at times.

"What's wrong with you?" Cal asked.

"My back. The sofa was too short for me."

"You slept on the sofa?"

"Didn't I tell you?"

"No."

"I meant to," Quint lied.

"Why would you—?" Cal stopped as soon as Quint opened the kitchen door. Thea was seated at the table, sound asleep with her head resting on her crossed arms. "Doesn't anybody around here use a bed anymore?"

Cal glanced back at Quint and noticed his condition for the first time. He grinned. "Never mind. I think I understand."

"You don't understand a damn thing. Can't you see she's asleep?"

"*She* is, but obviously you're not."

"I was asleep on the sofa and I had a dream."

"It must have been some dream. Do you want to tell me again how you hurt your back?"

"Go stick your head in a paper bag, Cal. And shut up."

Cal snickered.

Thea suddenly lifted her head. She looked at Quint and blinked. "Oh. Is it time for you to leave already?"

"Almost. Why aren't you in bed?"

"I couldn't sleep, so I thought I'd make coffee in case you wanted some before you left." She gestured toward the counter, where a fresh pot of coffee was ready.

"Thank you," Quint said softly, smiling at her.

"I can make breakfast, too, if—"

"We don't have time to eat," he interrupted. "We need to get going."

Thea glanced behind Quint for the first time and noticed Cal.

Quint had already seen the sheriff watching their exchange with interest. He wanted to tell Cal to wipe the smirk off his face and stop thinking whatever it was he was thinking, but didn't want to upset Thea, so he settled for a warning glance at his old chum instead.

"Hi, Thea," Cal said innocently.

She nodded.

Quint walked to the counter and poured two mugs of coffee. "Would you like some, Thea?"

"No, thanks."

He carried the mugs to the table and handed one to Cal, who had plopped himself onto the chair beside Thea. "Have you decided what to do about calling in the FBI?" he asked the sheriff.

"I thought I'd wait until we make one more search this morning. We might be able to find something in daylight. If not, I'll call them this afternoon."

"What about the Taylors? Have you talked to them yet?"

"I called just before I came over here. They haven't heard a word from or about Denise."

Quint glanced at Thea and noticed she had turned deathly pale. "Are you okay?" he asked her.

"Yes. It's ... this is just such a terrible thing."

"I know." He reached across the table and covered her hand with his own. "Why don't you go back to bed and try to get some rest?"

"I will, as soon as you leave."

"You promise?"

"I promise."

He squeezed her hand. To hell with Cal and whatever he might be thinking!

SHE HAD LIED TO QUINT. She had no intention of going back to bed. She had too much to do. She had to get her sons and herself ready to leave town, and she had to invent a lie to tell Aunt Maudie to explain their sudden departure.

She was still trying out ideas when Jacinda came in to ask about Aunt Maudie's breakfast. The girl volunteered to prepare it, but Thea said she'd do it, along with breakfast for the kids.

Betsy arrived before she could begin, however, and that settled the matter. When Betsy was in the kitchen, nobody cooked except Betsy. The housekeeper also brought news. The local school superintendent had announced on the radio station that all schools in the county were closed for the day. Parents were advised to keep their children at home.

"They said a child had disappeared, and they didn't know what had happened to her," Betsy repeated.

"The child they were talking about was Denise," Thea said.

"Alfie's friend Denise?"

"Yes."

Betsy whistled. "Does Alfie know about it yet?"

"Not yet. One of us has to go up and tell her."

"I think you'd better do it, Thea. She seems to like you more than anyone else."

That was a surprise. "Even Aunt Maudie?"

Betsy nodded. "I'll go with you, if you want me to."

"No. You fix Aunt Maudie's breakfast." Thea stopped by her sons' room on her way to Alfie's. They were both sleeping soundly. She watched them for a long, long time, thinking how dear and defenseless they were; this might be the last really good sleep they got in who knew how long. At last she backed out of the room and quietly closed the door behind herself.

She knocked on Alfie's door and waited. There was no response. She knocked again, louder. "Alfie? It's Thea. I have to talk to you about something."

After a couple of seconds she heard a muffled voice inside the room. "It's not time for me to get up yet. I have another ten minutes."

Thea knocked again. "This is important, Alfie. Please let me in."

After another few seconds, Thea heard the sound of the door being unlocked. Then Alfie flung it open. Clad in faded pink pajamas she must have owned since she was about seven, the girl glared at her with a belligerent expression on her face.

"What do you want?" she asked in a sullen tone.

"I already told you. I want to talk to you."

"About what?"

Thea hesitated. "May I come inside?"

Alfie frowned, then reluctantly stepped aside to allow Thea to enter her room. "Well?" the girl said.

Thea rubbed her eyes, eyes that felt as if they'd been sprinkled with red-hot pepper. "I don't know how to begin," she said.

Alfie merely looked at her, and Thea knew she'd receive no help from that quarter. She took a deep breath and plunged in. "It's about your friend, Denise. She . . . she hasn't been seen since early yesterday afternoon."

Alfie frowned but didn't offer any other response.

"Her parents are frantic," Thea continued.

Alfie did respond then. She snorted.

"Why did you do that?" Thea asked.

"They don't care anything about her."

"Of course they do. They're beside themselves, wondering if she's all right."

"They're putting on a big show. They don't care."

"You don't mean that."

"I do mean it! You just don't want to hear it!"

Thea wanted to argue with the girl, but stopped herself. After all, she didn't actually know whether Alfie might be right in her assessment of the situation; Alfie knew Denise and her parents, and she didn't.

"I'm sorry if that's the case, Alfie. And I didn't come to argue with you," she said gently. "I merely wanted to let you know about your friend."

That seemed to deflate the girl. She walked to the side of her bed and sat down, looking somehow lost and sad. "Do they know what's happened to Denise, or where she is?"

"No to both questions. Mrs. Taylor said she called yesterday afternoon to ask if you might know where she was."

"Yes, and I told her I didn't. Didn't you answer the phone?"

"That's right. The Taylors told the sheriff about it, and I think he might want to ask you some questions later." At that Thea saw a sudden fear on the girl's thin face. "Alfie, are you all right?" she asked anxiously.

"Why does he want to talk to me?"

"It's probably just routine. He'll ask you about Denise's habits and about her other friends. Maybe she said something to you."

"She didn't say anything."

"It could have been something you didn't think was important at the time."

"I told you! I don't know anything!"

Thea looked at her again. She was almost sure in her own mind that Alfie *did* know something. It would be pointless to try to question her about it, though, since Alfie was in such a hostile mood. Besides, Cal or Quint could do a much better job of it. They would know the right questions to ask and how to phrase them.

"Okay," Thea said, pretending indifference. She started for the door, then stopped abruptly and turned. "By the way," she said, making it sound like an afterthought, "you don't have to get up now if you don't want to. They've closed all the schools because of what happened to Denise."

Now she was convinced she had been right. The girl did know something.

The look on Alfie's face was one of sheer terror.

"THEA, I need to speak to you," Betsy said. She wore a worried expression on her normally placid face.

"Certainly. What is it?"

"Did any of you eat sandwiches yesterday?"

What a strange question, Thea thought. Betsy seemed completely serious, however. Thea concentrated, trying to remember. "No, I don't think so. We had pancakes for breakfast and leftovers for lunch. Then Quint made salad and scrambled eggs for supper."

"Did you have toast with your eggs?"

"No, we had rolls. Why?"

"It means we're missing a loaf of bread, too. That's in addition to a bottle of milk and a jar of peach preserves." Betsy hesitated. "I . . . I'm afraid I did the wrong thing, talking you into hiring Jacinda. I think she stole the food."

"Oh, no! There must be some mistake!"

Betsy shook her head. "I keep close watch on all the food in this house. I know there was a whole loaf of bread when I left Saturday night, and it's not there now. Could some of the children have made sandwiches without you knowing it?"

"I don't think so," Thea said slowly. "Quint took all the boys fishing yesterday afternoon, and Alfie was in her room."

"I couldn't find the peach preserves when I started to make Miss Maudie's breakfast this morning," Betty said.

"Are you sure there's a jar missing?"

"Sure I'm sure! I made them myself, and I saved them especially for Miss Maudie. They're her favorite." Betsy narrowed her eyes. "Who brought in the milk that was delivered this morning?"

"Jacinda did," Thea admitted. "But I don't see how she could have taken any of the food that's missing. She went home not long after the milk was delivered, and you and I were both here to watch her when she left."

"She was carrying a plastic sack," Betsy said with a significant look.

"Oh." Thea still couldn't believe that Jacinda was a thief, although the evidence seemed to point toward the girl. Another thought occurred to her. "Is any other food missing?"

"None that I know of so far."

"Could you check?"

"Yes, but I might not be able to remember everything we had."

"Do the best you can. Check especially on things like, uh, peanut butter...and crackers...and fruit and drinks. Will you?"

Betsy shrugged. "Okay, but I'm not sure it'll do any good."

While Betsy did an inventory of the pantry, Thea did the morning household chores and continued making preparations to leave. She also kept her fingers crossed that they might not have to go. If her idea proved correct... She didn't dare let herself hope too much, however.

She was putting a load of laundry into the dryer when Betsy approached. Thea caught her breath when she saw the housekeeper had an almost-empty jar of peanut butter in her hand. "Did you find anything missing?" she asked.

"I'm not sure," Betsy replied. "I was almost certain we had a new jar of peanut butter, but this is all I found."

Thea felt like applauding. "You looked everywhere?"

"Yes, this is all there is. Of course, I could be mistaken about—"

"I don't think you are," Thea interrupted.

"You have any idea what's happening?"

"Yes, but I'd like to think about it some more. Don't say anything to anyone else about this yet, will you?"

"How could I? I wouldn't know what to say."

Quint came home a little before noon, completely exhausted and utterly dejected. They hadn't been able to find a trace of Denise, and Cal had finally called the FBI.

Thea hated to approach him with her idea when he could barely stand on his feet, but what choice did she have? The FBI would be coming soon, and time was running out. She called Quint into the deserted dining room and closed the door. Taking a deep breath, she proceeded to tell him about her suspicions.

He reacted with disbelief. "You can't go jumping to conclusions because of an expression you imagined you saw on a ten-year-old's face. It's her best friend who's missing, so of course she's terrified."

Undaunted, Thea told him about the missing food and saw his expression grow skeptical, then shocked, and finally grim. He nodded. "I think you're right. Alfie is involved in Denise's disappearance in some way. At the very least, she knows where Denise is and she's taking food to her."

He rubbed a hand across his eyes. Thea had the feeling he wished he could wipe the whole ugly mess from his mind as easily. She wished there was some way she could comfort him, but knew there wasn't.

He dropped his hand and sighed. "Do you have any idea what we should do now?"

"No. I was hoping you would."

"We could bring Cal into this, but I'm not sure she'd tell him anything. Since she wouldn't tell you—and she damn sure won't tell me—maybe the best thing we can do is watch her. If she leaves the house we'll follow her, and hope she leads us to Denise."

"You think that might work?" Thea asked.

"I don't know. It's just that I'd like to keep this between us if we can, and not turn her over to...to—"

"I know," she interjected, placing a hand upon his arm. "We can do it. I'll help any way I can."

"Thanks," he said, covering her hand with his. He thought for a moment. "We need to figure out a way to get Alfie to go to Denise, right away if possible."

"It'll have to be something that alarms Alfie," Thea said. "I think Denise probably has plenty of food for a while."

Quint nodded his agreement.

"It's almost lunchtime," she said. "What if one of us casually mentions something then? Something like...the FBI is going to start a door-to-door search this afternoon?"

"That's not bad. It's plausible. Then as soon as lunch is over, you and I can set up lookouts. There's a storage room on the back porch where one of us can hide."

"How would it work if I took Aunt Maudie and Max out onto the front porch for fresh air?" Thea suggested. "Better yet, I could take the carom board out there and invite Alan and J.R. to play, too."

"That's a good cover. And I'll hide in the storage room and watch the back door."

"What should I do if she comes out the front?" Thea asked. "Tell the others I'm going for a stroll, and start following her?"

"I don't think she'll come out the front door. Even if she planned to, she'd change her mind as soon as she saw all of you out there." He thought again. "No, I think she'll come out the back door, and I'll be ready to follow her. I just hope this works and that we find Denise."

Thea fervently agreed with him, for many reasons.

THE PLAN wasn't going to work, Thea decided. She had been sitting on the front porch watching Aunt Maudie, Max, J.R. and Alan play caroms ever since lunch, almost two hours ago. From her seat she had a protected view of the stairs, and Alfie hadn't come down. She was still in her room; she obviously wasn't going to take the bait that Quint had thrown out at lunch.

Perhaps she had been wrong about the food, as well; perhaps Jacinda *had* taken it, as Betsy suspected. Perhaps Alfie didn't know where Denise was and she really had been abducted.

Whatever the real story, the fact remained that the FBI was arriving, and Thea and her sons had to leave. She'd decided to tell Aunt Maudie the truth. She was leaving because she was a kidnapper and was running from the police. Since Aunt Maudie wouldn't know where she was going—and wouldn't know she was a kidnapper until just before she left—the old lady wouldn't be criminally involved.

Thea wished she could explain things to Quint, too, so he wouldn't think too badly of her, but it was too dangerous. She didn't know why his opinion was important to her, but it was. She sighed.

Then she heard it—the unmistakable squeak that meant someone was coming down the stairs. Leaning back in her chair so Alfie couldn't see her, she held her breath and gave the girl plenty of time. Finally she leaned forward a little, then a little more. She saw Alfie at the far end of the hall. She was heading for the back door!

Thea quickly ducked into hiding again; she didn't want to spoil everything by having Alfie catch her watching. Counting seconds until she was sure that Alfie had had more than enough time to be out of the house, Thea finally got up and stretched.

"I think I'll get a glass of water," she said. "Anybody want anything?" There was no response; the carom players were clearly too engrossed in their game to reply.

After tiptoeing down the hall, Thea had a decision to make. She could either go directly onto the screened back porch or through the kitchen, where a second door opened onto the back porch. To be on the safe side, she decided to pass through the kitchen.

Betsy was busy making a pie for dinner and barely glanced at her. Thea casually walked to the sink and looked out the window. She spotted Alfie some distance away, slowly strolling along, glancing up at the pecan trees every now and then, as if to admire her surroundings. From time to time she also glanced behind herself, plainly making sure she wasn't followed. She was slowly but surely making her way to the barn! So that was where she'd chosen to hide Denise. Clever girl!

Alfie knew that the three boys had been banned from the barn ever since Max's accident and nobody else ever went there. The barn was close, convenient, and as safe a hiding place as there could be. Thea had to admire the girl's ingenuity.

She saw Alfie pick up a small rock and throw it toward one of the pecan trees. It missed. Then there was another movement. Thea gasped. Quint ducked behind another pecan tree. He was following Alfie!

"Did you say something, Thea?" Betsy asked.

"Huh? Oh, no. I was just getting a glass of water."

She continued to look out the window while she drew the water. She wanted desperately to help Quint, but couldn't think of anything else to do. If she went outside, Alfie might see her, and that would spoil everything.

At last, after what seemed like hours, the girl reached the door to the barn. She stopped there and this time made no secret of looking around to see if she was being followed. After scanning the landscape in every direction, including the spot where Thea could see Quint crouched behind another tree, Alfie opened the barn door and quickly stepped inside.

Thea hadn't realized that she was holding her breath until she suddenly released it. She immediately caught it again as soon as she saw Quint make a mad dash for the barn...right out in the open, completely exposed to any other eyes that might be watching!

As soon as he reached the barn, he stopped and pressed his ear against the door, obviously listening for any sounds that might be coming from inside. After a few moments, he, too, went inside and closed the door behind himself.

Thea watched and waited. When she couldn't bear the suspense any longer, she went onto the back porch. She was disappointed to find that she couldn't see any more there than she could from the kitchen. After debating with herself, she walked down the back steps and slowly headed toward the barn. Quint, along with Alfie and possibly Denise, had been inside it forever, it seemed.

What was going on? Was there something she could do to help? She stopped. Should she go back to the house and call

Cal? No. Quint had said he wanted them to handle it, if possible. She started walking again.

She'd taken only a few steps when the barn door was suddenly flung open and Quint emerged with the two young girls in tow, clutching each of them by the wrist.

"Quint?" she shouted.

He looked up and saw her. "Thea, I'm glad you're here," he shouted back. "I need you to make some phone calls for me. I'd do it myself, but I don't want to let go and have to chase these two down again!"

Chapter Eleven

Quint had Thea call the sheriff and Denise's parents. Cal Potts, several deputies and the Taylors all arrived at the same time. Thea escorted them into the parlor to confront a weeping Denise and a sullen Alfie.

Everyone talked at the same time while Quint and Thea explained how they had become suspicious of Alfie, followed her and found Denise. Then the tearful girl confessed how, following an argument she'd had with her parents, Alfie had helped her plan to run away from home.

According to Denise, it had been Alfie's idea to leave the bicycle by the side of the road, in order to make people think someone had kidnapped her. After abandoning the bicycle, Denise had simply taken a shortcut across the pasture to Aunt Maudie's barn.

Alfie never said a word, not even when Cal gave both girls a stern lecture that brought on more sobbing from Denise. Thea thought Alfie appeared close to tears, however, when Mrs. Taylor announced that she and her husband had decided it would be better if the two girls didn't see each other for a while.

At last everyone left, Cal with his deputies and Denise with her parents. Thea was about to leave, too, but was trapped when Quint began to lecture Alfie. She sank into the sofa cushions, wishing she were invisible.

She had never seen Quint so angry; she had never imagined that he could be so angry. He said a lot of things, but what most of it boiled down to was that he was initiating a new, "get tough" attitude with Alfie.

She was to take all her meals downstairs, on time, with the rest of the family, he said. She was not to lock herself inside her room. She was to do her studying downstairs, where he could see her. And she was to be polite to everyone, whether she wanted to or not.

"Any questions?" he asked when he had finished setting down the new laws.

"I hate you!" Alfie shouted. It was the first time she'd spoken since Quint brought her back from the barn.

Thea saw the muscles working in his jaw. "I'm sorry you feel that way, but it doesn't change things. This is the way it's going to be."

"You hate me, too," the girl muttered.

He took a deep breath before answering. "No, I don't hate you," he said. His voice was quiet and controlled, but the muscles in his jaw were still working. "I love you very much. But that doesn't change things, either."

At last, after eliciting her promise that she would go onto the front porch and tell Aunt Maudie and the boys exactly what part she had played in Denise's disappearance, Quint dismissed Alfie.

"Well, I did it," he said with a sigh after Alfie left.

Thea was instantly alarmed. "I hope you didn't do it because of what I suggested."

"No, I knew it had to be done, too," he said sadly. "I just didn't know how hard it would be to do it. And there are no guarantees it will help matters."

"If it's any consolation, I thought you handled it well," she said quietly. "You were fair, but firm."

"Thanks." He sat down on the sofa beside her. "I still find it hard to believe Alfie did such a thing. The anguish she helped put the Taylors through—I never imagined she could be so cruel!"

Seeing his hurt, Thea had to try to assuage it. "She probably didn't think that far ahead about the consequences, Quint. She's precocious, but she's still only ten."

"I don't know." He rubbed one hand across his mouth and the bearded stubble on his chin. "It's hard to know what she thinks anymore."

He turned his head away from her before he spoke again. "She blames me for her mother's death, you know, and for selling our house, breaking up our family."

Thea caught her breath. Suddenly she remembered Liz Bartlett talking about the grief and the guilt trips Sally had piled upon Quint while she was dying. "She made his life a living hell for more than two years," Liz had said. Thea remembered thinking at the time that Sally might be the cause of some of Alfie's problems, too.

"Why does she blame you?" Thea asked, choosing her words with care. "Did her mother suggest it to her?"

Quint turned back to her, his dark eyes flashing. "Sally wouldn't do—" He caught himself and turned away again. "I don't know. It . . . it's possible."

"That would explain a lot," she said quietly.

"Don't be too easy on me! I'm not without guilt here. There's a lot of merit in what Alfie thinks about me."

Thea studied his averted profile. "What merit? You had to sell your house. You had no other choice. And what about Sally? You stood by her all the way, did everything you could. Everybody says so."

"Yes!" He wheeled to face her again, his face contorted with anger and guilt. "And here's what everybody *doesn't* say, because they don't know the truth about me. I felt *relieved* when she finally died!"

Thea swallowed. "That was a natural reaction under the circumstances."

Quint leaned forward, propping his elbows up on his knees and staring at the floor. "She was my high school sweetheart," he said slowly. "She was my wife, the mother of my children, and the only thing I felt when she died was relief!"

Thea touched his shoulder. "Don't do this to yourself."

"I didn't work for eighteen months," he continued as if she hadn't spoken. "Her hair fell out. *Her hair fell out!* And I felt relieved when she died!"

He rose and loomed over her. "What does that make me?" he asked, his voice filled with anger and self-loathing.

"Human! It makes you human!" she said, getting to her feet to face him.

He shook his head, rejecting her defense.

"Yes," she insisted. "You're not Superman. You're human, like the rest of us. Maybe you and Alfie both expected too much of you."

He swung around, turning his back to her once more.

Thea kept her eyes on him, trying to think of some way to reach him, some way to comfort him. "Quint?" she said at last.

He didn't speak or move.

She reached up to touch his shoulder. "Look at me."

He turned, but kept his eyes averted. "Really look at me," she said.

He looked at her.

"You might not feel it was your finest hour when Sally died," she said, her voice very gentle. "It probably wasn't.

But what you felt is understandable. It's what anyone might have felt, and there's no reason for you to keep punishing yourself about it now. Let it go.''

She lifted her hands to his face, then, on impulse, briefly touched her lips to his. ''Let go of your guilt,'' she said. ''You've punished yourself enough.'' Then she kissed him again.

He made no move, but she could feel his response in the tightening of his jaw beneath her hands and the softening of his lips against hers. Then he opened his mouth in silent invitation.

She hesitated, then thrust out her tongue to meet his, letting it begin a slow, silent, tantalizing dance with his. His hands didn't move, but they didn't need to. His mouth was capable of creating plenty of excitement on its own. By the time she broke off their kiss, she was breathless and disoriented.

A myriad of long-suppressed emotions was racing through her body at breakneck speed. And what was he thinking? Did he think she'd kissed him out of sympathy? Or because she felt sorry for him? The expression in his eyes was deep, intense, unreadable.

She didn't exactly know why she'd had the impulse to kiss him, but sympathy or pity for him certainly weren't it. She suddenly felt a fierce need to be alone to sort everything out.

''I...I'd better go see about supper,'' she said. It was a lame excuse, because they both knew Betsy probably had supper already prepared.

He let her get away with it, though. He continued to gaze at her for a long moment, then nodded and stepped aside to allow her to rush out of the room.

QUINT LAY IN BED staring up at the ceiling. His body was completely motionless, but his mind raced wildly. He thought of his life as it had been before Thea Cameron returned to Planters' Junction—placid and predictable. *Be honest,* he told himself. Dull was more like it.

All that had changed, although he wasn't sure whether the change was for the better. Still, he felt more alert, aware…more *alive* than he had in years. Had she done that to him? Yes.

She'd also played havoc with his senses. This morning wasn't the first time he'd awakened fully aroused. It had happened a lot lately, more times than he could remember in a long, long while. It wasn't that she tried to excite him; far from it. She never flirted. Most of the time she either ignored him or tried to pick a fight with him.

Until this afternoon.

He couldn't believe he'd actually told her his deepest, darkest secret, the one thing he'd never told another living soul before. He couldn't believe her reaction when he'd told her about being relieved when Sally died, either.

She hadn't been shocked or horrified, or treated him as if he were some unfeeling monster. She had kissed him!

He still couldn't get over that.

After Sally's death—even before then—he had decided that he wasn't meant for marriage. He wasn't quite so sure anymore. Thea had said he was punishing himself because of the guilt he felt. Was he? He wasn't sure about that, either. He wasn't sure about anything, except one thing. He didn't want Thea to leave before he could find out exactly what his feelings were…and hers.

THEA LAY AWAKE in bed, staring up at the ceiling. She'd been wound tight as a drum for more than twenty-four hours, worrying about Denise's so-called kidnapping, making plans to escape to safety with her kids. Logically, now that the danger was over, she should be sound asleep. Why wasn't she?

Because love isn't logical.

"No," she said aloud. "No!" she said again, more forcefully.

She wasn't in love with Quint Richards. She barely knew the man, and love—other than the deep, abiding love she felt for her children—had no place in her life. Not now, and probably not ever.

Trying to be honest with herself, she admitted that she did feel something for him, something special. That was why she'd kissed him this afternoon. It was special, but it wasn't love.

What then? Friendship? That was it. What she felt for Quint was friendship, something that two people of any gender could feel for each other. It was something she'd missed for a long, long time.

Among other things, her ex-husband had become extremely possessive, insisting that she sever old ties. And later, after the divorce, she didn't have time for friends, what with working, taking care of her sons and running a household by herself.

She had missed sharing things with another human being. She had missed talking about troubles, sharing laughs and secrets. Quint had shared himself with her today; he'd told her something that he probably hadn't told another human being. That meant he considered her someone special, too.

She and Quint shared a special friendship, and that was why she had kissed him. With that comforting thought, she finally relaxed and closed her eyes.

SOMETHING had happened to Quint, and Thea couldn't figure out what it was. His mood was hard to describe. He wasn't exactly being mysterious; it was as if he knew a secret that no one else knew. And he was cheerful all the time, laughing and teasing everybody, not at all cautious and reserved, the way he sometimes used to be.

One day he even came home with two arm loads of flowers—a mixed bouquet for Aunt Maudie, another one for Thea, and still another for Alfie. "They were so pretty and looked so much like spring, I just couldn't resist," he explained a little sheepishly.

Thea saw Alfie's surprise and the shy smile on her face, and wanted to applaud Quint. Or hug him. Or both.

Another day he brought home fresh peaches. "They're the first of the season," he announced. Then he insisted that Thea, Aunt Maudie and all the kids join him in making a churn of homemade peach ice cream.

It was a lot of fun, Thea had to admit, and the ice cream was heavenly, but it was still strange behavior for Quint.

He brought home little gifts for everyone almost every day. They weren't big or expensive, mostly a special piece of candy, a single flower or a toy, but they *were* gifts. Why was he doing it? she wondered.

And why was he so happy? Maybe it was because Alfie's attitude had improved. It wasn't a dramatic change, but the girl was definitely less hostile, and that was a hopeful sign.

On Memorial Day, Quint suggested that they all pile into his station wagon and drive into town for the big parade. Aunt Maudie, who was able to get around with only a cane now, was a little skeptical about her ability to negotiate such a big crowd of several hundred people, but Quint insisted. The excursion turned out fine—no trouble at all—and Aunt Maudie had as much fun watching the parade as anybody, with the possible exception of Maxie, who had begun to chafe at being confined so long.

On the day school was out for the summer, Quint declared a holiday for everybody. They all piled into the station wagon again and he drove them to Paradise Lake for a picnic. Aunt Maudie pointed out that it would have been easier to have the picnic at the lake on her property, but Quint said he didn't want to scare the fish. "They probably wouldn't bite for a week if we all went swimming in their private domain," he said with a wink at Alan, who giggled in response.

Finally it was time for Max to have his cast removed, and Quint insisted on another picnic at Paradise Lake to celebrate the occasion. "Max didn't get to swim the last time we were there," he said by way of explanation.

A couple of days before the picnic, Quint asked Thea if she would take Alfie shopping for a new bathing suit. She was happy to oblige, having noticed on the previous picnic how droopy Alfie's old suit was.

Alfie tried on several and finally narrowed down the selection to a one-piece and a bikini. She wavered for several minutes and finally turned to Thea. "What do you think?"

Thea hesitated. "Wel-l . . ."

"I really want to know," the girl said.

"Okay," she replied, flattered by Alfie's confidence in her opinion. "I think they both look nice on you, but the one-piece is more becoming. You have such a marvelous slender figure and long legs . . . not many people can wear a suit like that, you know. At least, they *shouldn't*."

They both grinned, and Alfie accepted Thea's suggestion without hesitation.

While they waited for the clerk to ring up Alfie's purchase, Thea looked at suits and briefly thought about getting a new one for herself, but rejected the idea. With Max finally getting out of his cast, they would be leaving soon.

Though she'd carefully hoarded the money from the jewelry she'd pawned, along with the money Aunt Maudie paid her, and now knew she'd be able to work, she still wanted to hold on to her savings in case of another emergency. It also took a lot of money to get settled in to a new place. Sighing, she replaced the white suit she'd been admiring.

The day of Max's Coming-Out Party, as they'd all started referring to the day when his cast would be removed, dawned bright and hot and clear. He was so excited that he was already wide-awake and fidgeting by the time Thea came in to get him up. He urged her to hurry throughout breakfast and while she helped him get ready.

Quint volunteered to drive Max and Thea to the doctor's office and carried the squirming boy to his station wagon. Thea started to get into the car, then stopped and looked back to the front porch, where Alan and J.R. were playing.

"Do you want to bring Alan along with us?" Quint asked, apparently in response to her backward glance.

"No," she said after a moment. "He'd only be bored."

She saw Quint nod his approval. She was a little pleased with herself, too. Since the terrible scare she'd had when she left her sons with Betsy, only to find the sheriff there when she returned, she was reluctant to let either boy out of her sight.

After Max's cast was removed, he was a little shaky on his feet. The doctor assured him everything was fine and he'd be as good as new in no time. Quint drove Thea and Max home, then immediately left again, saying he'd be ready for their picnic as soon as he did a couple of errands.

When he returned, Thea and Alfie were in the kitchen, helping Betsy assemble their picnic lunch. He stopped inside the kitchen door.

"Alfie," he said quietly, "there's someone here to see you." He stepped aside, and Denise came into the room. Alfie's eyes widened and her mouth dropped open.

"I talked to Mr. and Mrs. Taylor, and they agreed to let Denise go on the picnic with us," Quint said.

Alfie didn't move. She looked from Quint to Denise and back to him again; her chin quivered. She still didn't move when Denise ran to her and hugged her. Quint walked toward his daughter, too, and tentatively reached out a hand to touch her shoulder. At that she uttered a small cry and threw her arms around his waist, burying her head against his chest.

"Thank you, Daddy," she said tremulously.

He picked her up then, holding her close and lowering his own head to her shoulder. Her thin arms came up to encircle his neck. "You're welcome, sweetheart," he said, stroking her dark hair. "You're so welcome. So very, very welcome."

His head was buried in Alfie's neck, so Thea couldn't see his face, but his voice was so choked that she was sure he was crying. She was crying, too, so hard she could barely see, and she could hear Betsy sniffling behind her.

What a grand and glorious day this was!

Quint had one more surprise. He handed it to Thea as soon as they were alone for a moment.

"What is it?" she asked, eyeing the gift-wrapped box.

"Why don't you open it and see? That's usually a good way to find out."

She made a face at him and opened the box. She gasped when she saw the white bathing suit she'd admired in the store. "How on earth...?" she began.

"Alfie told me she thought you might like it," Quint said. "She described it in great detail, even including the size you were looking at."

"I'm...I don't know what to say." She blinked. "And Alfie! To think that she'd... It's amazing."

"I know," he said with a grin.

"I'm so happy things seem to be working out for you two, Quint."

"Thank you."

"And I don't know how to thank you for—"

"I know how."

His mouth was on hers before she could blink an eye. He could move faster than any man she'd ever met. He could kiss better than any man she'd ever met, too. Reluctantly she pushed him away. "Someone's liable to come in," she said.

He released her with a long sigh.

PARADISE LAKE was man-made, right down to the white sand beaches, which the developers had brought in by the ton. It was nice, Thea thought, looking at the sparkling green water shimmering in the bright sunlight. The kids enjoyed the playground, water slides and paddle boats, too.

Betsy had packed lunch and supper for them, but it was still too early to eat when they arrived, so they dumped their picnic hampers and cooler on one of the covered picnic tables. Then the kids made a mad dash for the lake, except for Max, who was still a little wobbly from being in a cast so long. So Quint hoisted him onto his shoulders and carried him to the water.

Thea and Aunt Maudie watched from the shaded picnic table. "He's so good," Thea said without thinking. Realizing what she'd said, she tried to recover. "I mean—"

"He's not bad-looking, either," Aunt Maudie interjected.

"Let's not get off on that again."

"You're the one who started it."

Thea started to say more, but stopped when she saw Quint returning.

"How about us going for a swim, too, Thea?" he asked.

"You go ahead," she said quickly. "I'll stay here and keep Aunt Maudie company."

"I have a perfectly good book to keep me company," her aunt said, pulling a paperback romance from her bag. "You'd only make me nervous if you stayed here and watched me read. I'd be thinking I should be entertaining you, instead of enjoying my book."

"I'll set up your folding chair before we go," Quint said.

"That would be lovely, darlin'," Aunt Maudie cooed.

Later, walking down to the beach, Thea was conscious of several pairs of female eyes trained on the man walking beside her. She was pretty conscious of him herself, for that matter. He was tall, but not too tall; broad-shouldered, but not burly; confident, but not swaggering. She tried not to think about his other attributes. He was an almost perfect man. Almost? Whom was she kidding?

Reaching the water, he dived in immediately, but she waded in gradually, allowing her body to get used to the slight chill. Finally she dived in and swam underwater toward the spot where she'd seen Alan treading water. Opening her eyes, she spotted his skinny legs and grabbed one.

He yelped. She immediately came to the surface, laughing. "Gotcha!"

"Aw, Mom, I knew it was you."

"Oh, yeah?"

"Yeah. And I'm gonna get you now!"

She swam away from him, but allowed him to catch and dunk her for a few moments. Then she held up her hands in surrender. He immediately let go and she came up sputtering.

"Give up?" Alan said.

"You bet."

"You're too easy," he complained.

"Try to catch me, Alan!" Quint shouted from a few yards away.

"Come help me, J.R.!" Alan shouted, and a furious game of tag was underway.

Maxie, who'd been able to swim like a fish since he was three, joined in; now it was the boys against Thea and Quint. Then Alfie and Denise joined the game, too, and it was the kids against the grown-ups.

Thea finally had to plead exhaustion. Quint claimed he was tired, too, although she knew he was barely winded. He promised the kids they'd resume the game after lunch. "Let's swim out to that floating dock and rest a minute, Thea," he suggested. He set off, his powerful strokes propelling him smoothly through the water. She followed at her own pace.

He hoisted himself onto the dock in one long, fluid motion then held out a hand to help her up.

"Whew!" she said. "Those kids really gave me a workout."

"You look like a kid yourself," he said, yanking the long, single braid she'd made to keep her hair from getting tangled while swimming.

"Thanks a lot." She crossed her legs and sat down.

He immediately lowered himself onto the dock beside her, lying on his stomach and looking up at her. "Not that I ever knew any kids who looked *quite* like you when I was growing up." He let his gaze roam over the exposed parts of her body. "Especially like you in that swimsuit."

She felt herself growing warm. "Thank you. I think."

He propped himself on his elbows. "Did that remark make you uncomfortable? I didn't intend it to."

"No," she said, thinking about it. "I think it was the leer that did it."

He laughed. "Now *that* I can't control. A guy can't help it if his eyes automatically cross when he sees a beautiful woman." He crossed his eyes.

She gave him a quick, light swat on the head.

"Why don't you come on down and stretch out?" he suggested, stretching his arms in front of him.

"I think not."

"Why?"

"Little eyes on shore. Watching us with much interest."

He lifted his head slightly, made a circle with his fingers and peered through it. "Hmm. I see what you mean." He flipped onto his back, propping one hand behind his head. "Are you having fun today?"

"Very much."

"Me, too."

She squinted one eye against the glare of the sun and looked at him with her other eye. "You seem different lately," she commented, mentioning what she'd been wondering about for weeks.

"Me? How so?"

"It's hard to describe, but . . . you're more carefree. Less cautious or inhibited. Happier?"

He grinned up at her. "That's true. I am happier."

"Because of Alfie?"

"That, too."

"Oh?"

"Aren't you going to ask me what else?"

She hesitated. "What else?"

"Don't you know? Can't you guess?"

She shook her head.

"I'm in love with you."

Chapter Twelve

Quint hadn't intended to reveal his feelings to Thea so soon; he'd planned to give her a little more time. Judging by the look of distress on her face, maybe he shouldn't have planned to tell her at all. He pushed himself up to sit facing her.

"Look," he said, "I didn't intend to upset you."

She looked as if she were about to cry. "I didn't want this to happen."

"Maybe we can just forget I said what I did."

"It's not true?" she asked in what sounded like a hopeful tone of voice.

"Yes, it's true. But we could pretend I didn't say it."

"What good would that do?"

Not much, he had to admit. "Look," he said again. "Obviously you don't feel the same way I do, so—" He stopped when he saw the guilty look in her eyes; she turned her head away.

Wait a minute here, he told himself. Maybe he was being hasty again, jumping to conclusions. "Thea?" he asked, his heart beating faster. "How *do* you feel about me?"

"Does it really matter?" she asked, keeping her face averted.

"It's only the most important thing in the world. Tell me."

She didn't reply and kept her head turned away. His heart was hammering so hard he could hear it. He touched her chin with gentle fingers and slowly tilted her face toward him. Their eyes met and held.

At first he wasn't sure what he saw; then his heart stopped hammering. It seemed to stop beating altogether. "You love me!" he exclaimed.

"No!"

"Yes, you do! It's written all over your face. I couldn't be mistaken about that."

"Even if it's true—"

"Then it *is* true?"

"Yes," she whispered.

"Say it," he demanded.

"I love you."

He reached for her, suddenly as happy as he'd ever been in his life. Pulling her into his arms, he held her tightly and tried to kiss her.

She resisted. "Quint, stop it! The kids will see us." She pushed against his chest.

"I don't care." He let her go, but held on to her hand. "They'll find out sooner or later, anyway."

"No, they won't. We don't have to tell them."

"They'll see us . . . me. I can't hide the way I feel about you, not now."

"Please don't, Quint," she pleaded, distressed again. "Now that Max is out of his cast, we'll be leaving soon."

He stared at her, unable to believe what he'd heard. "All that's changed now."

"No. Nothing has changed."

"Of course it has. We love each other!"

She shook her head. "Listen, Quint . . ."

"No, you listen. This has been pretty sudden, for both of us. Why don't we talk about it later, after we've had time to digest what's happened?"

"Time won't change things."

"Sure it will. We'll be thinking more clearly. Let's meet tonight, after everyone else has gone to bed. We'll be able to discuss things openly when we have plenty of time and we're alone."

"Alone? An army lives in that house."

"I'll think of something. Will you do it—meet me and discuss the way we feel about each other and what we're going to do about it?"

She hesitated.

"Don't we both deserve at least that much?"

"I guess so," she finally agreed. "But I don't see how—"

He pressed a finger against her lips to silence her. "You can tell me all that tonight," he said, thinking that after she'd had a chance to review the situation calmly, she wouldn't be so eager to run away from what they had together. "Okay?"

She nodded and sighed. "I think we'd better go back," she said, glancing toward shore. "The natives seem to be getting restless."

He got up and held out a hand to help her to her feet. "Before we leave, tell me one more time, so I'll know I wasn't dreaming."

"I don't see what good that will do," she said. At least she didn't pretend she didn't know what he was thinking about, he thought wryly.

"Humor me. Please."

"I love you," she said a little breathlessly.

"And I love you," he echoed with certainty.

After lunch and another game of water tag with the kids, Thea and Quint joined Aunt Maudie at the shaded picnic table for a glass of iced tea. Thea tried to concentrate on the story Aunt Maudie was telling, but her thoughts kept returning to Quint and what they'd said to each other on the dock.

She'd known she was in love with him, but had never intended to let him know. Then when he'd pressured her about her feelings, she hadn't been able to lie to him. She owed him that much. By revealing her feelings, though, she would probably hurt him more when she left—and they *were* leaving.

In spite of what Quint hoped, and however much she wished it could be otherwise, that hadn't changed. She had no other choice, but how she dreaded saying what she had to say to him tonight!

"Hello, there!"

Thea, Quint and Aunt Maudie all turned as Liz Bartlett approached their table. In trim white linen slacks and an emerald silk blouse, she looked like a knockout, as usual, Thea thought. She was accompanied by a tall, blond man wearing reflective sunglasses. He was dressed in white slacks, too, although his were rumpled, and his Hawaiian print shirt looked decidedly foreign in Planters' Junction.

"What a pleasant surprise," Liz said. "I just finished giving Fletcher a tour of the town, which took an exciting thirty seconds, and we decided to come out for a swim. I didn't know we'd see anybody we knew."

"I thought I told you at lunch the other day that we were planning a picnic here," Quint said.

"Did you? I must have forgotten. This is Fletcher Cross," she continued without appearing to miss a beat.

While Liz made introductions, Thea wondered if the flirtatious divorcée and Quint had merely encountered each other at lunch, or whether they'd had lunch together. Then she chastised herself for worrying about such a thing.

"Fletcher's a free-lance writer," Liz said. "He's doing research for a magazine article about small-town Americana."

"How did you happen to choose Planters' Junction, Mr. Cross?" Aunt Maudie asked.

"I blindfolded myself and threw darts at a big map," he replied. "And call me Fletcher."

"Actually," Liz said, "Fletcher said he got the idea of coming to South Georgia because Jimmy Carter is from Plains, but it's become too well-known."

"What magazine are you writing for?" Quint asked.

"I'm hoping *National Geographic* will buy the idea and send down a photographer," Fletcher answered. "If not, I night try one of the regional magazines or the Sunday newspaper supplements. There are several possibilities."

While the others talked, Thea sat silently, watching and listening. Mostly she was watching and listening to Fletcher Cross. Something wasn't right about him. She couldn't put her finger on exactly what it was, but something didn't ring true.

She wished he and Liz hadn't come here today and that the two of them would leave, but apparently that wasn't going to happen. Liz finally excused herself to go change into her swimsuit; Quint went back to play with the kids in the water; and Aunt Maudie returned to her book.

Fletcher immediately sidled closer to Thea at the picnic table. "Aren't you going swimming?" she asked.

He shook his head. "Liz was the one who wanted to come swimming. I didn't even bring a suit...left it back at the motel."

"You're staying here in town?" she asked, thinking about the dilapidated tourist court that was the only motel in Planters' Junction.

"No, I'm at the Holiday Inn in Albany."

"Oh." That was at least thirty miles away. She only wished it were the Holiday Inn in Albany, New York.

"Have you lived here long?" Fletcher asked.

Taking a quick glance at Aunt Maudie to make sure she wasn't listening to the conversation, Thea nodded. "All my life."

"Must be pretty dull. At least, Liz says it is."

If he thought the town was dull, why did he want to write about it? "It's not to me," she said. "I have my children and . . . there's always plenty of work."

"What does your husband do?"

Thea was alarmed. Why was he so interested in her personal affairs? "I don't have a husband."

"You a widow?" he asked.

"Divorced," she replied curtly. "And why are you asking me all these questions?"

"It's my job," he said with a smile that he might have thought was winning, but which seemed sneaky and evil to her. "It's the way I do my research," he added.

"I think you should do your research somewhere else." She moved to get up. He reached out and grabbed her wrist, but released it quickly when she shot him a furious glance.

"You don't like me, do you?"

"I—" She started to deny it, but changed her mind. "No."

"Any particular reason?"

She shrugged and walked away. She held her shoulders straight and walked with an air of purpose, but she was trembling inside.

"YOU LOOK DIFFERENT from the last time I saw you," Liz said, glancing over the top of her compact at Thea.

They were in the bathhouse, where Thea had just changed into jeans and Liz had donned her immaculate white slacks before going home. Much to Thea's chagrin, Liz and Fletcher had attached themselves to their party for the remainder of the afternoon, and had even shared picnic supper with them.

"Do I?" Thea said noncommittally.

Liz nodded. "It's just what my intuition told me. You're in love with Quint."

Thea dropped her hairbrush with a loud clatter. "No, I'm not," she said, bending to pick up the brush.

Liz chuckled. "Tell me, do I look like an idiot or something? Of course you're in love with him."

Thea reluctantly rose to face her accuser. "Liz—"

"And of course he's in love with you, too. Has he told you so yet?"

She took a deep breath and nodded.

"I suspected it from the way he lit up at the mere mention of your name when I ran into him at lunch the other day. That's why I decided to follow you out here today, to see for myself and make sure."

"Liz, I'm so sorry. I wasn't lying to you when I said I wasn't interested in him the first time we met."

"I know that, and I think I knew even then that nothing was going to develop between him and me. We're good friends...but no spark."

"Maybe if you give it more time..."

"Are you crazy? You two have *found* each other. When that happens, you don't go around suggesting he spend time with another woman."

"He might as well spend time with you," Thea said sadly. "I'm leaving soon."

Liz's mouth dropped open and she shook her head in obvious disbelief. "You *are* crazy. How can you even think about such a thing?"

"It's true."

"Listen, I hope you're not letting what I said about this town influence you."

"No, it's not that."

"Is it your ex-husband?"

"Partly."

Liz took a deep breath and let it out in a long rush. "Don't you know how really special Quint is?"

Thea swallowed. "I know."

"It must be something terrible to make you give him up."

"Please, Liz."

"Okay, it's none of my business."

Searching through her beach bag for the compact that contained her eye makeup, Thea could feel the other woman's eyes on her.

"I don't know your ex-husband, but I'd be willing to bet my right arm that he's nothing like Quint."

"You'd win your bet," Thea agreed, still rummaging through her bag.

"What are you looking for?" Liz asked.

"My eye makeup. It's in a small compact, and I can't find it."

"Do you want to borrow mine?"

"Thanks, but our coloring is so different... I'll just go without."

"Quint's too much in love to notice, anyway."

"Liz..." She said, putting a warning note into her voice.

Liz held up her hand. "Just an observation." She continued applying her own makeup.

"How long have you know Fletcher Cross?" Thea asked after a moment, trying to sound casual.

"We only met today."

"Oh. Somehow I thought . . ."

"A friend of mine who works for the newspaper down in Albany called and asked me to show him around. I thought he'd make a good decoy when I came out to check on you and Quint, so I agreed."

Thea had to laugh at Liz's candor. She really liked her. Under other circumstances they might have become good friends.

Her thoughts returned to Fletcher Cross. She was relieved to learn it had been Liz's idea, not his, to come to Paradise Lake, but she still had her doubts about him. What were the odds that a legitimate free-lance writer would choose Planters' Junction—over all the places in the entire United States to feature in a story? Slim to none. And if he wasn't a free-lance writer as he claimed, who or what was he? A private detective?

He could have been hired by Alan to find her, to track her down like a wounded animal. And then do what with her? Did private detectives have the power to take fugitives into custody? More likely they simply reported them to the local authorities—to people like Cal. And Quint.

Cross hadn't done that so far, even though Quint had been introduced to him as the district attorney. That meant Cross wasn't positive she was the person he was looking for.

Also, perhaps her lie about having lived here all her life had thrown him off; he had seemed to believe it. And Cameron—her real father's name—was a name she hadn't used in years. George Morrison had adopted her when he married her mother, and she had been Thea Morrison when she met Alan. Maybe Alan didn't even remember that she had been born Thea Cameron. Maybe. So many maybe's.

One thing was certain. If there was a possibility, even a remote one, that Fletcher Cross was a private detective hired by her ex-husband to find her, she had to get her sons away from here as soon as possible.

They couldn't do it tonight. After a day of swimming and playing in the sun, she was too tried to drive. Their escape would have to wait until tomorrow.

In the meantime, she had promised Quint she would meet him tonight to talk about their feelings and the future—a future they could never have. She closed her eyes. He had become very important to her, very dear; he was everything she'd ever wanted in a man. How could she bear to leave him? Leaving him now would be like tearing out a part of her soul.

"I'M READY to talk when you are, Quint," Thea said. She'd just come downstairs after making sure her sons were asleep for the night.

He threw aside the newspaper and got to his feet. "We're only going to talk," he reassured her. "You said that as if it's the end of the world."

It *was* the end of any world they might have had together, she thought sadly. "Sorry," she said. "I'm a little tired."

"Too tired to talk?"

"No." In fact she was, and especially too heart-weary to talk about what they had to discuss, but this was their last chance. Suddenly a lot of "lasts" were coming up in her life. She started to sit on the sofa, but he put out a hand to stop her.

"Not here," he said. "Come with me. I have something to show you."

Holding Thea's hand, Quint led her down the hall, across the screened back porch and down the back steps. A bright, three-quarter moon was coming up over the pecan trees, and the air was heavy with the sweet smell of Aunt Maudie's gardenia bushes. After they'd taken a few steps, Thea realized they were headed in the direction of the barn. She looked at Quint.

"You'll see," he said, answering her unspoken question.

Hand in hand they walked along in silence until they reached the barn. He opened the door and waited for her to enter first, then closed the door behind them. The cavernous barn was cool, and was outlined in golden shadows by a light coming from above them.

"We'll need to climb up to the loft," he said. "You go first, and I'll be right behind to steady you."

"It hasn't been *that* many years since I climbed up there," she said. "I still remember how to negotiate the ladder."

"Humor me."

The ladder was smaller and shakier than she remembered it, and as she climbed, she was glad of Quint's comforting presence behind her. She stopped as soon as her head was above the level of the loft floor and she saw the cozy nest that Quint had arranged for them.

He had spread a thick quilt over a mound of hay. A kerosene lantern sat on an upturned bucket beside the quilt, and a bottle of wine was cooling in another bucket filled with ice. He had even arranged a colorful bouquet of flowers in a mason jar.

Quint had stopped on the rung below her, his arms holding the ladder on either side, and his head level with hers. When she turned around to look at him, his lips were only inches from her own.

"It's lovely, Quint! When did you do it?"

"Tonight. We needed a place to be alone, and this seemed the logical spot."

"You even got fresh flowers."

"I thought Miss Maudie wouldn't mind if I raided her flower garden, since it was for a good cause."

Thea, who never flirted, flirted. "And what cause was that?"

"Romance." His lips closed the distance between them and captured hers in a loving kiss.

After a moment she dared to release her grip on the ladder and brought up one hand to touch his cheek. His skin was warm beneath her fingers. His breath mingling with hers was sweet. He felt good, smelled good, tasted good. She wanted him.

There was nothing new about that; she'd wanted him for weeks. But this time there was an urgency to her desire that hadn't been present before. Time was running out. She'd be leaving in less than a day...in only a matter of hours...and she'd probably never see him again.

The thought of that brought a pain so sharp that she almost cried out. It wasn't fair! She'd finally met a man she both loved and respected—a wonderful man who loved her, too—yet she had to leave him.

Almost as painful as the thought of leaving was the realization that she couldn't even tell him *why* they could never be together. How that would hurt him! She'd almost rather die than cause him such pain, but there was nothing else she could do. Above all else, she had to protect her children. She'd willingly sworn to do so, and that hadn't changed, much as she loved Quint. She had to think of her sons' safety first—before Quint, before herself, before dreaming of the life they might have shared if things had been different.

She saw Quint lift his head and look at her solemnly, intently. This time she didn't try to hide the love she felt for him. She let it show, and saw his love for her shine from his eyes. So much love! She could almost drown in the vast, loving sea of his blue eyes. They gazed at each other for a long time.

He finally smiled. "I suppose we should climb into the loft now and have our talk."

"No," she said, making a sudden decision. Even though they had no future, they still had tonight. She didn't intend to squander it in a meaningless discussion that would only end in an impasse.

She wanted to spend the night locked in his arms, showing him her love in the most intimate and honest way there was. She wanted to receive his love, savor it, then lock the memory of it inside herself to keep for the rest of her life.

She knew she'd never loved Alan in the total, all-encompassing, unselfish way she loved Quint; she knew she could never love *any* man as much as she loved Quint. So the memory of this one night had to last her a lifetime, and if she was really, really lucky, it would sustain her through the empty years ahead.

"No," she said again. "Let's not talk now. Not yet. We have plenty of time for that later."

A lie. Another one, just like all the others she'd told him and led him to believe, she reflected sadly. Then she pushed the thought aside and scrambled up the ladder to the bed Quint had made for them in the loft of Aunt Maudie's barn—their own private world, where nothing and no one else could touch or harm them.

Quint was there in an instant, stretching his long legs beside hers. He propped himself on one elbow, looking down at her, then touched her cheek with a gentle finger. "A freckle," he whispered. "I see a freckle." He kissed the spot his finger had touched, and she shivered with pleasure.

"You see more than one, I imagine," she said a little breathlessly.

He narrowed his eyes to examine her face, studying it carefully. She lay still, studying him, too, memorizing each feature. She wanted to touch him, but didn't wish to spoil things by rushing.

"No," he said finally. "No more freckles. Just rosy cheeks." He ran his finger down her cheek and she shivered again. "Cheeks kissed by the sun...and now by me." He kissed her cheek, then trailed his lips along a path to her mouth.

At last, she thought, lifting her arms to wind them around his neck.

Disappointingly, he pulled back only seconds later. "Are you in a hurry?"

"Yes," she whispered.

He shook his head. "I want to savor you. I've wanted you so much for such a long, long time. I want to make it last as long as possible."

She forced herself to slow down, clenching her hands while he showered kisses over her face, her neck, along her bare arms, even the palms of her hands. When he teased the palm of her hand with his tongue, she cried out involuntarily. "You're trying to drive me crazy."

He grinned. "Is it working?"

"Yes," she muttered, reaching for him and starting to unbutton his shirt. "I can't stand it anymore. I have to touch you, too."

He sat back on his knees, remaining completely motionless, hands by his sides, while she removed his shirt. When she splayed her hands against his chest, though, he shivered. And when she ducked her head to capture a nipple between her teeth, he groaned and pushed her back into the soft quilt, burying his face against her neck and kissing the sensitive skin there before moving his mouth to hers.

Her lips parted, and they began to draw on each other hungrily. She moved her hands to his shoulders, then around his back, feeling his hard muscles, delighting in his solid strength, savoring his smooth warmth.

His hands tugged at her T-shirt, and she sat up to help him remove it, along with her bra. Their jeans and underwear followed. She'd never felt shy about her body before. It was a good body, she knew, and she'd always been comfortable with it. Why did she suddenly feel shy now?

Their eyes met and the shyness disappeared. The excitement that had been building inside her took a quantum leap. She caught her breath when he lowered his head to her breast. His mouth was warm and wet from their kisses.

She brought up her hands to touch his head, threading her fingers through his thick, dark hair, loving him with her touch. She heard a strange little sound and realized that it had come from her.

Then his lips were on hers again, hot and demanding; he pushed her down and into the quilt. His hard, bare chest was pressed against her breasts. He moved back and forth across her, eliciting an instantaneous response.

His hands, sometimes feather-soft, sometimes boldly aggressive, roamed over her entire body. His fingers tickled and teased, delighted and demanded. At last he pulled back to look at her, his eyes cloudy with desire. She wanted him so much that she ached. They looked into each other's eyes, acknowledging the specialness of the moment. And it *was* special. Not only her body wanted Quint, but her heart and soul wanted him, too.

He touched her lips lightly with his as he lowered himself and entered her slowly, inch by inch, his body becoming lost inside hers. He was losing himself in her.

Yes, Thea thought, straining toward him. This was what she'd been wanting, all her life, it seemed. Quint. Only Quint.

Chapter Thirteen

Quint lightly nipped Thea's earlobe with his teeth, then darted his tongue into her ear.

She squealed. "Quint, you'll make me spill my wine!"

He leaned back against the wall of the barn, but kept his arms securely around Thea, who was sitting beside him, her back resting against his chest. "I'd like some wine, too," he said. "But my cup's way over there on the other side of you."

She sat up to reach for his cup, but stopped. She placed her cup beside his instead, then held his head between her hands while she kissed him, long and deep. He tasted the tangy bouquet of the wine on her tongue.

"Mmm," he said finally. "Best wine I ever tasted." She snuggled against him with a long sigh.

"For a while tonight I thought I was dreaming," Quint said after a moment.

She tilted her head to look at him. "Why did you think that?"

"Making love to you was so much like some of the dreams I've been having lately. Only better, of course," he added.

She sat up and turned all the way to face him. "You've been having erotic dreams about me?"

"They were more like sensual dreams," he said. "And a little erotic."

He was surprised when she laughed. "What?" he asked.

"I've been having dreams like that about you, too," she admitted. "And mine were definitely erotic."

Her admission pleased him. "And, uh, how did reality compare with your dreams?"

"It was better. Definitely better."

That pleased him even more. "In that case, will you marry me?"

The sudden fear he saw in her eyes made him wince. "I know this is sudden," he said, hoping to allay her fears. "And I'm not suggesting we get married immediately."

He thought he understood a little of what was going through her mind. Until a couple of weeks ago he had been sure he wasn't meant for marriage and would never want to get married again. Thea had changed all that—first, by helping him let go of some of the guilt feelings he'd had about Sally, then by simply being Thea. He was in love with her, now and forever, and wanted to spend the rest of his life with her.

That was the way he felt, but it didn't necessarily follow that she felt the same. "We don't need to rush into anything," he said.

"I can't marry you, Quint. Ever."

She said the words quietly, almost whispering them, but they sounded like a giant PA system blaring into his ears and echoing through his skull. *I can't marry you...ever...ever.*

He swallowed. "That's a long time."

She looked as miserable as he felt. "I know. But I don't want to mislead you, not about something like this."

"Tell me one thing," he said, clutching at straws. "Be honest. Do you love me?" He held his breath.

"I . . . Yes."

"And you agree the sex is good between us?"

"Yes."

There was some hope then, he thought.

"That doesn't mean I'll marry you," she said, clearly reading his mind. "There's a lot more to marriage than love and sex."

"I know there is, but we have a lot more going for us, too. We respect each other. We like each other." He stopped as a sudden thought occurred to him. "Are you worried about living in a small town? We could move. I'm a damned good lawyer, Thea. I could practice anywhere. I'm almost out of debt now, too. We could move to Atlanta or some other city, or even back to California, if that's what you want."

"No! I never want to go back there!"

He was surprised by her vehemence. "Because of your ex-husband?"

"Partly," she said, averting her eyes.

He studied her. "Do you still care for him, Thea?"

"No," she said, still hiding her eyes from him. "That died a long time ago."

"You said he's a drug addict," Quint said, thinking out loud. "Are you afraid of him?" She didn't answer and still didn't look at him. He felt almost certain that he was on the right track.

He touched her shoulder. Her skin was soft and smooth . . . and vulnerable to pain, just as she was. He felt a great tenderness. He wanted to protect her, always. "I'd never let anything happen to you, Thea," he said gently. "Or to your children. Don't you know that?"

She looked at him at last, and the silent pain in her brown eyes almost broke his heart. "I love Alan and Maxie," he continued. "The same way I love my own children. I'd protect them—and you—with everything I have. With my own life, if necessary. Do you believe that?"

He waited and saw her hesitation. "Yes," she finally said.

"You can tell me what's troubling you," he said urgently, almost pleading with her. "Anything. I'll understand...and I'll try to help."

Again he saw her hesitate. He could almost feel her indecision. *Tell me what it is,* he silently willed her. He waited again.

"There's nothing troubling me," she said at last with a bright, false smile. "It's simply that everything has happened so suddenly, like you said. I need a little time."

He didn't believe a word she said, but didn't want to hurt her more by arguing about it. That didn't mean he was giving up. It would take a lot more than her flimsy protests to make him let her go.

"I love you, Quint. Can't we leave it at that for now?"

"Okay," he said, pretending to agree with her. "If you won't marry me on the spot...this very minute...you can at least have another glass of wine with me."

"I'd like that."

He heard the sadness in her voice, along with the relief. And later, when they made love again, she clung to him with an almost desperate intensity.

They sneaked back to the house in the early, predawn hours. Thea was quiet, although a million words were racing through her mind. There were so many things she wanted to tell him.

She wanted to tell him about her ex-husband and about kidnapping her sons to protect them from him. She wanted to tell him what it felt like to be a fugitive, frightened all the time, suspicious of everyone.

She'd almost told him a few hours ago. When he'd promised her that she could depend upon him and asked her to trust him by sharing her problems, she'd almost told him everything. Almost.

But she hadn't. She had been on her own for so long now—with no one to trust or depend on but herself—secrecy had become a habit with her. It was a hard habit to break.

Fear for her sons' safety was always uppermost in her mind, and that kept her silent, too. Quint had said he would do anything for Alan and Max, and she almost believed him. But even if there hadn't been a slight, remaining doubt in her mind, she wouldn't have allowed him to help them. The danger to Quint was too great.

He was a respected man, the district attorney. If she dragged him into the ugly mess of a kidnapping, his whole career could be ruined, his whole life turned upside down again. She couldn't do that to him. She loved him too much to involve him in her dangerous affairs.

Quint stopped outside the house. "I don't think the kids will be up at this hour," he said, "but there's always the outside chance Jacinda might be getting something for Miss Maudie, so we'd better go in separately." He kissed her lightly on the lips.

"Quint..." she began, not wanting to go inside. She didn't want to leave him now, for the last time. "I love you."

He smiled and kissed her again. "I love you, too, and don't look so unhappy. We'll see each other this afternoon."

She wanted to cry. They wouldn't see each other this afternoon, because she'd be gone by then. They wouldn't see each other again ever. She nodded, because she couldn't tell him that, and there was nothing else to say. Straightening her shoulders, she went into the house.

By ten o'clock that morning she was almost ready to leave. She had decided not to tell her aunt about the kidnapping, after all. She would simply say it was time for them to leave, without giving any explanation. That would hurt Aunt Maudie, but it wouldn't hurt as much as knowing the truth and worrying about them all the time.

"Tough Thea," Quint had teased her one time. That was what she would be. That was what people had to become in order to survive.

She hadn't told her boys they were leaving, either. She dreaded that almost as much as telling Aunt Maudie. Alan would be devastated to leave Quint, whom he adored. Maxie would hate to leave, too; he and J.R. were well on the road to becoming best friends.

She'd be unhappy to say goodbye to Alfie, as well, not only because she wanted to be around to see if the girl continued her progress, but because she'd come to love her. Alfie was special. J.R. was special, too. And Aunt Maudie. And Quint. Oh, Quint!

She brushed away a tear and started for the stairs, but stopped when she saw Liz Bartlett coming up the front steps. Slightly surprised, she went onto the front porch to meet her. "You're out and about early," Thea said with a smile.

"I have a zillion errands to do today," Liz replied. "It's the curse of unemployed children like me to be stuck with chores their parents don't want to do."

Thea wondered briefly why Liz didn't simply go out and get a job. "Won't you come inside for a cup of coffee?"

"No, thanks. I just came by to return this." Liz looked into her purse and pulled out Thea's compact. "Fletcher found it last night and thought it was mine. I told him it wasn't, and then I remembered yours was missing, so…here you are."

Thea's suddenly shaky fingers grasped her compact. "Why… why didn't Fletcher return it himself?"

"He didn't know where you lived and he had an early plane to catch."

Thea's mind whirled. "He's leaving?"

Liz gave a short laugh. "He decided Planters' Junction didn't have what he was looking for, after all. His words, not mine."

Thea struggled to breathe. Fletcher Cross had given up? He'd left town? Because he hadn't found what he was looking for? "Will he be back?" she asked.

"I doubt it. Why would anybody voluntarily return here?" Liz said, turning to leave. "Well, see you later."

Thea didn't come out of her stupor until the other woman was already down the steps. "Goodbye," she finally called. "And thanks!"

Liz waved.

Thea watched her get into her car and drive away. She still couldn't believe what Liz had told her. But it must be true. Fletcher Cross had left town! That meant . . . what?

It could mean he really was a writer, and had decided Planters' Junction wasn't the place he wanted to write about, as he claimed? Or, if he was a private detective as Thea had suspected, he hadn't found anything suspicious about her. And that meant . . .

"Oh, dear Lord!" she said, collapsing into one of the white wicker chairs. That meant she and her sons were safe!

For now, said a tiny, cautioning voice inside her. She thought about that. It had been weeks since she'd left California. Alan had had plenty of time to alert the police that she'd disappeared with their children. He'd had plenty of time to hire private detectives, if he wanted to. And nobody had come looking for them, with the possible exception of Fletcher Cross, who had left.

She didn't dare delude herself into thinking that Alan hadn't tried to find them, but maybe they'd eluded him. She *had* gone to great extremes to cover their trail to Georgia. Maybe she'd been successful.

She took a deep breath and exhaled slowly. She looked up at the sky, which suddenly seemed brighter, bluer. What a gorgeous day this was! What a beautiful day to stay home and not go anyplace at all unless she wanted to go, which she didn't. She grinned. Then she got up and went inside the house to unpack.

The more she thought about it during the next few hours, the more excited Thea became. Suppose...just suppose...she and her sons could be safe here for a long, long time, as she'd hoped when she first thought about Aunt Maudie's home as a refuge. What if, by some miracle, she and her sons could live here with Aunt Maudie and Quint and his children happily ever after, or a reasonable facsimile thereof?

She frowned. To be completely happy, she and Quint would have to be married. On a whim, she went to the phone in the hall and found the number for the county clerk's office.

"What are the requirements for getting a marriage license?" she asked as soon as the clerk answered the phone. She nodded as the clerk recited the requirements—a blood test, twenty-nine dollars in cash and a birth certificate.

Uh-oh, she thought, hearing the last item. She hung up. There was no way she could produce a birth certificate, or even use her legal name. It would be too easy to trace by a routine computer check.

Thinking more about it, she called back. "What do you do if you don't have a birth certificate and still want to get married?" she asked.

"Well..." the clerk answered, "the requirement is mainly to screen out underage applicants. If you're legally of age—"

"How does thirty sound?"

"In that case, you simply sign an affidavit."

Bingo! Thea hung up again, barely able to contain her excitement. She got up and started pacing the hall. Was it possible? Could they marry and mesh their families—his children with hers? Her children. There were still problems with Alan and Max—school, for instance.

Would she be able to enroll them in school, not only here, but also any other place she might take them? She went back to the phone book and got the number for the local school system. Even though school was out for the summer, the administrators should still be working.

They were. Thea gave a false name and asked about requirements for enrolling in school. "Well..." the secretary said, "you'll need a birth certificate."

"I've lost their birth certificates," Thea said, already anticipating that question. "But I'm their mother. Couldn't I simply sign an affidavit or something?"

"Sure. No problem."

"What else will they need?" Thea asked.

"Immunization records—you know, a doctor certifying that they'd had all their shots."

Poor Alan and Maxie. They'd have to take all those shots again, but it was for a good cause. "We have those," Thea lied. "Anything else?"

"You'll need their school records from previous schools they've attended."

Thea thought furiously. She didn't dare write for her sons' school records; that would be like announcing their whereabouts to the entire world. Could she get away with making up a fictitious school?

"Uh," she said, stalling for time, "I'll be honest with you. My sons attended a private school and I don't have their records. Is there any way around that requirement?"

"Hmm," the secretary said. "As a parent, you could apply for a waiver and sign another affidavit to the effect that your children have completed such and such a grade. In the meantime, the school board will write to their former school, requesting that their grades be forwarded to us."

"What if their former school doesn't respond?"

"Well, the waiver's good for four months." There was a slight hesitation, then the secretary giggled. "To tell you the truth, if everything's working out with the students, the school board rarely follows up with another request for the previous records."

"Thank you," Thea said with feeling. "Thank you very, very much."

Hanging up the phone, she felt better than she had in days. In months. In years.

"Thea, could I speak to you a moment?"

She turned and saw Quint standing inside the open front door. She'd obviously been so engrossed in the phone conversation that she hadn't heard him come in. She smiled and started toward him. "Certainly."

Her smile faded when she noticed the expression on his face. "Is something wrong?"

Instead of answering, he took her arm. "Let's go outside."

Stepping onto the porch, she stopped and gasped. Quint's car was parked in the driveway and so was Cal's. And standing beside the sheriff's car were Cal and Fletcher Cross.

She glanced at Quint. His expression was unreadable. Her palms were suddenly wet and her mouth was dry. She allowed Quint to lead her down the steps and across the drive to the other two men.

"You seem surprised to see me," Fletcher Cross said to her.

She swallowed. "Liz told me you'd left town."

"I told her that to throw you off."

"Cross paid a visit to Cal this morning," Quint said. "Cal brought him to me, because he thought I should hear what he has to say."

"Everything I said was true," Cross said defensively. "She's a kidnapper!"

Thea clamped one hand over her mouth to stifle her cry.

"Is that true, Thea?" Cal asked quietly.

"No! He's . . . he's lying. Or else he's mistaken."

"Oh, yeah?" Cross said, whipping a photograph out of his pocket and waving it in her face. "What do you say about this?"

Quint grabbed the man's arm. "She can't say anything about it unless you let her see it."

Cross calmed down and handed her the picture. She didn't want to take it; she didn't even want to touch it. Finally she did.

The photo was several years old and dog-eared from being carried around in Fletcher Cross's pocket, but she recognized it instantly. She remembered when it was taken. She even remembered when the four of them had been that smiling, happy family in the picture.

She took a deep breath and handed the photo back to Cross. "What does this prove?"

"You don't deny that it's you in the picture, and your husband and sons?" Cross asked with a sneer.

"Ex-husband," she corrected him. "And no, I don't deny it." She wondered briefly how her voice could sound so calm when she was quivering like Jell-O inside, and her knees felt as if they would collapse at any moment.

"Alan Kirkland is the man who hired me," Fletcher Cross said to Cal. "He has joint custody of the kids and he wants them returned to California. Pronto. You should throw her in jail for kidnapping.''

"Listen, Cross," Cal said, his face growing red. "You don't tell me what to do. I decide for myself, understand?''

"I'm just saying—''

"Understand?''

The man nodded. Cal turned to her. "Did you take the kids without your ex-husband's knowledge, Thea?''

"I . . . yes.''

"Why did you do it?" Quint asked.

"Because . . . because I was afraid for Alan, Junior, and Maxie. I told you Alan's a drug addict and—''

"He said you'd say that!" Cross interrupted. "He's been through treatment and he's clean now. He warned me that you'd—''

"Shut up and let her finish, Cross!" Quint said. He turned to her. "Exactly what did he do to make you afraid, Thea?''

"It . . . it happened the last weekend the boys visited him. I went to pick them up on Sunday and . . . Alan was high on something. He threatened me with a knife.''

"That's a lie!" Cross shouted.

"It's the truth!" she shouted back. "And later, while I was driving the boys home, Alan, Junior, started crying. He said he was afraid of his father, too.''

She looked from Quint to Cal and back to Quint again, imploring them to believe her. "Don't you see? I had to do something. The judge had awarded Alan joint custody, but I knew he was capable of . . . of anything. I couldn't take the chance that he might go off the deep end again . . . and . . . I just couldn't! I had to get my sons away from him! I had to!''

She hadn't realized that she was crying, but suddenly Quint handed her his handkerchief. "I think we've heard enough for now, don't you, Cal?"

"Plenty," Cal said grimly. "Come on, Cross. I'll drive you back to your car."

"No! You can't let her get away with this!"

"I said come on."

"Are you going to believe that lying—?"

"Now!" Cal shouted. "Unless you'd rather I drove you to jail instead."

Fletcher Cross threw one last venomous look at Thea, then got into the car with Cal.

She felt stunned as she watched them drive away. "That . . . that's all?"

"For now," Quint said. "What did you expect?"

"You mean Cal isn't going to arrest me?"

He stared at her for a long time. "There's something you need to understand. Cal's job—and mine, too—is upholding the law, and it's also seeing that justice is done. What would be the justice in arresting a mother for trying to protect her children from a madman?"

She opened her mouth, but no words came out.

"Didn't you say you had joint custody?" he asked.

She nodded.

"Then you probably had a perfect right to take your kids to visit your aunt."

"That wasn't exactly the way it happened."

He shrugged. "A technicality. I'll discuss it with Cal later. I need to look up several points of law, too, and I might want to talk to a judge."

"A judge?"

"In case your ex-husband tries to have you extradited."

"Oh!"

"Don't worry," he continued when he saw her alarm. "It won't happen. Cal and I won't let it happen. He's on your side, too, you know."

She shook her head. "I can't believe things are happening this way. I've been so scared for so long, and you make it all sound so easy." She took a deep breath. "Thank you, Quint. Thank you."

"For what?" He almost exploded. "Didn't I tell you I loved you and loved your kids? Didn't you believe me? Did you think I'd turn them over to a dangerous drug addict? Don't you know me better than that?"

"I knew you were the district attorney! The district attorney! I thought you'd have to do it."

"And *you*—did you think I'd send the woman I love to jail because it was my job?"

"I . . . I wasn't thinking straight."

"I'd sooner cut off my right arm—both arms—than let any harm come to you or your children! I thought you knew that."

"I'm sorry."

"Why didn't you tell me? Why couldn't you trust me?"

"When I first came here, all I knew was that you represented the law. I couldn't take a chance with my sons' safety."

"And last night," he said quietly. "When we were lying in each other's arms...couldn't you trust me enough to tell me then?"

"I wanted to, Quint." He knew she'd had the opportunity to tell him. He'd almost begged her to tell him what was troubling her. "I almost did tell you. Then something stopped me."

"What?"

"I don't know. Fear, I guess. Cowardice."

"I thought we loved each other."

"I do love you! With all my heart!"

"If you really love someone, you trust them. Why couldn't you have trusted me, Thea?"

She could hardly bear to look at him, to see the hurt and sadness in his eyes. "I don't know," she whispered.

He looked at her a moment longer. "I'm going downtown to talk things over with Cal. He should be back in his office by now."

He took a few steps toward his car, then suddenly stopped. "Oh, by the way. If you're thinking about running away again, you might want to reconsider. The next place you run to might not be a town where you have both the local sheriff and the district attorney on your side."

She knew she deserved the barb, but it still hurt.

Chapter Fourteen

Thea answered the phone when Quint called that afternoon to say he'd be working late with Cal and tell her not to hold dinner for him. "Everything's looking good," he said. "I don't think there'll be any problems."

After he'd hung up, Thea stared at the receiver in her hand for a long time before replacing it. In spite of what Quint had said, there *was* a problem. It was between the two of them, and it was all her fault.

She knew he still loved her; the way she'd hurt him hadn't changed that. But the special bond between them had been somehow weakened by her refusal to trust him with her secret. She sighed. It was too late now to try to make it up to him; the damage had already been done.

Everyone was already in bed when he came home that night. Thea heard the squeak of the front door when he opened it. More than an hour later, she heard the squeak of the stairs as he came up to his room. She never slept at all.

The next day was Saturday, Betsy's day off, so Thea made breakfast. Later she was a little surprised when Quint told her that he and Cal were taking the boys fishing.

"We've done all we can until Monday," he reassured her. "Why don't you come along with us? It'll help you to relax."

She attempted a smile. "Thanks, but I promised Aunt Maudie I'd drive her to her bridge club."

Alfie, who sometimes went fishing too, now that she wasn't invited to Denise's house every Saturday, decided to stay home with Thea and finish the mystery she was reading.

After the men and boys left, Thea wandered around the house feeling dislocated, alienated and restless. She should do something constructive, something to help her relax, as Quint had suggested, but her mind kept returning to all the bad things that had happened and could still happen.

She thought about the danger from Alan, who now knew where she was. Quint seemed confident that she wouldn't be extradited to California, but what if he was wrong? What would happen to her children if she *were* sent to jail?

One thing was paramount. She couldn't allow Alan, Junior, and Maxie to fall into her ex-husband's hands. Above everything else, she had to make sure that never happened. She thought more about it, and decided to write Quint a letter, to make sure there was no misunderstanding.

She went upstairs to her room and took out a pen and notepad. After several false starts the words began to flow.

My darling Quint,
I know you're confident that everything will turn out right and I won't be sent to jail on kidnapping charges. I share your confidence, but on the remote chance that something does go wrong, I have an important favor to ask of you. Please take care of Alan and Max. I know you love them, and they love you. They'll be safe and happy living with you and your family. Please forgive me for the hurt I've caused you.

Thea

It wasn't perfect, but she'd have to leave it for now, because it was time for her to drive Aunt Maudie to her bridge club. She would work on it more when she got back.

Aunt Maudie was ready and waiting impatiently downstairs. "Would you like to ride with me, Alfie?" Thea asked as they were leaving.

"I'm just at the most exciting part," the girl said, looking up from her book. "But I'll go with you if you want me to."

"No, finish your book," she said, waving her hand. "I'll be right back."

When Thea returned about twenty minutes later, she was surprised to see a strange car parked in front of the house. Who could it be? The first person who popped into her mind was that loathsome Fletcher Cross, and she certainly didn't want to see him. To be on the safe side, she drove around to the back and parked behind Quint and Cal's cars.

Entering the house through the kitchen, she crossed the room and peered into the hall. She didn't see anything, but could hear voices coming from the living room. One of them was a man's voice.

It must be Fletcher Cross, returning to harass her again. Or maybe it was merely some salesman. She sighed. Either way, it wasn't fair to leave Alfie to handle him by herself. Reluctantly she started down the hall.

She halted after a few steps, listening as the man spoke again. Her eyes widened. It couldn't be! She heard him say something else and gasped. It was him! Alan, her ex-husband! Why was he here?

She knew the answer, of course. He'd flown here because Fletcher Cross had told him where she was. He'd come to get his sons.

She shivered, then clenched her teeth. He couldn't have Alan and Max; she'd never let him have them. Never!

What should she do? Should she run down to the lake and warn Quint? He would help her get the boys to safety. And Cal was with them, too! She started to retrace her steps to the kitchen, but stopped abruptly.

She couldn't leave. Alan had Alfie!

Thea closed her eyes, her mind racing furiously. *Think. Think.* She had to save her boys, but couldn't leave Alfie alone with her dangerous ex-husband. Before she did anything else, she had to make certain Alfie was safe. After that, she wasn't sure, except for one thing. Alan would never get their sons unless he killed her first. Squaring her shoulders, she walked to the living room. Both Alan and Alfie looked at her as she came through the door.

Alfie, obviously agitated, spoke rapidly in her high-pitched voice. "Thea!" she exclaimed. "This is Maxie and Alan's dad! Oh, but I guess you already know each other."

Thea looked at her, wondering whether the girl was scared or merely nervous. If Alan had done something to frighten her...

"Hello, Thea," he said. "You've led me a merry chase."

There was no trace of agitation in *his* voice; it was deadly calm. Too calm. And although he was dressed in an expensive business suit, he didn't look well. He was very pale, and much thinner than the last time she'd seen him. "Why are you here?" she asked.

"To see my sons, of course."

"I told him I'd show him the way to the lake where—" Alfie began.

"No!" Thea interrupted. She knew she couldn't allow Alfie to go off alone with him; she had to handle that. But for Alan's benefit, she had to make it seem like the natural thing to do.

"Alfie can't leave now," she said to Alan, then turned to face the girl, looking her straight in the eye, trying to impress her with the importance of what she was about to say. "Her friend Denise—the sheriff's daughter—is due here any minute."

Please, Alfie. Use that good, quick, clever mind of yours now to figure out that something is terribly wrong.

She waited as long as she dared for the coded message to sink in. "Isn't that right, Alfie?" she asked, holding her breath for the answer.

After what seemed to be an eternity, Alfie replied. "Yes. Denise is coming. Her dad's bringing her over."

Thea breathed again and permitted herself a brief smile in Alfie's direction before she turned back to Alan. "I'll take you to the boys. It's about a thirty-minute drive from here," she added, thinking that that should be plenty of time for Alfie to run to the lake and warn Quint, and for him to get the kids to safety.

"Thirty minutes?" Alan asked with a frown. "What's the name of the place?"

"It doesn't have a name," Thea replied, attempting to be calm and also trying to remember whether she'd covered as many bases as she could. "It's just a little lake with fish in it."

He narrowed his eyes. "You'd better not try to pull anything," he said in a threatening tone.

"Like what? Didn't I say I'd take you to the boys?"

Alan hesitated and looked back at Alfie for a moment before he took Thea's arm. "Okay. Let's go."

The note! Thea suddenly remembered the note she'd written to Quint. "Oh, by the way, Alfie," she said, lingering at the door, "I wrote a note to Denise's parents, telling them about the medication you're supposed to take. The note's on the dresser in my room. Would you please get it and give it to them?"

Alfie stared at her for a moment, then nodded.

Thea didn't dare say more than that. She only hoped it was enough.

Once outside, she headed for the passenger side of the car Alan must have rented. "No," he said, giving her arm a jerk that made her wince with pain. He pulled her to the door on the driver's side. "You drive. That way I'll be able to keep tabs on you."

He got in first, holding on to her arm to pull her in behind himself as he scooted across the seat. "Close the door," he said. After she'd done as he instructed, he handed her the car keys. "Now drive."

He didn't say anything else, and neither did she until they were on the country road and well away from the house. "Alan, what do you plan to do with the boys?"

"I plan to take them back to California with me, of course. Back where they belong."

"This is their home now. They're happy here."

He gave a harsh laugh. "And how about you, Thea? Are you happy here, too...with your new boyfriend?"

"I—"

"Don't lie to me! Fletcher Cross already told me about you two!"

"I wasn't planning to lie."

"This time you've made a big mistake. When I tell the judge about you two living together, he's going to give me *sole* custody."

"It's not that way at all! My aunt lives there, too. And the children—"

"Exactly! What's the phrase they use? Bad influence on the children? Bad role model? Immoral behavior?"

"You know that's not true! I'd never do anything to... Oh!" She cried out in pain when he suddenly grabbed the back of her neck and squeezed it hard.

"Didn't I tell you not to lie to me? Didn't I?"

The pain was excruciating. "Yes! Yes, please..."

He released her, but the pain didn't go away immediately. She raised a shaky hand to wipe away the perspiration that had formed above her top lip. She knew the car must have swerved when he grabbed her, but luckily no other cars were in sight.

On the other hand, maybe it would have been better if another car had been coming and... *Stop it!* she told herself. She glanced at the clock on the dashboard to check the time. She wanted to allow Quint a full thirty minutes before backtracking and taking the old logging road that led to Aunt Maudie's lake.

Alan shifted in his seat. She knew he was watching her, and her flesh crawled. She tried to concentrate on driving.

"Fletcher Cross said your boyfriend is the local district attorney."

"I... Yes."

"It won't help you any. I'm still going to have you put in jail for kidnapping my sons."

"Our sons."

"You'll still rot in jail for taking them."

"I'm not going back to California, Alan. My...my friends here won't let me be extradited."

He gave another mirthless laugh. "Oh, I think you'll go back, all right...willingly. Once I have the boys out there, you'll be begging to come to California to see them."

She shook her head. "It's not going to happen. I'm not going to let the boys go back with you."

"You don't have a choice, Thea." Out of the corner of her eye, she saw him reach into the pocket of his suit. "No choice at all," he said, pulling something out.

She glanced at him to see what he'd taken from his pocket and caught her breath. The revolver in his hand looked small, dark and very dangerous.

"See what I mean?" he said, with a laugh that sounded like a madman's.

It took all the willpower she had to direct her eyes back to the road and away from the fearful object Alan held in his hand, pointed directly at her. Her heart beat erratically, and she breathed rapidly, almost panting. She hadn't expected something like this, not even from Alan.

What should she do now? Should she change the rough plan she'd formulated earlier? Her idea had been to have Alfie alert Quint to the danger, so he could get the children to safety. After that was done, she'd hoped that he and Cal could intimidate Alan to the point where he'd leave quietly, with no harm to anyone.

The deadly revolver Alan carried changed everything. Guns terrified her; they always had. She shivered again and tried to think coherently. In a way she was responsible for the gun her ex-husband held now. If she led him to Quint, and Alan used the gun to hurt him, she'd be responsible for that, too. Yet if she refused to take Alan to the lake, he would use the gun on her, then start looking for the boys by himself. He might still harm not only Quint, but her children, as well. She couldn't allow that to happen!

The best chance for everybody was for her to stick to her original plan by leading Alan into the trap she'd set. Cal was with Quint, too. Wouldn't the sheriff be able to deal with an armed man? He might even have had time to arm himself.

She glanced at the clock again. It was time to head back to the lake. She closed her eyes for a moment. When she made a right turn at the next intersection, her palms were so sweaty that they slipped on the steering wheel.

"Haven't we been by here before?" Alan asked a few minutes later.

"I made a wrong turn a little while ago. It's okay," she added quickly when she saw the anger flare in his eyes. "I know where I am now."

The old logging road that led to the lake on the side farthest from Aunt Maudie's house was deeply rutted and overgrown with weeds, because it was rarely used. Thea slowed the car to a crawl as they bumped along it.

"This road looks like nobody's used it in years," Alan said. "Is it the only way to get to the lake?"

"Yes," Thea lied. "It's the only way."

She stopped the car and killed the engine as soon as the lake came into view several hundred yards ahead. "What now?" she asked Alan.

"We get out." He waved the gun back and forth a couple of times, and finally pointed the barrel straight at her head. "And we don't try anything cute. Understand?"

She swallowed. "Yes."

He got out on the passenger side this time, but kept the gun pointed in her direction. When she got out, she slammed the door. Hard. Alan was beside her instantly, grabbing her throat with one hand, holding the gun against her cheek with the other.

"Dammit! I told you not to try anything! I should kill you right now."

What did he mean? Kill her now...instead of later? She thought about struggling with him for the gun, but knew that with his superior strength, he'd be the one to win. Maybe she should go ahead and get it over with. The sound of the shot would warn Quint of the danger, if he was here.

She clenched her fists, thinking about it...thinking. But she didn't want to die. She wanted to live. For Quint. For her sons. For herself. If there was the slightest chance that she could protect the ones she loved and also survive, she wanted to be around to take that chance. She unclenched her fists.

"I'm sorry," she whispered. "I didn't know it would make so much noise."

"Don't make another mistake," he threatened, relaxing his grip on her throat and lowering the gun.

She nodded.

"Let's get going," he said. She'd barely turned around when he gripped her arm to stop her again.

"I don't trust you," he muttered, half to himself. "I think we'll walk to the lake . . . this way." Before she could move again, he'd crooked one arm around her neck and jabbed the revolver into her ribs.

"Yeah," he said with a maniacal laugh. "This is the way we should walk . . . ladies in front, and gentleman following closely behind." He laughed again while he pushed and prodded her along.

She didn't see Quint at the lake or anywhere around it. She didn't see anybody. Surely Alfie couldn't have misunderstood her message!

Then Quint emerged from the woods on the same side of the lake they were on. He must have been in hiding; he must have decided to expose himself when he saw them. She had to warn him that Alan had a gun!

"Is that your boyfriend?" Alan suddenly asked. "Is that the guy I'm going to kill today?"

She shook her head. "No!" she said in a low, urgent voice.

Alan glanced at her for a brief moment. "You never were a very good liar."

As he brought up the gun to take aim at Quint, he slightly relaxed his grip around her neck. Using all the strength she possessed, Thea tore herself free and lunged for the gun.

"No!" she shouted. "Quint!"

She heard a loud explosion, then she felt white-hot pain sear her forehead. She saw Alan drop his hand, saw him drop the revolver. He stared at her. "Oh my God," he whispered. "I've killed you!"

Thea touched a hand to the place that burned on her forehead. It felt sticky. She lowered her hand and looked at it. It was bright red with blood. She felt more blood oozing down her face now, into her eye, down her cheek, rapidly making a puddle on the green grass at her feet.

Almost as if she were watching a movie in slow motion, she saw Alan fall to his hands and knees. He was crying. "I've killed her," he said over and over. "I've killed her."

Then Quint was there, holding her in his arms, his face as white as she'd always imagined new snow would be, and Cal was right behind him. She looked at Quint, saw the tears in his eyes, and suddenly she knew. She *was* dying. Alan *had* killed her.

She tried to think of something to say to Quint, something to make him feel better. "I love you. I wish we could have had more time . . . time to get married and . . ."

And then there was nothing.

Chapter Fifteen

She wasn't dead, after all. She was alive. The doctor in the emergency room said that the bullet had only grazed her, and that head wounds always bled a lot. He even said she didn't have to stay overnight, because she didn't have a concussion. She had merely fainted.

Thea wasn't sure she believed the doctor. He was too cheerful; maybe there was something he wasn't telling her. "I've never fainted before," she said to Quint as they climbed into his station wagon for the drive home.

"Yes, you have," he contradicted. "You did it the first day you came here."

"Well...this was only the second time. And the first time, I hadn't had much to eat in a couple of days." She stopped when she saw the fierce look on Quint's face. "I didn't mean to tell you that."

"Why not? Because it's the truth? Because lying to me has become a habit with you?"

"I had my reasons for—"

"And those reasons don't exist anymore. From now on I expect you to tell me everything, Thea. No lies. And no evasions or half truths, either."

"Yessir," she said, giving him a snappy salute.

His mouth twitched, but his voice was firm. "You have to promise me."

She sighed. "I promise."

"That's better." He started the car.

"When are we going to get the kids?" she asked.

"We're on our way there now. Then we'll stop by and pick up Miss Maudie before we go home."

"Where did Cal's deputy take the children, anyway? I forgot to ask you before."

"He took them to jail."

"To *jail*?"

"We figured it was the safest place around."

She laughed. "I can't believe it. Max is going to absolutely adore it!"

"Yeah. J.R. will, too."

She suddenly sobered. "What will happen to the boys' father now, Quint?"

"I'm afraid his jail stay is going to last a lot longer than the kids' visit. It won't be nearly as pleasant, either. Assault with a deadly weapon is a serious crime."

"It's all so sad," she said, shaking her head.

"Well, at least your ex-husband will get the drug treatment he needs. He won't have a choice this time."

"I still find it hard to believe that he actually did such a terrible thing." She shuddered.

Quint reached out his free hand to squeeze her knee reassuringly. "I know, but it's over now."

"Tell me honestly, Quint," she said, studying his profile while he watched the road. "Before...before what happened today, were you really so sure that I wouldn't be sent to jail for kidnapping, and that Alan wouldn't be able to gain custody of the boys?"

He thought for a moment. "I was pretty sure," he said slowly. "But crazy things happen in the law sometimes."

She shuddered again.

"You don't have to be afraid anymore," he said, squeezing her knee again. "From now on, he'll never be able to harm you or your children again. Ever. And that's a promise."

"Speaking of my children," Thea said, "I've been wondering what or how much to tell them about what happened today. What do you think?"

"You're asking me? I don't have a very good track record dealing with kids."

"That's not true!" she protested. "Remember whose daughter it was who saved all our lives today!"

Quint frowned while he thought about that, then grinned. "Alfie *was* pretty spectacular today, wasn't she? By the time she ran down to the lake and found us, she already had planned exactly what everybody was supposed to do. She gave orders like a drill sergeant."

Thea snickered. "Did she really?"

"You better believe it. She told me to take your boys to safety, because their father had gone off the deep end. She ordered Cal to run up to his car immediately and radio for backup help. In the meantime, she said, she'd take care of hiding J.R. and herself."

Quint chuckled. "We did almost everything she ordered, except we did send Alfie and J.R. along with your kids. She protested a little, but I think she was secretly relieved."

"Maybe I should ask her advice instead of yours," Thea suggested.

"Probably so," he agreed. "But seriously, since Alan and Max already know as much as they do, I'd fill them in on the rest of the bare essentials of what happened today, without going into details. If they want to know more later, you can answer their questions when they ask them."

Thea nodded her agreement. "I like that. It's a good way to handle it."

Quint guided the station wagon into a parking space in front of the jail and killed the engine.

"How do I look?" Thea asked before he got out of the car.

He turned to her and smiled. "You look pretty damned good to me."

She smiled back at him. "You look pretty damned good to me, too, but I'm talking reality here. I don't want to scare the kids."

"Haven't you looked in a mirror since you were wounded?"

"No," she admitted. "I was afraid to."

"Thea," he chided, "and you were so brave today."

"I used up all my bravery."

"Then touch yourself. Put your fingers on your forehead and feel it."

"Do I have to?"

"Trust me."

She touched her forehead with one finger, then two, then with both hands. "It's so *small*!" she exclaimed.

"It's a butterfly bandage."

"Butterfly bandage? What's that?"

He laughed. "It's a fancy kind of Band-Aid."

"A Band-Aid! You mean I went through all that, getting shot and losing all that blood and thinking I was dying . . . And you thought so, too. Don't deny it! And that's all I wound up with? A Band-Aid?"

"Look on the bright side," he said. "You won't have to worry about whether my homeowner's insurance will cover a stay in the hospital for you."

"How do you feel?" J.R. asked.

Everyone else in the family had talked constantly in the

car, and had crowded around Thea as soon as they got home. J.R. was only making his hesitant approach to her now, while they were waiting for Quint and Alan to return home with a carryout order of fried chicken for dinner.

"I feel fine," Thea replied. That was true. She felt more than fine, in fact. She felt as if the weight of a country the size of China had just been lifted from her shoulders. She had tried to persuade Quint that she was willing and able to cook dinner by herself, since it was Betsy's day off, but he'd insisted on getting carryout, even if he had to drive twenty miles. Alan, Quint's shadow, had volunteered to go with him.

"Did you really get shot?" J.R. persisted. "With a real gun and all?"

Thea leaned into the soft sofa cushions in Aunt Maudie's living room. "I sure did," she said.

He moved a step closer. "That's not a very big bandage," he said. "It looks like a Band-Aid."

She laughed. "It does, doesn't it? And I'll be able to take it off in only a few days."

J.R. shook his head, marveling at it all. Thea held out her hand. "J.R., come here."

He hesitated, then placed his little hand in hers. She pulled him closer. "J.R., there's something you have to know and remember. It's very important, so listen closely."

He nodded.

"Not everyone who gets sick or everyone who's injured will die. Most of us get well again. Aunt Maudie did. And I did, too."

He bit his bottom lip while he thought about what she'd said. "I'm glad," he finally declared.

"Me, too, honey," Thea said, pulling him closer for a huge hug. "Me, too."

She released him after a long moment and looked around for Alfie. "You," she said with a grin. "How does it feel to be a heroine?"

Alfie blushed. "It was your idea. That was neat, the way you gave me the message to go tell Dad and the sheriff what was happening."

"It wouldn't have worked if you weren't so bright. You picked up on it immediately."

Alfie's blush deepened and she shrugged.

"I don't want to make you uncomfortable, Alfie, so I won't get all mushy," Thea said. "But I do thank you, from the bottom of my heart."

Alfie's smile was sweet and shy and totally endearing. "You're welcome."

"And I owe you a favor. A big one. If there's ever anything I can do for you, please ask me. Will you?"

The girl nodded. After a moment she smiled again, this time less self-consciously. "You can teach me your special recipe for pancakes."

Thea laughed. "It's a deal."

"Is anybody ready for dinner?" Quint shouted from the hallway.

"We have tons of chicken!" Alan added.

Maxie, J.R. and Alfie made a run for the kitchen. Aunt Maudie, who had been unusually quiet since she heard what had happened that afternoon, got up from her chair and waited for Thea. "You should have told me just how dangerous that man was," she said.

"I know," Thea admitted. "But I didn't know myself that he'd go as far as he did...to such extremes. I would never have knowingly put you all in such danger, Aunt Maudie. You, and Quint's children, and..."

"And Quint?"

"And Quint."

"It's over now, thank heavens," Aunt Maudie said, reaching for Thea's hand and patting it. "The thing now is to put it behind you and get on with your life."

Thea nodded.

"So what are your plans?"

"Plans?" Thea blinked. "Well, I, uh...I haven't thought that far ahead. I mean . . . so much happened so fast this afternoon and . . ."

"Hogwash!"

"What?"

"You heard what I said. You've had plenty of time to think about your future plans *before* what happened this afternoon. So are you going to marry Quint Richards or not?"

Thea tried to speak, but only single syllables came out. "I, uh, I . . . I . . ."

"You might as well know right now," Aunt Maudie declared, "that he has already asked my permission to marry you."

"He did what?"

"Since your mother lives all the way across the country, and I'm your closest nearby relative, Quint did the proper thing and asked my permission to marry you."

Thea's head spun so fast that she wondered if she might not have a concussion, after all. "And . . . uh, what did you say?"

"I said yes, of course."

"Of course," Thea whispered.

"Naturally, the final decision is up to you."

Thea barely nodded her agreement.

"But if you have half the sense you were born with," Aunt Maudie continued, "you won't give him a chance to change his mind. You're not getting any younger, you know."

Thea couldn't even nod this time and she certainly couldn't speak. What was there to say?

"ARE YOU SURE you're all right?" Quint asked. "You barely said two words during dinner."

The two of them were alone in the living room; everyone else was in bed. At last. "I'm all—" Thea began. Her words came out as a croak, so she cleared her throat and started again. "I'm all right. I'm fine. Dandy. Hale and hearty. Super. Terrific. Couldn't be better. Have I forgotten something?"

"You're furious."

"You're darned right I am!"

"At me?"

"Do you see somebody else in this room?"

"Why?" he asked innocently.

"You have the nerve to ask me that!"

He nodded his head. "Yes, I have the nerve to ask you that. What the hell is going on?"

"You and Aunt Maudie have been conspiring behind my back! That's what's been going on!"

"Oh," he said, belatedly beginning to see the light. "She told you about giving me permission to marry you."

"Exactly! How could you do that to me, Quint? Go behind my back and—"

"Whoa! Hold on a minute here. I didn't go behind your back and I didn't conspire with your aunt."

"Did you or did you not ask her permission to marry me?"

"I did, but—"

"Isn't that conspiring?"

"In a sense, but you have to know exactly what happened to understand why I did it."

"Okay," Thea said, crossing her arms and glaring at him. "What exactly *did* happen?"

"Well..." Quint began, "first of all, she knew about the two of us being alone together in the barn that night, and she had a pretty good idea about what we were doing."

Thea uncrossed her arms and put one hand to her mouth. "Oh, no...."

"Oh, yes. It seems that Miss Maudie never sleeps through the entire night. And it also seems that one of her bedroom windows has a view of the barn. She saw lights out there that night, and thought about calling me... or the police... but finally put two and two together."

Thea moved her hand from her mouth to her eyes and groaned.

"Remember how you came into the house first the next morning?" Quint continued. "Well, when I came in...Miss Maudie was waiting for me."

"Oh, dear!"

"She told me she knew what we'd been up to. Then she asked me what my intentions were."

"She didn't!"

"I told her they were honorable, of course. 'Does that mean you intend to marry my niece?' she asked, and I replied that yes, it did. 'In my day, a gentleman asked *permission* to marry a young lady of quality,' she told me, a little huffily, I thought, so I said, 'Miss Maudie, may I have your permission to marry your niece, Theodora Cameron?' She said, 'Yes, and it's about time, too.' And that's the way it happened, so help me!"

Thea laughed so heartily that it was hard to talk. "Oh, Quint. *Poor* Quint. Poor darling."

Quint laughed, too. "If it hadn't happened to me, I never would have believed it."

Her laughter eventually subsided, and she scooted from her end of the sofa to his. She snuggled against his chest. "Was it horrible?"

He wrapped his arms around her. "Well . . . it was different."

She snickered one more time and uttered a long sigh. "I love you very much, Quint Richards."

"And I love you, Theodora Anne Patricia Cameron."

She snuggled closer and he hugged her tighter. They both sighed. "I did think you were dying this afternoon, you know," he said after a moment. "I saw all that blood, and I saw the horror in your eyes. . . . I felt as if I were dying, too."

He took her hand and brought it to his lips to kiss her palm. "The best part of me *would* die, Thea, if anything ever happened to you."

"I feel that way, too," she said. "If anything should happen to you . . ." She left the sentence unfinished.

"Nothing will happen to me," he vowed. "To either of us. We've going to have a long, happy life together. Very, very long." He kissed her nose. "And very, very happy." He kissed her lips.

"And very, very together," she whispered when they broke apart.

"Definitely," he said with conviction.

"Quint," she said after a moment, dreading to bring up the subject, but knowing it needed to be said, "I'm so sorry I hurt you. I hated telling you all those lies, keeping the truth from you. I'm especially sorry I didn't trust you enough to tell you the truth the other night when you asked me. When you begged me to . . ."

He placed a finger across her lips to stop her. "Shh. That's in the past. Besides, you've more than made up for it."

She tilted her head to look at him. "I don't understand."

"You risked your own life to save mine today."

"That was—"

"And you did something even more significant than that, if it's possible."

"What?"

"Your note to me. Remember? You said if something happened to you . . . that you wanted me to have your boys. Your precious babies."

He stopped. After a moment he continued, his voice choked with emotion. "You don't know what that did to me, Thea. I wanted to cry. I know how important Alan and Max are to you, more important than breathing. And you were entrusting their care to *me*!" He blinked. "If that's not trust—and love—I don't know what is."

He tightened his arms around her, burying his face in the softness of her neck, telling her with his gentle touch that he loved her forever. She wound her arms around him, pulling him close, telling him with her fierce embrace that she'd never stop loving him.

Neither spoke. They simply held each other for a long, long time.

Quint was the one who finally broke the spell. He relaxed his arms, cleared his throat, and gently but firmly disentangled her arms from around him. "I suppose it's time I finally did the right thing by you," he said.

Before Thea could guess what he meant, he'd already slipped off the sofa, grasped her left hand and knelt in front of her. "This is the way they did it in old movies, so I think it's what Miss Maudie had in mind."

Thea suppressed a snicker.

"Ms. Cameron, will you do me the honor of becoming my wife?"

For some reason she suddenly felt as shy as a schoolgirl. "I'm the one who's honored, Mr. Richards."

He blinked. "Is that a yes?"

"Yes. Oh, yes! Definitely yes!"

He was back on the sofa beside her immediately. His arms closed possessively around her; his lips fiercely claimed hers. She kissed him back, just as fiercely and possessively. Had there ever been a woman happier than she was at this very moment? No. It wasn't possible.

By the time Quint lifted his head, they were both breathless. "How do you feel about short engagements?" he whispered.

"Love 'em. The shorter, the better."

"Me, too. How about if we tell the kids and Miss Maudie the news first thing tomorrow?"

"I'm sure that will take a load off my aunt's mind," Thea said with a giggle. Then she sobered as another thought occurred to her. "How do you think your kids will react to the news?"

"They're not getting married. *We* are."

"It's a package deal, Quint. You know that. Neither of us could be completely happy if one—or more—of our kids was miserable. So tell me the truth. How do you think Alfie and J.R. would feel if we got married?"

"Not *if*," he insisted. "*When*."

"Okay. But how would they feel about it?"

He thought for a moment. "J.R.'s no problem. He'll love having you for a mother. I can't say for sure about Alfie, but I think—I honestly believe—she cares very deeply about you. I think having you as a mother will be the best thing that ever happened to her. And that's the truth."

Quint paused and took a deep breath. "But what about your boys? What will they think about the idea?"

Thea placed her hand against his cheek. "You don't even have to ask. They both adore you."

"Really?" he asked with a grin.

"Absolutely. Especially Alan. I think he loves you almost as much as I do."

His grin broadened. "No kidding?"

"Quint," she chided, "you're just begging for compliments. Have you no shame?"

"None at all. Tell me again how much you and your boys adore me."

She shook her head and laughed, but kissed him anyway.

"I think we should apply for a marriage license first thing Monday morning," Quint said when they broke apart. "I don't know exactly what we'll need to get one, though."

"A blood test, twenty-nine dollars in cash and a birth certificate," Thea responded immediately.

Quint raised his eyebrows. "Oh?"

"But if you don't have a birth certificate, you can simply sign an affidavit."

"And how did you happen to come by that information?" Quint asked, his eyes sparkling with amusement.

"Would you believe a wild guess?"

"No."

"I didn't think so. Actually, I was sitting around the house the other day with nothing to do, and I just happened to call the county clerk's office."

"Really? How fortuitous."

"Wasn't it, though?" she said.

Quint tightened his arms around her. "It sounds as if you've been conspiring behind my back, too."

"A little," she admitted. "Do you mind?"

"Not me. Not about something like that. Have you figured out yet where we should live after we get married?"

Thea blinked. "No, it never occurred to me. I suppose I assumed we'd stay here. But Aunt Maudie might not like that. Having four kids in the house, and at her age..."

"I think she'd love it. And if we decide it's what we want, we'll simply ask her. We can count on her to be brutally honest. But I wasn't talking about that. I meant whether we'd live in Planters' Junction or somewhere else."

"Somewhere else?" she asked blankly. "Where?"

"Well...Atlanta maybe. Or New York or Washington. Someplace like that."

Thea was aghast. "Is...is that what you'd like to do? I always thought... But I guess I was assuming again. Do you want to live in a city?"

"I don't mind," he said slowly. "And I thought you'd probably want to."

"Why would you think that?"

"Because you've *always* lived in a city. Small-town life can be awfully dull to some people."

"Liz Bartlett," Thea said, remembering how much Liz hated Planters' Junction.

"Yes, but we're not talking about Liz. We're talking about us. Where would you like to live?"

Right here, Thea wanted to say, but didn't. She didn't want to force Quint into a major career decision based merely on where she wanted to live. "I think we should consider where you need to live to pursue your career," she said at last, hedging.

"I can practice law anywhere. I'm already a member of the Georgia and the New York State bars. I told you I've paid off almost all my debts, so...there's nothing to force us to stay here."

Did that mean he *wanted* to move on, now that he could? She much preferred life in a small town, but knew in her heart she would be relatively happy anywhere, as long as Quint Richards was living in the same place.

"So where would you like to live?" he asked again.

"Anyplace is okay with me," she replied.

"That's no answer."

She knew he was irritated. What did he expect of her, anyway? Then she remembered. He expected honesty. "No more lies or half truths," he had said.

She took a deep breath. "Okay, I'd prefer living right here in Planters' Junction. I love it here and always have. Plus it's a wonderful place for kids. But if you—"

"You mean that?" he interrupted. "You really mean it?"

"Certainly. I promised I'd be honest with you."

"Ah, Thea," he said, giving her a huge bear hug. "You make me so very happy."

"That's nice." He squeezed her so hard that she could barely breathe. "But what did I do?"

"Living here is what I wanted, too, at least for the time being."

"Then why didn't you say so?" she asked.

"I didn't want to force you to live someplace you'd be miserable. And I knew I'd be happy anywhere, as long as you were there, too."

"Quint." She shook her head. "Oh, Quint, that's exactly the way I felt. What a pair we are. We were each **trying** to do what we thought the other wanted."

He nodded. "It's settled, then. We'll live here in Planters' Junction, and I'll announce my candidacy for district attorney. Okay?"

"Only if you're sure it's what you want to do."

"Let's not get started on *that* again."

They both laughed. "Seriously," he said. "I admit I originally took the D.A.'s job because I was in a bind. But

I really like it. It's the most satisfying job I've ever had, even if it doesn't pay as much as private practice."

"I think you found the key word, Quint. Satisfying."

"At the risk of sounding conceited, I'm good at the job, too."

"I never doubted that, not for an instant."

"In that case, will you be my campaign manager?"

She laughed.

"No, I mean it," he said. "I've never run for office before, so I'll need somebody to keep me from stumbling over my own feet. With your marketing skills, you should be able to help present me in my best light." He turned his head to the left, then to the right. "Which side is best for a campaign photo?"

Thea laughed again.

"Or would it be better if I put a paper bag over my head?"

She captured his head between her hands, holding him immobile. "You look wonderful from any angle," she said with certainty. "You *are* wonderful."

"See? I knew you'd be a terrific campaign manager...."

She silenced him with a kiss.

"Does that mean you accept the job?" he asked a long time later.

"I suppose so, if you really think I can help."

"I'm sure of it. We'll make a great team, Thea." He gave her another light kiss. "And now, to show my appreciation, I'm going to pamper you."

Before Thea knew it, Quint was already standing and pulling her to her feet. "I'm going to give you a bath."

"A bath!"

"Not just an ordinary bath. A very special bath. How long has it been since someone pampered you, Thea?"

Forever, she thought, or at least a long, long time. "No, Quint," she said, shaking her head. "We can't. The children might hear. Or Aunt Maudie."

"We'll be quiet."

"But—"

"Shh!" He tugged at her hand, pulling her along with him across the living room, down the hall, up the stairs, across the upstairs hall and into his bathroom. It wasn't precisely *his* bathroom; everyone used whichever one of the upstairs bathrooms was available during rush times. Thea always thought of this particular bathroom as Quint's, though, because it had a private entrance from his bedroom, in addition to the one from the hall.

Quint guided her into the bathroom from the hall entrance, then locked the door behind them. "Now," he said briskly, "I'll start running the bathwater while you step out of your clothes."

"That's insane!" she said in a fierce whisper.

Quint was already on his knees, adjusting the flow of water into the huge, old fashioned, claw-footed tub. He swiveled his head to look at her. "You take a bath with your clothes *on*?"

"I'm not taking a bath in this room, period. If I decide I want to take another bath tonight, I'll go to the other..." She stopped because she'd forgotten what she intended to say. She looked at Quint instead. He had gotten to his feet, extracted a foil-wrapped box from the linen closet and now poured something into the tub.

"What are you doing?" she asked.

"Bubble bath," he explained. "I bought it to give to Miss Maudie last Mother's Day, but by then she was in the nursing home, so I got her some flowers and candy instead."

Thea's lips twitched. "The box has already been opened," she observed.

"Yes . . . well. I had a really rough time in court one day, and . . ."

"How was it?"

"Wonderful. Very relaxing." He grinned a little sheepishly.

Thea unbuttoned her blouse as Quint watched her. "That's an awfully big tub," she said, dropping the blouse to the floor, then unhooking her bra. "I might get lonesome in there." She threw her bra on top of the blouse.

Quint's eyes were twin dark agates. Thea saw his Adam's apple bob up and down when he suddenly swallowed.

"Are you suggesting I should join you?" he said in a low, slow drawl.

Two steps moved her close enough to reach up and place her hands on his shoulders. "I don't see why not," she whispered.

He cupped both her breasts with his two big hands. She caught her breath to keep from crying out with pleasure. "Besides," she said when she was able to speak again, "if you're going to pamper me, you probably expect to be pampered in return."

He ducked his head to capture her lower lip between both of his, taking a couple of quick nibbles. "It crossed my mind," he murmured as his fingers began a slow circular motion around her nipples.

Thea moaned and closed her eyes, reveling in the outrageous pleasure his touch gave her. She slid her arms around his neck, then stood on tiptoe to search for his mouth with her own. Finding it, she released a long sigh of satisfaction when their lips met.

Right offhand, she could think of about a dozen ways she'd like to pamper him, and that was only for starters.

This pampering business could turn into something really terrific.

QUINT'S PARENTS, now retired and living in Florida, were too frail to attend the wedding, but Thea's mother and stepfather, Ginger and George Morrison, flew in from Arizona. As soon as Thea and Ginger saw each other, they both burst into tears and rushed into each other's arms.

Quint looked on in alarm. Then he heard George Morrison's low chuckle beside him, before the older man put a hefty arm around his shoulders.

"They always do this when they haven't seen each other in awhile," George said. "Not that I haven't been worried about Thea, too. Until she called to tell us you two were getting married, we'd only had one quick phone call from her since she left Arizona."

Quint nodded. Thea had already told him about driving straight to her parents as soon as she'd left California with her children. It was George Morrison who had pointed out that, much as he and Ginger wanted to protect Thea and her boys, their house was the first place Alan would look. George had then helped Thea devise a plan of escape and had given her as much money as he could spare, which hadn't, however, amounted to more than a few hundred dollars.

"Miss Maudie has told us what a fine, upstanding fellow you are," George continued. "From what she says, you're the greatest thing since sliced bread."

George had moved a couple of steps away and was studying Quint with narrowed eyes. He felt himself start to sweat. "She, uh, she exaggerates sometimes."

"I hope she's not exaggerating this time," the older man said earnestly. "Thea has had a rough time of it . . . and for a lot longer than these last few months. She deserves something better, a lot better."

Quint swiped a hand across his forehead. "Mr. Morrison—"

"George. Call me George."

"Okay," Quint said, nodding. He was as tongue-tied as a green lawyer trying his first case, or a lovesick teenager about to ask the prettiest girl in school for a dance, even though he knew he was a lousy dancer and his new shoes were killing his feet.

"George," he began again. "I'm not perfect, but..." He stopped, wiped his wet palm on his trouser leg and started again. "I'm in love with Thea. I love her as much as it's possible for one human being to love another. She loves me, too. We respect each other. We love each other's children and we're friends, as well. I sincerely believe we'll have a wonderful life together."

He held his breath as he waited for the older man to respond. Finally George broke into a broad grin and swung his arm around Quint's shoulders once more. "I believe you will, too," George said. "I really believe you will."

Quint started breathing again.

ALAN AND MAX gave the bride away; J.R. was best man, and Alfie was maid of honor. Miss Maudie held the wedding reception afterward in the rose garden at her house, and everyone in the county attended.

"I read in the paper that you two were going on an extended honeymoon," Cal said as he approached the newlyweds in the receiving line. "What exactly does that mean?"

"It means we don't want any visitors coming around for several weeks," Quint whispered.

Thea held her hand over her mouth to suppress a snicker.

"The paper also said you were going abroad," Cal said. "What country?"

Thea laughed out loud.

Quint looked around to make sure nobody else was listening. "Can you keep a secret?"

"You know me," Cal said.

"Yes, but will you keep this a secret, anyway?"

"Sure, I will," Cal replied indignantly.

Quint looked around again. "We're going to the nearest motel with room service and a swimming pool. Miss Maudie has the phone number, so she can reach us immediately, in case there's some emergency with one of the kids."

Cal frowned. "You call that a honeymoon?"

"Yes, I do," Quint said with a broad smile at his new bride.

"We most certainly do!" she agreed, returning his smile.

Epilogue

"Wait!" Quint said.

Thea, who had been about to step through the open doorway, turned to look at him. "What's wrong?"

"I have to carry you across the threshold," he said, scooping her into his arms, "just like last time."

"Quint." She shook her head and laughed, but secretly she was pleased right down to her toenails, utterly charmed by him and by his romantic gesture. She shouldn't be surprised that he remembered everything about their honeymoon; he always remembered important things. How lucky she was!

Once inside the motel room, he kissed her. That had happened last time, too. The kiss was even better this time, she decided, because she wasn't nervous, as she'd been on their honeymoon. She could relax and enjoy it more now.

"I can't believe it's been an entire year since we spent our honeymoon in this room," she said when Quint lowered her to the floor.

"Me either," he agreed. "Fifty-two weeks. Three hundred and sixty-five days. How many minutes is that?"

"A lot."

"Yeah. Especially the ones when we weren't together. If I'd know you were going to work so hard on my campaign, I might not have asked you to be my manager."

"I helped you get elected, didn't I, Mr. District Attorney?"

"You sure did, Ms. Campaign Manager." He touched her cheek tenderly, then kissed her again. "I couldn't have done it without you," he murmured against her neck. "Would you like me to show you how much I appreciate your good work?"

"Don't you think you'd better close the door first?" she asked innocently.

Looking at the open door, Quint made a face. "Right. And maybe I'd better get our luggage while I'm at it."

Thea snickered. "Good idea."

She wandered around the motel room while he brought in their bags. "Everything looks just the same," she said, running her finger along the dresser. "Same pictures. Same drapes." She walked over and sat on the bed. "Same hard mattress, too."

Quint groaned. "I was hoping that *would* have changed."

"Be brave. Like you were the last time we were here," she added coyly.

He leeringly wiggled his eyebrows at her.

"Do you think I should call home now, and see if everything's okay?" she asked.

"You think that much could have gone wrong in thirty minutes?"

"Stop it, Quint. We've been gone more than an hour. I know you think I'm a little overprotective...."

"A little?"

"A lot. But with J.R. just recovering from chicken pox—"

"He's almost completely well, Thea. And between them, Betsy, Miss Maudie and Jacinda can handle anything."

Quint was probably right, Thea knew. Betsy knew almost everything there was to know about children. Jacinda, who was living in the house while they were on their second honeymoon, was levelheaded, too.

Jacinda also knew how to drive. Aunt Maudie had bought a new car when she'd decided to hire the girl permanently as her driver-companion. Then she'd asked Thea to teach Jacinda how to operate it. Only a few people knew that Aunt Maudie was also paying Jacinda's tuition to study computer programming at the nearby community college, and allowed the girl to use her car to commute.

"I consider it an investment," Aunt Maudie had explained to Thea. As soon as she graduated and got a good job, Jacinda would help her next-younger sibling attend college or technical school. That youngster would in turn help the next brother or sister, and so on down the line.

"Everyone will benefit," Aunt Maudie had said. "Especially me. What with all the children in Jacinda's family, I'll have nice young people to drive me around for years and years."

Thea sighed. "I suppose you're right, Quint. Aunt Maudie and her two cronies can handle things just fine. The kids probably won't even miss us."

"Don't look so forlorn," he said, sitting down beside her and putting an arm around her shoulders. "I said they'd be okay. I didn't say they wouldn't miss us. If you weren't there, who'd go with Alfie to the Girl Scout Mother-Daughter Dinner next Tuesday?"

Thea brightened at that. "I still can't believe it. Alfie actually asked *me* to go to the mother-daughter dinner with her!"

"Why not?" Quint said. "I find it completely reasonable. What I can't believe is that Alfie finally did something like joining the Girl Scouts. It was a complete turnaround for her... and you made it happen."

"Me? I didn't—"

"Yes, you did. Remember that night at dinner when you were talking about how much fun you used to have in the Scouts?"

"I don't remember."

"I do, and Alfie must have remembered it, too. She joined only a few weeks after that."

"Well..."

"Don't you understand? Alfie admires and respects you. You're her role model."

"You're embarrassing me."

"Why? I'm only telling you the truth."

"Don't make me sound like some kind of heroine, Quint. I'm not. I have plenty of faults."

"But you're still a heroine. To the kids...and to me, too. You're the best kind of heroine."

She narrowed her eyes. "What kind is that?"

"A real, live, flesh and blood heroine. One with faults, sure, but also with more than enough good points to make up for them."

"Personally," he said, dipping his head to kiss the most sensitive spot on her neck, "I prefer a flesh and blood heroine." He brushed back the loose-fitting neck of her cotton T-shirt and touched his lips to her shoulder, sending a delicious shiver down her spine. "Smooth, soft flesh," he said, "and warm, warm blood."

"Blood getting warmer all the time," she said, winding her arms around his waist.

"Hmm."

Somebody knocked on the door. "Damn!" Thea said. "Just when we were getting to the good part."

Quint laughed. "Hold that thought," he said, getting up and heading for the door.

A room service waiter wheeled in a cart with hors d'oeuvres, wineglasses, and champagne chilling in a bucket of ice.

"You remembered," she said to Quint after the waiter had gone.

"How could I forget? You were wearing that beige lacy thing. It was the same color as your skin...."

Quint's eyes, dark as midnight blue, were fastened on hers. She swallowed. "I brought it along. It's in my bag...."

His features relaxed, not actually into a smile; it was more like a softening. "Why don't you put it on now?" he said quietly. "I'll pour us some champagne."

She nodded and went into the dressing room. All her movements felt as if they were in slow motion, but her fingers were deft and sure of what they were doing.

When she came back into the bedroom, Quint was in bed, his bare torso propped against the headboard, his lower body covered by a pastel sheet. If he remembered everything about their honeymoon, as he seemed to so far—and if *she* did—he was completely naked beneath the sheet. Her beige "lacy thing" would soon disappear, as well. She felt a little giddy at the thought of what would happen after that. She smiled.

He returned her smile and patted the bed beside him. She walked to the bed and sat down, but didn't crawl beneath the sheet. Not yet. "Quint," she said. "I have something to tell you."

"You're pregnant."

Her eyes widened. "How did you know? How could you know that?"

"It's what we decided, isn't it?"

"Yes, but that was only a little over a month ago! I thought it would take months and months."

"Thea," he chided, reaching out to capture her hand, and gently pulling her over to him. "It would never take us months and months to get pregnant, not with the chemistry we have. All those estrogens and progesterones and neutrons and protons flowing back and forth and—"

"Quint!" she said, laughing. "You don't know what you're talking about. You're making up words as you go along."

"Whatever. You know what I'm talking about."

Yes, she did. They did have a chemistry between them that had nothing to do with organic matter and everything to do with life, love, sex, and being together.

"I know," she said.

"When did you find out?"

"This morning. I would have told you earlier, but—"

"You did the right thing. This is the time. And the place." He tightened his arms around her, holding her close. "I can't think of a better one."

"I love you, Quint Richards," she said.

"And I love you, Theodora Anne Patricia Richards," he said.

Cradled against his chest, feeling his strong, steady heartbeat vibrating against her cheek, inhaling the sweet male scent of him, Thea was happier than she'd ever been in her life. She had the sensation that she had been on a long, perilous journey, from which she had finally, miraculously returned. She was home at last.

Once, long ago and a lifetime away, she had thought that the special bond she and Quint shared had somehow been weakened because she hadn't had the courage to tell him the truth about her past. Now that same special bond was back, stronger than ever.

And it was still growing. Like the new life inside her.

HARLEQUIN
American Romance®

COMING NEXT MONTH

#341 IMAGINE by Anne McAllister

Frances Moon was a woman of the '90s. The 1890s, that is. At least she was convinced she'd have been more comfortable back then. She had everything she needed in the wilds of Vermont. And if she'd wanted a man, she could create one. Then Jack Neillands showed up. Inch-for-masculine-inch he embodied her perfect man. But fantasy heroes were safe and predictable . . . and Jack was anything but!

#342 LUCKY PENNY by Judith Arnold

Syndicated columnist Jodie Posniak got all sorts of household hints, recipes and questions from her readers. Until now she'd never gotten a love letter. Into Tom Barrett's missive, Jodie read an aching over lost love. Though his words were simple, she envisioned a man who would charm her with his tenderness . . .and ignite her with his passion.

#343 SPIRITS WILLING by Leigh Ann Williams

New Yorker Angie Sullivan flew off to the Coast to collaborate with a Hollywood living legend on her autobiography and found her employer distracted by a New Age mystic who'd spellbound Tinseltown. Angie suspected she was being hoodwinked California-style. Angie's own mental energy was being diverted by guru biographer Lance Wright, who definitely enhanced Angie's aura—on a purely sensual plane.

#344 BEST BEHAVIOR by Jackie Weger

Willa Manning longed to give her beloved adopted daughter the grandparents she dreamed of, but not at the risk of losing her forever. Nicholas Cavenaugh understood Willa's reservations, but he'd promised to bring his friends the child their lost daughter had borne so far from home. Fate, which had brought Nicholas and Willa together, had put them on opposite sides in the only struggle that could tear them apart.

In April, Harlequin brings you the
world's most popular romance author

JANET DAILEY

No Quarter Asked

Out of print since 1974!

After the tragic death of her father, Stacy's world is shattered. She
needs to get away by herself to sort things out. She leaves behind
her boyfriend, Carter Price, who wants to marry her. However, as
soon as she arrives at her rented cabin in Texas, Cord Harris, owner
of a large ranch, seems determined to get her to leave. When Stacy
has a fall and is injured, Cord reluctantly takes her to his own ranch.
Unknown to Stacy, Carter's father has written to Cord and asked
him to keep an eye on Stacy and try to convince her to return home.
After a few weeks there, in spite of Cord's hateful treatment that
involves her working as a ranch hand and the return of Lydia, his ex-
fiancée, by the time Carter comes to escort her back, Stacy knows
that she is in love with Cord and doesn't want to go.

**Watch for *Fiesta San Antonio* in July and
For Bitter or Worse in September.**

JDA-1